Malcolm MacRae
Jocelyn MacRaine

Two Nights with the Duke

The Silver Dukes
Book 3

by
Meara Platt

© Copyright 2025 by Myra Platt
Text by Meara Platt
Cover by Dar Albert

Dragonblade Publishing, Inc. is an imprint of Kathryn Le Veque Novels, Inc.
P.O. Box 23
Moreno Valley, CA 92556
ceo@dragonbladepublishing.com

Produced in the United States of America

First Edition February 2025
Print Edition

Reproduction of any kind except where it pertains to short quotes in relation to advertising or promotion is strictly prohibited.

All Rights Reserved.

The characters and events portrayed in this book are fictitious. Any similarity to real persons, living or dead, is purely coincidental and not intended by the author.

ARE YOU SIGNED UP FOR DRAGONBLADE'S BLOG?

You'll get the latest news and information on exclusive giveaways, exclusive excerpts, coming releases, sales, free books, cover reveals and more.

Check out our complete list of authors, too!

No spam, no junk. That's a promise!

Sign Up Here

www.dragonbladepublishing.com

Dearest Reader;

Thank you for your support of a small press. At Dragonblade Publishing, we strive to bring you the highest quality Historical Romance from some of the best authors in the business. Without your support, there is no 'us', so we sincerely hope you adore these stories and find some new favorite authors along the way.

Happy Reading!

CEO, Dragonblade Publishing

Additional Dragonblade books by Author Meara Platt

The Silver Dukes Series
Cherish and the Duke
Moonlight and the Duke
Two Nights with the Duke
Snowfall and the Duke
Starlight and the Duke
Crash Landing on the Duke

The Moonstone Landing Series
Moonstone Landing (Novella)
Moonstone Angel (Novella)
The Moonstone Duke
The Moonstone Marquess
The Moonstone Major
The Moonstone Governess
The Moonstone Hero
The Moonstone Pirate

The Book of Love Series
The Look of Love
The Touch of Love
The Taste of Love
The Song of Love
The Scent of Love
The Kiss of Love
The Chance of Love
The Gift of Love
The Heart of Love
The Hope of Love (Novella)

The Promise of Love
The Wonder of Love
The Journey of Love
The Dream of Love (Novella)
The Treasure of Love
The Dance of Love
The Miracle of Love
The Remembrance of Love (Novella)

Dark Gardens Series
Garden of Shadows
Garden of Light
Garden of Dragons
Garden of Destiny
Garden of Angels

The Farthingale Series
If You Wished For Me (Novella)

The Lyon's Den Series
Kiss of the Lyon
The Lyon's Surprise
Lyon in the Rough

Pirates of Britannia Series
Pearls of Fire

De Wolfe Pack: The Series
Nobody's Angel
Kiss an Angel
Bhrodi's Angel

Also from Meara Platt
Aislin
All I Want for Christmas
Once Upon a Haunted Cave

Chapter One

Arbroth Inn
Arbroth, Scotland
August 1817

"Lass, ye have to the count of three to tell me who ye are, how in blazes ye got into my bed, and who gave ye permission to sleep in my shirt?" demanded the big, angry Scot who had just roused Lady Jocelyn MacRaine in the middle of the night with a light shake of her shoulders.

Jocelyn's heart pounded as she struggled awake and stared into this stranger's piercing green eyes. She noted the huge scar across his cheek that was illuminated by the candle he held above her head. But the scar did not make him look twisted or ugly. Quite the opposite—it added character to his nicely formed features.

Not that she was studying the man or considered him handsome.

"What are *you* doing here?" Jocelyn shot back, trying to appear resolute and not show her fear that she had been caught dead to rights by this man. She suspected he was foxed because she caught the scent of whiskey on his breath.

But he seemed to be sobering fast as he glowered at her. "Me, lass? Ye dare to question *my* right to be here?"

Not really, since it was obviously his room, and a lovely one it was, too—the inn's most expensive, and filled with many convenient luxuries.

Having been caught, Jocelyn had no choice but to brazen it out. She returned his glower with one of her own. "Yes, I dare! I distinctly heard one of the maids state that you would not be returning tonight. Did you or did you not mislead her?"

"Of all the outrageous gall," he said, his voice a deep growl. "And ye think this gives ye the right to stake a claim to the room *I* paid for? Then ye have the gall to order a bath and a meal, and then take over my bed? I suppose ye charged everything to my account."

Jocelyn nodded. "Yes, well…the innkeeper's son was on duty and *might* have assumed I was your wife."

"My wife!" He sighed and shook his head. "The bloody *idjit*."

"It wasn't his fault. He trusted me…as you should, too. I shall pay you back in full, sir. Upon my honor, I shall." She cleared her tightening throat. "But I haven't the funds with me at the moment."

He gave a curt, bitter laugh. "How convenient for ye."

"It's the truth," she retorted, indignant that he did not believe her. Never mind that he had absolutely no reason to trust her, a stranger in his bed. "I was exhausted and bedraggled. I needed a place to hide. I will pay you back every last groat, I promise. And I haven't touched a single thing of yours other than this shirt. Um…and your comb, since I had to brush out my hair after washing it."

He set the candle on the night table beside the bed. "Lass, why did ye need to hide?" he asked with surprising gentleness, taking a seat at the foot of the bed and making no attempt to approach her.

"It is a long story." Running away from a wedding, especially one's own, was a tiring business. After three days on the run, she'd found herself in desperate need of a meal, a bath, and a good night's sleep, not necessarily in that order. But she did not dare spend more than one night in any place for fear that her family and her reprehensible cad of a jilted bridegroom, the Earl of Ballantry, would find her and force her to the altar.

Luck had finally come her way when she overheard one of the

maids at this elegant Arbroth Inn mutter something about a man called MacRae—she hadn't caught all of his name at the time, but noted it later when peeking at the inn's register. "Och, he will no' be returning to his room tonight for certain," the maid had said to another as they chatted while walking off duty.

"Lass? I will no' harm ye," he said now, regaining her attention. "But I need to know the entire truth."

She nodded. "I ran away from my wedding because I could not bring myself to marry the Earl of Ballantry."

"Ballantry? That rat?"

"Oh, you know him?"

He raised the candle again to study her face. "Aye, I can see how ye're pretty enough to attract that knave."

She shook her head. "He was never interested in me."

"Ah, yer wealth, then."

She pinched her lips, afraid she had just made a monumental blunder in being honest with him. Would this rogue now claim to have compromised her and attempt to marry her, too?

He must have sensed her thoughts, for he sighed. "Lass, do ye know who I am?"

She nodded. "Malcolm MacRae. That's the name you wrote in the inn's register."

"Aye, because I dinna want to make a bloody announcement about my true identity. The innkeeper knows, of course. I've stopped here many a time."

"And claimed the inn's best room. I thank you for that," she said, daring a small smile.

He chuckled. "What's yer name, lass?"

"If I tell you, will you promise not to give me away?"

"No, I canno' promise ye that. However, if it's Ballantry that's asking, I will consider no' telling him anything."

"You cannot tell my parents either."

He remained silent a long moment before finally responding. "Sorry, lass. But I am no' negotiating with ye on this. Either ye tell me yer name or I turn ye over to the local magistrate this very night. Well, whatever is left of it. And I'll take my shirt back, if ye please."

"No! You mustn't." She let out a deflated breath. "My name is Jocelyn MacRaine. Lady Jocelyn MacRaine. Isn't it a coincidence that our surnames are so similar?"

"No, lass. Almost everyone in Scotland is a MacSomething. Do not attempt to weave connections between us when there are none."

"I was merely attempting to be cordial," she said with a purse of her lips and a chiding frown. "There, I've told you everything. Runaway bride. No funds. Not ever going to marry that toad of an intended bridegroom."

"What did he do?"

"Other than seduce my maids, my odious cousins, and even the vicar's wife within days of our supposed wedding ceremony? The vicar's wife was that very morning."

"Ah, he was a busy fellow, wasn't he? Sounds like Ballantry."

"So there you have it. I thought marriage to him might provide an escape from the pressures of my family, but all I was about to do was exchange one unhappy situation for another. So I came to my senses and escaped. Are you satisfied? And you are not getting your shirt back until my gown and undergarments are returned to me properly freshened and cleaned. I'll have them back in the morning. So you are stuck with me until then."

"Lass, you seem to have matters backward. This is *my* room. *My* bed. *My* shirt," he pointed out again. "I give the orders here, no' you."

She tipped her chin up. "Are you a gentleman?"

"Aye, by rank. But no, if ye are referring to my manners."

"Oh." She tugged the covers more securely about her body. "Well, you had better behave like a gentleman around me. Not that I am all that tempting, or so my family finds it necessary to tell me. I am a twenty-seven-year-old spinster with a sour disposition. Certainly too old and too much trouble to interest the lascivious likes of you."

He laughed. "Jocelyn MacRaine, ye say? MacRaine? As in the Earl of Granby's daughter? I heard ye were a bit of a harpy."

Her eyes widened. "Who said so?"

"Well, ye just admitted it yerself. So why are ye in a dander over who else might have said the same thing?"

"It is entirely different. It hurts to know others outside my family also think the worst of me. Why would any of them bother to talk about me behind my back? I am well beyond my prime and mean nothing to any of them."

"Och, Jocelyn. Ye're a fat coin purse, just as I am. Otherwise, no one would care if either of us lay sprawled in a gutter gasping for our last breath. But wealth and title? Everyone wants to grab a piece of us. Who cares what others think? It's nice to meet ye, lass," he said, casting her a dangerously appealing smile. "If ye want the truth, ye hardly look a day over twenty-six and a half."

His teasing caught her by surprise, and she laughed in spite of wanting to be angry with him. Not that she had a right to be angry, since she was the usurper here. "You mentioned you were a gentleman. Am I to assume you are titled? Who are you?"

"I am Camborne."

"Who?"

He chuckled. "As in *the* Duke of Camborne."

She regarded him blankly. Where had she heard that name before? Associated with something...gold...silver. She inhaled sharply. "Are you one of the notorious Silver Dukes?"

"Aye, that I am."

"Thank goodness." She let out the breath she had been holding and relaxed against the fine, downy pillows piled against the headboard of the large bed. Everyone knew Silver Dukes were men who did not marry. They were known to cavort. Seduce. And no woman resisted their advances because these Silver Dukes were gorgeous.

She studied this man beside her. Yes, he was quite handsome. Exquisitely good looking, actually. About forty years of age, or perhaps a few years older if the dusting of gray upon his chestnut-brown hair was any indication. Goodness, he was quite nicely formed. And he had a manly face, the sort one might trust because of the squareness of his jaw and the sharpness of his gaze. Oddly, the scar on his cheek enhanced his appeal.

This was a man who knew what he wanted, and then took decisive action without ever doubting his decisions.

As a Silver Duke, he was also never going to marry. Which meant he was not going to scheme to get her to the altar and gain control of her wealth.

"Now that we have been introduced, what are we to do about this situation, Jocelyn?"

She liked the rugged timbre of his voice and his Scottish burr. Having been raised in England and schooled in England, she had never acquired much of a Scottish accent or manners, even though she could claim Robert the Bruce as one of her blood ancestors, or so her father had often boasted. "What do you suggest we do, Camborne?"

"I'm not of a mind to think clearly at the moment," he said, raking a hand through the glorious waves of his hair that seemed to have a tinge of red amid the brown by candlelight. "Let me sleep on it and we'll come up with a plan in the morning. How does that sound to ye?"

"Fine, so long as you intend to sleep on the floor and not in this bed beside me."

He arched an eyebrow and cast her a rakish smile. "There ye go thinking ye are in a position to make demands, lass. Well, ye are not. I dinna have the makings of a pallet. There's only one coverlet and it is on the bed. If I take it, ye'll be cold. If ye keep it, then I'll be cold."

He began to remove his clothes, starting with his jacket and his neckcloth.

No, no, no. They had gotten off to such a good start, and now he was ruining it. "Camborne, you cannot undress!"

"I can and I will. However, I will keep my trousers on for the sake of yer modesty. Although I've been told I have a very fine arse."

"Ugh! Is that supposed to make me shiver with delight?" Was he serious? Were all dukes this deluded about their looks?

"No, lass. If I wanted to send thrills and tingles through ye, then rest assured ye'd be thrilling and tingling right now."

"Ha! Doubtful."

He yawned. "I'm too tired to prove it to ye tonight. Move over, lass. Ye canno' take up all of the bed."

"But it is my bed!"

"Wrong again, Jocelyn. It is *my* bed, and I am letting ye stay in it out of the goodness of my heart. I promise not to touch ye, if that's what ye're afraid of. I have no interest in good girls."

"I'm hardly a girl. And how do you know I am good?"

"People would no' be calling ye a harpy if ye were liberal with yer favors," he said, having the audacity to settle on the bed beside her. "So that's an end to it. Ye're a good girl and I will no' touch ye. Nor do I have any desire to do so at the moment. I hope this does not disappoint ye."

"Disappoint me?" She wanted to shove him out of her bed, but it really wasn't hers, although she had planted herself in it and was not about to leave its comforting warmth. Besides, he was too big and muscled to push around. Not to mention he had the manners of a jungle cat and felt no remorse in claiming half the bed as his territory. "Oh, is that what you think? That I am some repressed, never-been-kissed, pathetic spinster yearning for a torrid night of passion with you?"

"Aren't ye? Shall I kiss ye and find out?"

Chapter Two

*B*LESSED SAINTS! The lass was beautiful, to be sure. However, Malcolm had no intention of kissing her...not tonight, anyway. For all he knew, her every word could have been a lie. What if she wasn't Granby's daughter? What if she did not know Ballantry?

Well, her description of his dallying with every woman he could get his hands on was accurate. She had gotten that much right. Besides, his gut instinct told him that she was telling the truth.

"Goodnight, Jocelyn. Sweet dreams," he said, interrupting her while she was in the midst of berating him for his unspeakable gall in believing she might ever want a kiss from him.

Having vented her spleen, she huffed in indignation and then sighed. "Goodnight, Camborne. Just remember to keep to your side of the bed."

"Need I remind you that it is *all* my bed," he said, sitting up a moment to remove his shirt and then stretching his large frame atop the mattress once more. His trousers chafed, for he preferred to sleep wearing nothing at all. However, he had promised to keep them on for Jocelyn's sake, and he always kept to his word. "I think it is quite generous of me to give ye half of it even though my shoulders are twice as broad as yours."

She huffed again, but ended with another sigh. "I do appreciate your sacrifice. Thank you for letting me stay."

"Ye're welcome, lass." All he could see of Jocelyn was the back of a head of silky hair that was almost as black as a raven's feathers. It fell across her shoulders in captivatingly soft waves, in stark contrast to their white coverlet.

Malcolm decided he would not mind running his fingers through her lush tresses. Nor would he mind kissing her impertinent mouth when the time was right.

Perhaps it was foolish of him to allow her to remain with him, but would a thief have been polite enough to mutter a thank you? Well, he was a light sleeper and had slipped his dirk under his pillow to keep it at hand in the event he needed to defend himself.

But as the sun rose and his sleep had not been disturbed at all, he rose quietly, drew aside the curtains to fully allow the morning light to shine into his quarters, and set about readying himself for the day.

Jocelyn was asleep, no doubt exhausted from all those days on the run. That she slept so soundly was a sign she trusted him.

He liked that she trusted him. And she looked quite pretty in sleep, he noted upon taking another moment to study her features.

A soft knock at the door distracted his attention.

He had just finished washing and shaving, and had yet to don his shirt, but he strode to the door, expecting the innkeeper or one of his boys. It was one of the inn's young maids instead. Her eyes widened and she smiled at him seductively.

"Ah, my wife's clothes?" He took the neatly pressed bundle from her hands.

The lass batted her eyelashes at him. "Aye, sir. Will she be needing my assistance?"

"No, I'll attend to her."

"And you, sir?" She cast him another inviting smile as her gaze raked over his bare chest. "Will you be requiring my services? I'd be happy to oblige ye. Ye need only ask for Molly—that's m'name."

"No, lass. No obliging necessary. My wife is quite enough for me."

"Och, 'tis a pity," she said, glancing at the figure of Jocelyn fast asleep in his bed before sauntering off.

"Remarkable," he muttered, shutting the door and shaking his head. But he was not commenting on the maid's propositioning him, for that happened often enough and came as no surprise. What he considered remarkable was how easily those two never-before-mentioned words had tripped off his tongue.

My wife.

The mere thought of being bound in marriage ought to have put his stomach in a churn, but he felt not a single, unsettling roil at the moment.

Was this not odd for a man who had spent his life avoiding matrimonial commitment?

Not only did he feel perfectly fine, but a gentle warmth spread through his body now that he'd referred to Jocelyn as his wife.

He shrugged it off. Perhaps he was still a little drunk.

But he knew that he wasn't.

Well, she had told the inn's staff that she was his wife, and he was not going to give her away as a liar. Aye, it was a dangerous thing to do, because they were in Scotland and he would be trapped if Jocelyn refused to declare this marriage falsehood merely a jest.

Oddly, he trusted the lass.

After donning fresh clothes and slipping into his boots, he debated whether to head down to the common room for breakfast or wake Jocelyn and assist her in dressing. He wasn't quite certain she would allow his assistance, since she was wearing nothing under his shirt, a circumstance that had left him tossing and turning a bit before he finally drifted off to sleep.

Nor was she going to remove his shirt and prance naked in front of him, another circumstance that seemed unlikely because Jocelyn was, despite last night's bluster and feigned bravado, a modest young woman.

He decided to head downstairs and send a maid up to attend her. But he did not want to disappear without advising Jocelyn of his whereabouts.

He knelt beside her and shook her lightly. "Jocelyn, lass," he said in a whisper. "I'll be having my breakfast downstairs. Will ye join me when ye're ready?"

She pursed her full, lovely rose-petal lips. "*Mmm. Go away.*"

"Jocelyn, I'm going for breakfast," he repeated, silently resolving to kiss her beautiful lips before they parted ways. "I'll bring ye up a few scones if ye're no' down there by the time I finish."

"I like scones," she mumbled. "And tea."

"All right, lass. I'll return with a pot of tea, too."

Suddenly, she sat up. "*You.*"

The word sounded like an accusation. "Aye, me. This is my chamber, if ye will recall."

She groaned as she brushed back her hair and blinked several times to wipe the sleep from her eyes. "I recall," she said, yawning as she stared up at him. She regarded him with the most incredible crystal-blue eyes framed by the longest black lashes. "Oh, you're already washed and dressed. You move about with the stealth of a cat. I did not hear a thing."

"I wasn't that quiet. You were exhausted." He reached out to tuck back a wayward curl that had remained upon her cheek, all the while staring at her eyes because they were as beautiful as her lips and impossible to ignore. "How do ye feel after a solid night's sleep?"

"Hungry," she said with a surprisingly genial smile.

"Well, the maid brought back yer clothes a few minutes ago. Care to ready yerself and join me in the common room? I'll buy ye a proper breakfast."

A light blush stained her cheeks. "That is generous of you, Camborne."

"It is nothing, lass." He brushed another stray wisp off her lovely face, liking that her skin was soft and warm. "See ye downstairs. I'll send up a maid to assist ye. Dinna be long."

He strode out, not daring to look back at her for fear of losing his resolve and falling back into bed with her, for she looked remarkably pretty in the morning light.

Perhaps there was something to the notion of waking up with a woman in his bed. But he did not think he would be feeling quite as pleased if it were someone other than Jocelyn curled beside him under the coverlet.

First of all, the women with whom he consorted were not soft or sweet. Quite the opposite, they were mercenary and predatory, which suited him just fine, since he sought them out for one thing only, and that was to fulfill his manly needs.

It was mutual satisfaction, of course. Once his needs and those of the lady in question were satisfied, he would leave her bed because there was no purpose to staying. Most of his liaisons were with married women, for they were generally safest. He always chose the ones whose husbands no longer cared what they did or with whom they did it. Even though there was little chance of discovery in those situations, he never stayed the night. Why risk any awkwardness in being found in a married woman's bed come morning?

Waking to find Jocelyn beside him felt nice, however. When had he ever simply slept with a woman? No sex. Just sleeping.

The answer was *never*.

Could it be this was what he had been doing wrong all his life? He'd never spent an entire night into morning with any of his conquests, not even any of his mistresses. He would entertain them for an evening, satisfy himself, and then leave.

Come to think of it, this was probably why his arrangements often turned sour. The ladies wanted more attention than he was willing to give them. The gifts he provided usually appeased them. After all, taking on a mistress was purely a business arrangement for him, and he had been quite clear about this when negotiating terms.

The nicer his gifts, the louder their purrs and panting breaths whenever they coupled. None of it was real, and he'd never really cared. Everyone lied to him. How could he ever know whether their mews of pleasure were real or fake?

But somehow, he and his fellow Silver Dukes had become known for their sexual prowess. It was mostly myth. He, Bromleigh, and Lynton often met at their club over drinks and laughed about the rumors of their skill. Yet, for the sake of their pride, they all hoped much of it was true.

But how could any of them ever know?

He could not speak for his friends, but he knew his own actions were to blame for his situation. Was it not mostly his fault that he had never found love when he purposely chose women who were mercenary and not going to get attached to him? Nor was he in any danger of getting attached to them.

But this was the very reason he had returned to Scotland, his need to get away from London and think deeply about what he had become. There was no better place on earth for a man to dig deep into his soul, to spend his hours fishing and contemplating the changes he needed to make in his life.

Those changes included the possibility of taking a wife.

But if he could not handle a mistress, how was he ever to be a proper husband to the woman he married? How did one choose wisely?

He strode into the common room and was immediately greeted by the innkeeper, Mr. Farrell. "Is all well, Yer Grace?" he asked in a furtive whisper, regarding Malcolm anxiously. "And yer *wife*, did she find the accommodations to her satisfaction?"

Malcolm chuckled. "Yes, she was most pleased. I'm grateful to ye for accommodating her in my absence."

The innkeeper's eyes widened and he released a breath. "Then she really is yer wife?"

"Yes," Malcolm said without hesitation because he did not want to shame Jocelyn. "Very recently wed."

"Good. Good," Mr. Farrell said, releasing another breath. "I wanted to hit my son about the head when he told me this morning that he had given her access to yer quarters."

"No harm done," Malcolm assured the man. "It is my fault that I did not leave word of the possibility of her arrival. In truth, I did not expect her to join me until tomorrow at the earliest, if at all."

"Blessed saints, that's a relief." The innkeeper mopped his brow as he led Malcolm to a quiet table off to the side of the common room that would soon be bustling.

"No, I'll have this one," Malcolm said, preferring a table that gave him an unobstructed view of the doorway. He did not trust Jocelyn to join him, and feared she might sneak off once she was washed and dressed.

Then again, she had to be hungry.

But she also had to be worried someone would recognize her and report her whereabouts to Ballantry and her family.

Even so, that someone would have to be aware she had run off on her wedding day, and then be willing to go out of their way to tattle on her. The chances there would be a problem were slim.

He had just finished his eggs and kippers, and was nursing a cup of coffee, when Jocelyn entered the common room looking as fresh and lovely as the breath of spring. It did not escape his notice that every man was gawking at her. Discreetly, of course. No one would dare openly ogle her because she was thought to be with Malcolm, and no one was going to dare tangle with him. He was rough looking, not at all elegant, as one might believe a duke to be. Not that anyone besides the innkeeper knew of his true identity.

But Jocelyn carried herself like a proper duchess.

Her hair was drawn back in an artfully braided bun, no doubt styled by one of the inn's maids, who obviously had a good sense of fashion. Perhaps Jocelyn had instructed her on what she wanted.

No matter—the effect was extraordinary.

She wore her only gown, the one she was meant to be married in. It was a pearl silk confection that was far too light for the raw Scottish weather and far too elegant for ordinary morning activities.

He wondered how she had not yet taken ill, for it could not have been easy for her once the sun went down and the night's chill spread through the Highland glens and dales.

Her eyes sparkled as she spotted him. He rose as she approached and cast him a beaming smile.

A horrifying notion struck him in that moment. He did not want to lose this lass.

Not yet, anyway.

He offered her the seat beside him. "Ye clean up nice, Jocelyn."

She laughed as she settled in her chair. "How did you ever gain your Silver Duke reputation, Camborne? I 'clean up nice'? Is this how you flirt with all the ladies?"

He grinned while settling back in his chair. "I'm no' completely sober yet. But just say the word and I'll be happy to seduce ye and conquer yer heart."

He was surprised when she actually gave the jest consideration. "Perhaps the seduction part," she said quietly. "At my age, when am I ever to have the chance again?"

His heart shot into his throat.

Was she serious?

She was beautiful and would likely remain so into her dotage. Some women just had that look about them, an inner glow, something soft and appealing that simply would not fade.

"However, I do not wish my heart to be conquered. Is my situation not bad enough? My family hates my independence, and they grow more desperate every year to see me married off."

"Even to a wretch like Ballantry?"

"That was my mistake more than theirs. I chose him."

"Och, lass! How could ye? He's a knave."

"I know, but I am well into my spinsterhood, Camborne. I could not bear to listen to my parents—my aunts, uncles, and even my insufferable cousins—bemoan my fate. Well, my cousins were probably mocking me rather than pitying me. I know it is not right to speak ill of my own blood kin, but they are truly lacking in warmth or kindness." She emitted a ragged breath. "I finally resolved to accept the next man who came along. Utterly stupid on my part, I will own."

"And Ballantry was that next man?"

She nodded. "I held my nose and accepted him. As it turns out, he would not care if I died three minutes after we exchanged vows. In fact, I know he would prefer it."

"I'm glad ye ran, lass."

"So am I. But my already waspish reputation is certainly in complete tatters now that I have jilted my bridegroom on our wedding day. No one decent is going to come near me after the gossips get through annihilating me."

Malcolm placed a hand over hers. "Lass, ye're with me now, and I will no' allow anyone to harm ye."

She cast him a surprisingly vulnerable smile. "You are a better man than I deserve, Camborne. But do not let the compliment go to your head. I am not likely to give you another."

"Because ye are a wicked harpy?" He laughed. "I'll keep that in mind."

Having just assured Jocelyn that he would protect her, Malcolm resolved to take her to the local shops and buy her some sturdier gowns. Shawls and stockings, too.

She inhaled deeply and emitted a soft sigh of pleasure that would have had his heart beating faster if she were making that delicious sound over him and not the aroma emanating from his coffee. "That smells heavenly," she said.

"Aye, it is very good. I'm on my second cup. Care for one?"

"It does stir one's senses, but tea is my morning drink." She inhaled again. "Did you just have eggs and kippers? I prefer my eggs with sausages. But I like kippers, too."

He grinned as he summoned one of the serving maids. "Order whatever ye like, lass. The innkeeper knows to charge all to my account, as ye so helpfully instructed his staff last night. There's no reason to change that standing order. I'll have him bring out every last morsel in his kitchen, if ye like."

She blushed, obviously aware she had no funds of her own, which meant he had to pay for everything anyway. "I'm sorry, Camborne. Make note of what I owe you. I *will* pay you back in full."

"I dinna want repayment, Jocelyn. It is my pleasure to have ye with me."

Her blush deepened. "Now I feel worse about abusing your generosity."

"Dinna feel bad. Ye know it is mere pocket change for me. In truth, I'm glad ye're safely under this roof and have food and warmth available to ye. Those first few nights on the run must have been very difficult for ye."

She nodded. "They were. I do not frighten easily, but there were moments when I questioned the wisdom of what I was doing. I hid in churches those first two nights. The wooden pews weren't the most comfortable, and there were no warming fires nearby, but I thought I would be safest in a house of the Lord. Thank goodness it is August, the hottest month of the year."

He nodded, knowing she probably would have frozen to death that first night had she run off a month or two later.

"I had a few coins in my shoe, a silly wedding tradition that ultimately proved useful. I found my way to a coaching inn and used those coins to take a mail coach as far away from Lord Ballantry as I could. This is how I came to be in Arbroth yesterday. The fare was enough to buy my passage as far as here."

"And then ye overheard those maids talking about my unoccupied bedchamber at this inn?"

She nodded. "I was cold and starving. I needed a place to warm myself and think about what I was to do next. The bankers in Aberdeen know me, and I must get to them before Ballantry and my family do. Several accounts are mine outright, so I am able to do exactly as I wish with them. But I am an unmarried woman. The bank managers might not allow me to access my own funds if my father ordered it so."

Malcolm frowned. "Do ye think yer parents and Ballantry are there already? Waiting for ye?"

"I hope not, but it is a possibility. It is a risk I'll have to take."

He leaned back in his chair. "Lass, ye're still a two- or three-day ride by carriage to Aberdeen. Ye haven't the fare for another mail coach. Walking there will take ye two weeks, if not longer. This assumes yer legs dinna give out along the way or ye dinna die of starvation since ye haven't the wherewithal to pay for a meal. Not to mention ye haven't the clothes to keep yerself warm, either."

"Which is why I need your assistance, Camborne." She cleared her throat. "I was hoping you might see your way to escorting me to Aberdeen. Were you on your way there by any chance?"

"No, lass. I wasn't."

"Oh." She glanced down at her clenched hands. "Would you consider taking me there? The bankers might not dare block my accounts if you are there to growl at them. And I can pay you back on the spot. I'll gladly pay you double whatever it is I owe you."

"Ye dinna owe me anything, Jocelyn," he said, trying to keep the annoyance out of his voice. "I dinna want yer blunt." How could she think he would demand repayment from her?

She let out a breath. "Then you'll take me there out of the goodness of your heart?"

He was spared the need to respond when the innkeeper scurried toward them to take Jocelyn's order. "My wife will have eggs and sausages, and toss on some kippers," he said, intentionally speaking for her since he did not want her to skimp for his sake. "Lots of bread, too."

"And a pot of tea," Jocelyn added.

The innkeeper hurried off.

Jocelyn smiled at him. "You did that on purpose."

He arched an eyebrow. "What did I do?"

"Made certain I would have plenty to eat. Thank you. By the time we part ways, you'll have me fat as a Christmas goose."

He shook his head and chuckled. "I told ye that I would look after ye. I keep my word. Eat to yer heart's content, and afterward I'll take ye shopping."

"But I—"

"Ye can settle up with me once we reach Aberdeen, if ye're insisting on it," he said, although this was merely to appease her. He had no intention of accepting any reimbursement whatsoever from her. Not for food. Not for clothing. Not for shelter.

Her eyes widened. "Then you'll take me there?"

"Aye. But ye need more sensible clothes before we head off or ye'll freeze to death. My carriage cracked a wheel just as I reached Arbroth, which is why I had to stop here for the night." He eyed her with a hawkish gaze. "Perhaps it was fate, and I was meant to provide a room for ye. Well, anyway…my carriage won't be ready until tomorrow morning. We'll leave once it is brought to the inn."

She nodded. "All right. Thank you, sincerely."

"My pleasure, lass. We'll now have the entire day to get ye some proper clothes."

"But nothing extravagant. Don't forget, my accounts might be blocked and I may not have the means to pay you back immediately."

He waited for her food to be set before her, and they were once again left to themselves before he resumed their discussion. He did not want to make an issue of his paying for her things, but neither did he want her stinting on her purchases. Perhaps it was best just to be honest about his intentions and clear the air. "Jocelyn, I will no' accept repayment for whatever I spend on ye today—or any other day, for that matter."

She had just taken her fork in hand but now set it aside. "No repayment at all?"

"None."

"Are you suggesting I can purchase anything I need and you will not put a limit on my spending?"

"That's right."

"What if I buy expensive trinkets?"

He shrugged. "I can afford it. Nor am I worried about yer spending too much, because ye are obviously a thrifty lass. Ye're only thinking of yer minimal needs, not even giving a thought to what ye might want beyond these urgent items. And ye've not stopped calculating down to the last farthing whatever it is ye think ye owe me. Once again, let me make myself clear. Ye owe me *nothing*."

"So, you do not want my money." Her hand trembled as she set it on the table.

"Lass, I have so much of my own that it is coming out of my ears. Why would I need yers when I could no' spend mine in a lifetime of trying?"

"That is beside the point."

"I think it is entirely the point," he countered.

"No, it isn't."

Botheration, what had he said to overset her? He thought he was being kindly and generous. Obviously, the lass did not think so.

She nibbled her lip and regarded him fretfully. "Camborne, if you do not want my coins, then what is it you want from me?"

Chapter Three

"Wʜᴀᴛ ᴍᴀᴋᴇs ʏᴇ think I want *anything* from ye?" Camborne replied with a low growl.

Jocelyn shivered as his gorgeous green eyes bored into her, for her question had made him angry. But he was a Silver Duke, and she was not so naïve as to believe he was helping her merely out of the goodness of his heart.

She was glad he did not want her money. That was a convenient circumstance, since she did not have a ha'penny to give him anyway.

But was it not odd that he seemed to want nothing in return?

Growing up the daughter of an earl, she had learned early on that everybody wanted something from those who were rich and titled. Just because Camborne happened to be rich and titled himself did not mean he wasn't out to claim something from her for himself.

He appeared to approve of her body, if his languid gaze was any indication. He made her tingle every time he looked at her, but he was mostly discreet. Still, she had noticed the flash of heat in his eyes a time or two, especially when she slid her tongue along her fork in order to savor the delicious fare.

Did he believe she was subtly seducing him?

Her fault, of course. Had she not brazenly admitted she might desire a night of passion in his arms? Lord, how could she be so foolish as to confide such a thing to a Silver Duke? Did he now think she was sending him signals?

To her dismay, she hoped so.

After all, her life was in ruins now that she had jilted Ballantry. Why not enjoy a memorable night in Camborne's arms? Despite the rugged look of him, she sensed he would be gentle with her.

She stuffed a chunk of sausage into her mouth while she contemplated what to say next.

Fortunately, he was not awaiting a response from her. "Lass, I will no' claim to have a sterling reputation, but I am no depraved hound," he insisted, continuing to sound offended by her insinuation that he had to want something from her. "I am not expecting *anything* in return for my assistance. Are we clear?"

She nodded as she stuffed more sausage into her mouth, because she truly did not know how to respond to his kindness, nor did she understand why she felt such an aching need for a night of splendor in his arms.

"I'll never be asking ye to do something against yer will," he went on, still indignant. "However, if ye ever wish me to seduce ye, I will gladly do it. But the choice is completely yer own. *Completely* up to ye, Jocelyn. It will not change how I treat ye or what I do for ye in order to protect ye."

She swallowed her last bite, knowing she now had to respond. "I owe you an apology, Camborne. You have been kinder to me than I deserve. I am very grateful."

"Apology and gratitude accepted," he said with a grunt. "And there's nothing more to be discussed about it, lass. Again, ye owe me *nothing*."

She shook her head. "I think I owe you my honesty and my friendship, if you will accept it. Please do. I never meant to insult you. It's just that—and you will certainly understand my feelings, since you experience the same—people always want something from us, don't they? In my heart, I know you are different. But I've protected myself by being wary all of my life. And then I slipped up and made that horribly stupid mistake in accepting to marry Ballantry. I'm just so scared to make another. But I know you are nothing like that awful man. So, please accept my offer of friendship."

The glint of anger in his eyes melted away and he smiled. "Gladly, lass. I've never been friends with a woman before."

The admission surprised her, for he had behaved so kindly toward her, and not with any lascivious intent. She sincerely believed him and trusted that he would never force her into his bed unless she were willing.

Dear heaven.

She was more than willing, but so ashamed to admit it.

How was she to accomplish it when she also wanted to gain his respect? She had lain in his bed last night, and he'd slept beside her. But he hadn't attempted anything. Was this not the mark of a man who could respect a woman? The proof of a man who could honor a wife and consider her a friend and confidante?

Not that he would ever marry her. He was a Silver Duke and had sworn off marriage, hadn't he?

"Are you serious, Camborne? You haven't ever been friends with any woman before?"

"No, lass. Ye'd be the first." He nodded toward her plate, silently urging her to continue her meal. "I'm generally an arse around the fairer sex. I keep away from good girls, as I mentioned to ye last night. I make certain to escort the cold, calculating ladies of the *demimonde* so there is no question my heart will ever be at risk."

She had just taken a sip of her tea, but swallowed hastily in order to respond. "That sounds awful!"

He shrugged.

"Why would you subject yourself to those awful ladies?" She set down her teacup, more interested in hearing him out than finishing her breakfast. "Well, the better question is, why are you so afraid to put your heart at risk? Please tell me. And do not insist on my taking another bite while you talk. My stomach will explode if I so much as nibble on another sausage."

His smile was devastating in its warmth. "All right, lass. The truth is, I came north to do a bit of fishing and contemplate the changes I need to make in my life. And it is in desperate need of changing."

This surprised her, for he appeared so confident and comfortable in the life he had chosen for himself. He also seemed to be a man who had everything—wealth, title, and good looks. Not to mention ladies eager to leap into his bed at a mere nod. Even she was shockingly eager to do this very thing. "What is it that you do not like about your life as it is now?"

"Everything." He arched an eyebrow in response to her look of confusion. "For one, I dinna like myself much."

She inhaled lightly, for this admission was quite a surprise. "Camborne, if you treat others as kindly as you have treated me, then you are a fine man."

"No, lass. I am not so fine as ye think. Ye are unmarried and innocent, so I canno' speak to ye about what men do."

"Yes, you can. Camborne, I am not a naïve goose. I know men keep mistresses and frequent houses of ill repute. You are a bachelor, so who are you hurting by seeing to your urges in this fashion? Or do you hurt these women? Indulge in depravities?"

His eyes widened. "Never! I've never raised a hand to a woman. Nor have I engaged in anything unspeakably foul. Blessed saints, what do ye think I am?"

"I did not say I thought this is what you were. I am merely trying to figure you out." She could tell by the way he treated her that he was no brute. Irreverent and brash, perhaps. Not averse to a night of naughty indulgence. But never cruel. "Tell me more about yourself. What have your engagements with ladies been like up to now?"

"It is better described as purposeful lack of serious engagement." He raked a hand through his hair. "I've kept mistresses on occasion, rare occasion. But never more. In truth, it was always a terrible arrangement. I chose the mercenary ones because I knew I would never grow attached to them. As for falling in love with them? Utterly impossible."

"But you knew that you were capable of loving. Is this not a good thing?"

"No, Jocelyn. Just because I might fall in love with someone does not mean I would know how to treat her properly as my wife. I do not know what a good marriage is or what having a proper family life involves."

"And your own family?" she asked gently.

He shrugged and gave a light snort. "Hardly knew them. I was the youngest and only six years old when I lost my parents and all three older siblings to illness."

"I am so sorry." She took his hand in both of hers. "Who took care of you afterward? And…goodness, does this mean you became a duke at the age of six?"

He nodded. "Well, I had to wait until I came of age to obtain full control and come into all the rights granted unto my title. In the meantime, I was raised by my two uncles. They were more of a board of directors than loving mentors. Neither of them ever married, so there were no women in our lives." He glanced at his hand that she was still holding. "Are ye going to release me, lass?"

In truth, she liked cradling his hand in both of hers. "Do you want me to?"

He chuckled. "Surprisingly, no."

She smiled, for this meant he did not mind her touch.

Well, it could not mean very much, since women often had their hands all over his impossibly fine body. But this was more than mere physical touching. She hoped it was an acceptance of her friendship.

"My family life is not the best at the moment, but I did grow up in a fairly happy family setting," she said. "I could teach you about the benefits of a home life with women in the household. Would you consider allowing me to guide you about this?"

Having to rely on him to pay for everything had left her feeling ill at ease. Not that he made her feel this way, but she was used to taking care of herself, especially during these past five years that her family had grown desperate to marry her off. She had not expected her father to become so angry with her or remain so insistent on her heading to the altar. Yet when she had finally taken the leap and agreed to marry Ballantry, she sensed he was suddenly trying to undermine her every step.

She shook her head, for her father's erratic behavior these past few years still confused her. First, he considered her willful and combative because she would not marry, then he accused her of the same when she finally took the leap and accepted Ballantry's offer. He'd called her stubborn and unreasonable.

Of course, she wasn't going to change. She was the same person she had always been.

Rumors began to circulate that she was mean-spirited, unreasonable, unmanageable, and obviously a harpy. She expected her odious cousins were to blame, for she could not imagine her father ever speaking ill of her to others.

No matter how strongly they disagreed, there had always been love between them. Same for her mother, who was a wonderful woman and had a lot of common sense.

Could she not teach Camborne about growing up in a happy home? Should she not contribute something in exchange for his kindness?

Despite having gained an awful reputation, she was actually a good and kind person. She had plenty of compassion for those who deserved it, often taking the lead in charitable works to help those in need in the Granby area. Surely Camborne could use her assistance.

"You've spent a lifetime dealing with people who wished to manipulate and control you," she said, understanding the toll his childhood losses had taken on him.

"Aye, lass. That is a fact."

"No wonder you have avoided the parson's mousetrap all these years. If you ever took the leap and chose badly, your life would be a misery from then on."

"Ye're right again, lass. This is my dilemma. For all my supposed prowess with women, I dinna know them or understand them."

"I can help you sort it out. Won't you please let me help you? I'm a good listener, and I like to think I am fairly intelligent. Ask all the questions you wish about the fairer sex and how we think, what we worry about, what our hopes and goals are, and I will answer them as best as I can."

Both of his eyebrows shot up. "The idea has merit."

"Yes," she said, giving his hand a light squeeze. "I may not be the woman of your dreams, but I will give you honest answers, and you can trust me to keep our discussions confidential." She cast him a wry smile. "Besides, who am I going to talk to now that my entire family is so furious with me that not one of them will ever speak to me again?"

"Lass, let's get ye some proper clothes and then we can talk into the night, if ye wish. I'll ask the innkeeper for the recommendation of a local modiste."

She nodded. "Do you think they have stylish ladies' shops here?"

"Canno' hurt to ask. We aren't all that far from Aberdeen, and even closer to Dundee. They are both popular cities with an established Society. Nothing as fancy as London, of course. But still sufficiently elegant, and close enough to here that the innkeeper ought to know what a modiste is."

"Care to wager on it?" Jocelyn asked, casting him an impish grin.

He laughed. "No. Ye are far too confident. I only accept the bets I know I can win."

"Drat, too bad," she muttered, casting him a smile. "I was sure you'd be an easy mark. Oh, here comes Mr. Farrell. Care to test this out?"

Camborne arched an eyebrow. "All right."

"What's a modiste?" the innkeeper responded when Camborne asked him.

Jocelyn stifled a grin. Hadn't she just warned him there would be no such fancy establishments here? As beautiful as the town of Arbroth was, life was hard for most, and there was no time for frivolity. No one could afford to toss their coins about freely, paying twice as much as necessary because the shop had an elegant name.

"A modiste is a good seamstress with a sense for fashion and design," she explained to the innkeeper.

"Och, why dinna ye say so? My niece is the best seamstress in town. Even owns her own shop, and all the ladies flock to it. Ye'll find fabrics and notions, everything a fine lady will need. Her shop is just down the high street."

"Thank you, Mr. Farrell," Jocelyn said.

He smiled at her. "Just tell her I sent ye, and she'll treat ye right."

There was an unexpected bite to the wind as she and Camborne walked along the high street a short while later. Well, unexpected for her, since she had lived most of her life in England and rarely came north to these Highlands. It was beautiful here, but quite rugged and cold.

Much like Camborne, she mused.

Except he was not cold at all, not to her. But she sensed he could be ruthless if pushed to it.

Still, was he not as beautiful, and perhaps as wildly dangerous, as this glorious nature? He fit these surroundings and embodied them.

They were close to the North Sea and the strong winds that constantly blew off it. They were also close to mountains and valleys that would become impassable in winter but were stunningly beautiful in summer, with their array of wildflowers, and just as stunning in autumn in their blankets of purple heather.

There was no water bluer or fresher than the waters of the North Sea, and nothing more breathtaking than the deer and goshawks that dotted the landscape just outside of town.

They had not walked two steps down the street before Camborne removed his jacket and wrapped it around her shoulders. "Canno' have ye shivering, lass."

"What about you? Won't you be cold?"

He laughed. "This is hot for me."

She smiled, for did this not just prove her point? He was an embodied spirit of the Highlands. She thought he would look quite magnificent in a kilt. "If you say so."

The scent of him lingered on his jacket, a delightful mix of musk and maleness that she enjoyed breathing in as they walked toward the shop. It was not long before they reached the seamstress's obviously thriving establishment. A pleasant woman who looked to be about ten years older than Jocelyn approached them with a smile. "How may I help ye?"

"Miss Farrell?" Jocelyn asked.

"Aye, that's me."

"Yer uncle at the inn sent us over to ye," Camborne said. "I'm Malcolm MacRae, and this is my wife. We're hoping ye can help her out. Her luggage has not caught up to us yet, and we fear it might be forever lost. She is in dire need of everything."

Warmth curled in Jocelyn's belly when he referred to her as his wife. In truth, it felt so very nice and natural, as the words easily tripped off his tongue. This was not at all the curdling feeling she got whenever Ballantry, that toad of a cheating earl, drew near. But she had only herself to blame for allowing things to progress to their actual wedding day before she came to her senses and ran off.

She also realized Camborne must have wanted to maintain his anonymity, since he did not reveal his title. The inn's proprietor knew who he was but must have been paid handsomely to keep his secret. There was the fact that this man beside her was the handsomest, most commanding, splendid male she had ever encountered. He walked like a duke and spoke with the authority of a duke.

Still, she would respect his wishes and not give him away to any of these shop patrons or its owner.

"Let me have a look at ye, Mrs. MacRae," said Miss Farrell, nodding in approval when Jocelyn handed Camborne back his jacket and then slowly twirled around for inspection. "Och, ye are a pretty thing. No wonder yer husband appears besotted with ye."

She and Camborne grinned at each other.

Miss Farrell then scurried behind a curtain into the back room and returned with an armload of fabric bolts that she spread out on a long table in the center of the shop. The ladies who had come in to purchase ribbons and buttons looked on in curiosity as Jocelyn and Camborne approved all the fabrics Miss Farrell had brought out, including two sturdy muslins—a sapphire blue and an emerald green—and two soft wools in a midnight blue, and another in a dove gray with the palest hint of blue that Camborne claimed captured the crystal splendor of her eyes.

"Can ye have them ready by today?" he asked.

The seamstress immediately advised that it was impossible, and Jocelyn readily agreed. "*Husband*," she said, "you obviously do not realize what goes into sewing a gown."

"Aye, I am quite aware. How much will these cost, Miss Farrell?" He then placed triple the quoted price on the table. "It's all yours if ye deliver the gowns to the inn by suppertime tonight. I'll double it if ye have them ready by teatime."

The seamstress hustled her patrons out of the shop. "We are closed until tomorrow!"

After shutting everyone out but her and Camborne, she scurried once again into the back room and shouted to the ladies who had been sewing in her workroom, "Drop everything! We are going to work on Mrs. MacRae's gowns."

Wasting not a moment, the seamstress steered Jocelyn back there while Camborne was left to wait in the front of the shop. In a trice, she was undressed to her shift, thoroughly measured, fabrics were cut, and then those fabrics were pinned to her shape.

Miss Farrell then began to ask questions about use of lace, silk trims, and preferences for style designs. "Oh, I think just plain will do," Jocelyn answered, only to be immediately overruled by Camborne, who had overheard the questions.

"Dinna listen to my wife," he called from the doorway of the workroom, then simply marched in, muttering something about marrying a skinflint. "She's to have lace, silk, beads... Whatever is needed to fashion a lovely gown."

Having said that, he politely turned his back, stilling Jocelyn's protests. Not that she could have protested, since they were supposed to be husband and wife. He'd seen her wearing nothing but his shirt, anyway.

And how dare he refer to her as a skinflint! She wasn't a miser. Did he not care that she was being considerate of his expenses?

No one thought twice about his invasion of their workroom, since Camborne was wickedly handsome and had been ridiculously generous in offering triple the fee. If he wanted to strip down to his own undergarments and have them measure *him*, they would have done so without qualm or hesitation. Indeed, they would probably enjoy putting their hands all over him, since he had a very fine body. Men his age should not look this good.

Of course, he kept his clothes on and made no such inane suggestion.

But Jocelyn was now wearing only her shift, and it was all she could do not to blush. Camborne, to his credit, did not turn around to ogle her. He kept his gaze to the wall or turned only to speak to the seamstress. "Tell me what ye propose by way of design for these gowns."

Jocelyn had to admit that the innkeeper's niece had a good eye for style. So did Camborne, it turned out. Between the two of them, they came up with some beautiful designs. Once the initial fittings were completed, Camborne asked about undergarments, shawls, gloves, stockings, and hats. They were referred to the haberdasher's next door for all but the undergarments and stockings, which Miss Farrell also carried in her shop.

"Do ye have undergarments of silk and lace?" Camborne asked.

Jocelyn blushed furiously. "Absolutely not! Durable linen will do."

"Not on yer life," Camborne shot back, his eyes gleaming and his grin rakish.

The seamstresses could not hold back their titters. Camborne was enjoying this far too much, as he winked at the ladies, which only encouraged more titters. They compromised and Camborne purchased two of each.

"Honestly," she muttered, shaking her head.

He leaned close and whispered in her ear, "Does no' matter—I'll have them off ye, whichever ones ye're wearing."

Her face burned, for the ladies had heard and were thoroughly charmed by this gorgeous man who appeared to be a devoted husband.

While the seamstress and her helpers worked on her gowns, Jocelyn and Camborne walked next door, where they selected two shawls, a pair of gloves, and two hats. *Dearest,* Jocelyn intoned when Camborne saw another shawl he liked and wanted to buy it for her, "I do not think I need more."

The haberdasher was not about to lose this handsome sale, however. "Mrs. MacRae, this one is silk and meant for evening wear. I'm sure ye and yer husband travel in the finest circles and will be invited by the best families. Ye canno' arrive wearing one of these sensible, but quite plain, woolen shawls. It will shame yer husband, since everyone will think he canno' afford anything better. Ye dinna want that, do ye?"

She turned to Camborne, who was taking far too much pleasure in shopping for her. "Are you certain, *husband*?"

"Aye, Mr. MacGregor is right. In fact, I think ye need two silk shawls."

The haberdasher promptly agreed.

Camborne shot her a conquering grin as he paid for the purchases. "Deliver these items to the Arbroth Inn. But we'll take one of the woolen shawls with us now."

"As ye wish, Mr. MacRae."

They returned to the seamstress's shop, where Jocelyn was once more measured and fitted. Camborne then arranged for the seamstress and her workers to come to the inn at three o'clock for her final fittings. Any alterations would be completed on the spot and the finished gowns left with Jocelyn to enjoy.

"A productive morning's work," he said, obviously pleased with the results.

"I am keeping track of these expenditures, Camborne. You are far too generous. And I am not wearing those silk and lace undergarments, so you may as well save them for your next mistress."

He frowned at the remark.

Jocelyn realized she had insulted him, which was unfair in light of his generosity. "Sorry, that was inconsiderate of me. You have been beyond kind, and I did not mean to sound ungrateful. I should not have said what I did just now. I've never worn silk under my gowns before."

He shrugged. "Do what ye wish with those unmentionables, but ye'll not be repaying me for any expenditures. That discussion is closed."

She and Camborne now had several hours on their own to wander through the quaint town that he seemed to know fairly well. He led her to a beautiful abbey that lay in ruins atop a rise that had a magnificent view of the sea. He showed her where historical documents had been drawn up and signed. Finally, he led her to a local tea shop as the church bells rang to signal the one o'clock hour. "Let's grab a quiet spot and we can talk," he said.

Yes, she was eager to talk to him and get to know him better.

Not that it would ever go beyond these next few days of friendship, because they would part ways once they reached Aberdeen and she got her funds. He would go off fishing, and she… Well, she wasn't certain where she would go, but the world was open to her. Ballantry might chase her as far as London, but hardly beyond.

In truth, once the desperate hunt for her died down, she could settle in Devon or Cornwall and create a new identity, that of a genteel widow who wished to live out her life in quiet comfort. Not that she wished for this outcome, but it might be necessary if her family refused to forgive her and did not accept her back into the fold.

This would sadden her terribly, because she loved her parents. But why not start afresh in a lovely cottage by the sea?

However, none of it would be possible until she got hold of her bank accounts.

There was only one other table occupied as they entered the charming tea shop just off the high street. Two elderly ladies who appeared hard of hearing were talking to each other while sipping tea and nibbling scones, neither one understanding a word of what the other said, since they were merrily chatting away at the same time and talking over each other.

Perfect. Jocelyn and Camborne would not be overheard as they conversed.

Once they had comfortably settled at a corner table, she said, "I think you enjoyed yourself far too much this morning."

"Aye, lass." He chuckled. "Didn't ye have fun, too?"

She nodded. "I felt quite pampered. You really did not have to purchase four gowns and all those accessories for me."

"It was my pleasure," he said with unexpected affection. "I have no one to spend my coin on other than myself, and I have no need of anything."

"You know, if you treat a wife as nicely as you treated me today, you will have no problems in your marriage."

He shook his head. "Och, lass. I hate to disappoint ye, but I must disagree. This is what I do best."

"What do you mean?"

"I buy my way into everyone's good graces. I'm very good at it."

"Oh," she said, dismayed that he thought so little of himself. "But that is not so. People would like you for yourself. You've shown so many fine qualities in the short time I've known you. You never *needed* to bribe me to win my favor. I would have been just as pleased with one sturdy woolen gown and paying you back for it."

"I know, lass." His expression turned serious. "This is why I was more generous with ye than I would have been otherwise. Ye aren't looking to grab something from me."

"How can you say such a thing? I took your room, and obtained a meal and a bath on your account," she said with a gentle laugh. "Don't tell me you have already forgotten?"

He chuckled. "No, lass. Finding ye in my bed is not something I will soon forget. But ye offered to pay me back. In fact, ye're still insisting on it and are obviously put out by my refusing reimbursement. No one else would be. They'd be scheming how to squeeze more out of me."

"I would never do that. However, the amount of money you so casually tossed around made me wonder about your financial acumen," she teased. "Although you surely pleased Miss Farrell and Mr. MacGregor. It was fun to watch their eyes pop wide. It was also nice knowing they were going to make a healthy profit off you and perhaps be able to do something generous with it for themselves and their families." She took his hand into hers.

He grinned. "Ye're holding on to me again. Do ye do this with all yer husbands?"

She laughed lightly once more. "Need I remind you that I am a harpy and no one else will have me? So, no other husbands. But I do like holding your hand. It is big and warm and roughened, the hand of someone not afraid to work. Let's put in our orders and then we can talk further."

"All right, as ye wish. What would ye like to have?"

Jocelyn ordered tea and an apricot tart. Camborne ordered tea and a slice of lemon cake.

After they were served, Jocelyn regarded him for a long moment.

"What are ye thinking now, lass?"

That he looked quite handsome with the hint of a smile on his nicely formed lips and a warm shimmer in his eyes. "I'm trying to take the measure of you."

"Och, I am not all that deep. What ye see is what ye get."

She nodded, although she did not agree that he was someone easy to know. There were hidden depths to him, and he took pains to keep his intimate thoughts and feelings behind a carefully constructed wall.

There was a reason beyond simply being raised by an inept, but well-intentioned, pair of uncles that had him determined never to marry.

Had he ever been in love?

Had someone hurt him deeply?

"All right," she said. "Let's get to it. What would you like to know about these elusive and enigmatic creatures known as women?"

Chapter Four

"Ah, lass. Where do I start?" Malcolm could not recall a time spent with a woman that he had enjoyed more than this day with Jocelyn. There was something comforting and enlivening about her company. Yes, she had an achingly beautiful body and a lovely face, so that he wanted to bed her.

But it was not at all the same feeling as he had with other ladies of his acquaintance. He did not want to bed Jocelyn and leave. In fact, he did not care if they ever went near a bed again. He just wanted to be with her.

Well, that bed *was* important. He could not deny it.

But Jocelyn was someone he would consider a *forever* lass, the sort one came home to night after night, never tiring of seeing the smile on her welcoming face. He'd never felt this way about anyone before, and did not understand why he considered her different from the others.

But she was. There was a compelling difference, although he did not know how he could form such an opinion upon a few hours of acquaintance.

"It isn't so much about the women, Jocelyn. It is more about me and why I dinna want to take a wife. I am nothing like Ballantry. Yes, I have a reputation with the ladies. But it is exaggerated. I dinna chase skirts. They chase me. Sometimes, I am in the mood to be chased. Sometimes, I am not. And I am a man of my word."

She nodded. "So when you take a vow and promise to be faithful, you intend never to break it?"

"Aye, lass. Exactly."

"Unlike that toad, Ballantry," she muttered. "Oh, Camborne. I can never go back to him. I have not stopped berating myself for ever considering him. I may have left him at the altar, but that does not free me of him. What if he wants me back?"

"Do ye think he will?" He cast her an affectionate smile. "Could be he decided ye are more trouble than ye're worth. But seriously, lass, it is all about gaining access to yer wealth for a man like him. If yer wealth does not meet his expectations, he'll drop ye faster than a hot potato. Just how much do ye have?"

She blushed. "Honestly, I don't know the full extent of my assets. This is partly why I wanted to present myself in person at the Aberdeen bank. I should have about ten thousand pounds spread out in various accounts in my name alone, but I've received no information on them for several years now. My father claims all is well and those bankers keep him apprised, but I am starting to have my doubts."

"Why, lass?"

"He refuses to show me any correspondence about them, and will not give me any information on my dowry, either. Should I not have been told more details about the fifty thousand pounds Ballantry was to receive upon our marriage? Yet my father merely tells me not to concern myself with any of it. This is a bad sign, is it not?"

Camborne nodded. "Possibly."

"But it could be a way out of my betrothal if it turns out I am not as wealthy as my father represented to Ballantry." She let out a long breath. "That would be a relief. Ballantry would never want me, if that were so. Of course, I would have to face impoverishment if it turns out my father mismanaged everything and lost the dowry. Truthfully, I do not care. I wouldn't really be impoverished, since I have enough within my own control already to allow me to live out my days in modest comfort."

She stopped and stared at him, grimacing. "Oh, but I am talking about my problems and not yours. I'm so sorry. Some friend I've turned out to be, thinking of myself when it is you that needs the help."

"Dinna be sorry, lass. I think it does not matter what we talk about, but that we talk to each other."

She regarded him with obvious surprise. "That is a very good and enlightened, husbandly thing to say. Did you know that?"

He arched an eyebrow. "No."

"Camborne, you are a man who cares for others, keeps to your word, and does what you feel in your heart is right. Any woman would be fortunate to have such a husband. So it isn't a matter of your not being suitable. It is something else that is holding you back."

"Lass, ye are assuming I need to marry in order to be happy and lead a fulfilled life."

She shook her head. "No, this is obviously something *you* feel you are missing. And yet you will not take that step to commit to any young lady. Oh, but I see your concern. You don't know what qualities will make for a good wife. Having never been in a traditional household, you cannot understand what a wife needs to do to make it function properly."

He pursed his lips. "Do ye not have a housekeeper for that?"

"Yes, a requirement in a large and active household. But I don't mean proper attendance to chores. I am speaking of the subtler values of love and devotion. Sacrifice. Caring. Consideration. A wife who is proud of you and supports you. Who is good and caring to your children and those in your domain who depend on you."

"Aye, these are the qualities I should be looking for. But how do I judge when someone truly holds these values or is just pretending until the knot is tied and I am stuck with her forever?"

"You strike me as a man with good instincts."

He did take pride in his ability to discern cheats, but of the male variety. "They've kept me alive while fighting Napoleon. They've allowed me to invest wisely and increase my wealth. But…"

"You have doubts about your ability to detect fraud and malice in a woman? It is not very different from how you detect it in men. That greedy, calculating look in one's eyes is the same. Pettiness is also easily detected. One merely has to see how the object of your desire acts or reacts when she does not think you are observing her."

He nodded, liking the sound of Jocelyn's voice and her obvious common sense.

"I do not think those natural instincts can be hidden, Camborne. Selfishness, jealousy, and pettiness will eventually come out. What traits do you look for in a good friend?"

"That's an easy question, lass. Honor. Support. Honesty. Someone I can trust will always have my back."

"It is similar to the qualities you ought to seek in a wife. Of course, there's the bedroom aspect to a marriage. One hopes you and your wife will also be compatible in…um, the bedchamber."

"The bedchamber isn't the problem for me. Women leap into my bed." He raked a hand through his hair. "Well, who knows what is real and what is feigned even with that?"

She shook her head. "There are ways to tell if a woman is being honest with you. Your problem is that you never look at them outside of the bedchamber. How are you ever to know their true character if you do not observe them in all aspects of their lives? For example, a young woman might be all smiles for you, but haughty and disdainful of your servants or others they deem beneath their station. The converse is also true—some people are naturally kind and considerate. Forgiving. Willing to make sacrifices to help another. Can you not tell when you walk into a happy household? Or one that is dour and the servants all appear stressed?"

"Go on," he said, fascinated.

"I think these qualities of loyalty, kindness, and trust are a must for a successful marriage, unless the parties have no intention of living under the same roof. Then all of it becomes irrelevant, doesn't it? But a marriage in name only cannot be what you wish for."

"It isn't," he agreed. "What is the point of getting married if ye are gaining nothing but a stranger to add to yer obligations?"

"So, I think it must be a love match for you, Camborne. Or at least a match where there is deep caring by both of you. *Both* must care and be invested in the marriage. Having it all go one way is not good. The sacrifices do not have to be entirely equal, but they cannot be so one-sided as to be unfair."

"Ye seem to know a lot about this, lass."

She nodded. "My parents have a loving relationship, which is why I dread finding out that my father has wasted the dowry funds or misused them. I am not going to do anything about it, no matter what I discover. I would never shame him."

Her declaration surprised him. "Even if he outright stole from you?"

"How can I ever think of it as stealing when it is he who has given me all I have? He has loved me all of my life. If he took something from me, he must have been desperate to do it. I would rather help him through his problems than condemn him."

"Will ye allow me to pose a hypothetical question, Jocelyn?" He now understood why she stood out as different from the others. She had the ability to forgive, to not condemn or pass judgment but look at a situation with compassion.

How far did her compassion extend?

This had always been his worry, that he would make mistakes and hurt those he had pledged to love and protect. A wife. Children.

No one was perfect. Did not everyone make mistakes at some point in their lives?

Perhaps this was what he feared most, to make a misstep, even a small one, and lose everything that mattered to him because of it. This was the helpless feeling he never wanted to experience again. Even now, the recollection of losing his entire family within the span of days because of a ravaging illness tore at his soul.

He had gotten sick first and passed it on to his entire family. With their dying breaths, his parents had insisted it wasn't his fault.

Still, their loss haunted him. Why had he survived when no one else had?

And now, all these years later…was it the pain of loss he was running from?

Aye, perhaps. Losing his loved ones had ripped his heart to shreds. That feeling of loss had never left him. But it had shaped itself into something a little different, something that left him feeling helpless and dreading being put to the test again. What if he still could not save those he had grown to love?

How better to handle this worry than never to love again?

But this was no solution for him, he was coming to realize.

He was ready to open up his heart and fall in love if the right woman came along. But it would be no easy task, for he was now above forty years old and quite cynical. He was well beyond his childhood, but still unable to reconcile losing someone he loved, of having that love destroyed and suddenly taken away. Not only because of illness or sudden death, but because of a mistake he might make.

A disappointment he might cause.

A blame that would never be forgiven.

Was this not what had prevented him from ever moving forward? Having to watch his every step. Never wanting to be trapped in a lifetime prison sentence, always wary of making an innocent error and losing his family's love and trust forever because of it.

Jocelyn might consider it illogical, perhaps irrational, on his part. But there it was…the giant stumbling block he faced.

"Ah, we are to speak in hypothetical terms?" she asked with a delicate arch of one eyebrow. "All right, ask your question and I will answer it as best as I can."

"Assume you and I are married…"

Her eyes, those pretty eyes of hers that were always so expressive, widened. "Married to a Silver Duke?"

"Aye, lass."

"Oh, I am all giddy and elated," she teased, not realizing how serious he was about getting to the heart of his troubles.

Or was she aware and purposely attempting to keep their discussion light?

"Very well." She cast him a soft look. "We are husband and wife. What is it you wish to know?"

"In your opinion, what might I do that ye would deem unforgivable?"

"Unforgivable," she repeated softly, and studied his stoic expression. There was a long pause before she spoke again. "I think a lot would depend on the circumstances. It is not an easy question to answer."

"Give it yer best, lass."

She nodded. "Much would have to do with honesty and expectations, I think. Honesty because even if we did not agree on a matter, we would know where each of us truly stood. Being truthful about our opinions and feelings then allows the other person to make a choice. For example… May I speak about myself again?"

"Aye. Go on."

She shifted in her seat, obviously feeling uncomfortable as their discussion turned more personal. "I knew Ballantry was never going to be faithful to me, but I did not realize just how indiscreet he would be or how disrespectful of my feelings. I assumed a certain level of honor and decorum between us. Well, he promised this to me, and it was written into our betrothal contract because I had insisted on it. Within the hour, he was chasing skirts and hadn't a single care whether my feelings would be hurt. I ought to have begged off my betrothal then and there."

"Why did ye hold on, lass?"

"After the years of fuss and daily hounding about my never marrying, I thought finally becoming a bride might solve the problem. I realized quickly that it wouldn't, but still stubbornly held on." She swallowed hard. "So I lowered my expectations and convinced myself I could endure and lead my own life with as little contact with Ballantry as possible. But as I neared the altar, I knew I was about to throw my life away."

"Ye could not do it, and so ye ran."

"Straight into your bed, fortunately. Well, you could not have been too happy about it. I shudder to think what might have happened to me had the room belonged to someone else. What does this say about me? I was too stupid to plan for the eventuality of becoming a runaway bride even though I knew I could not go through with the wedding. As for Ballantry, there is not enough treasure in the world that would sway me to ever being his wife."

He reached for her hand, and she willingly entwined her slender fingers with his. "I'm glad ye ran from him, Jocelyn."

She nodded again. "I've given thought whether the outcome would have been different had he just been honest with me from the start and simply told me he was going to be a skirt-chasing arse and not give a care about my feelings."

"And?"

"I would not have agreed to a betrothal or a marriage, but I would not have hated him as I do now. He is a liar and a miserable toad. One cannot build a marriage on lies and mistrust."

"So, it is the lies that are unforgivable?"

"Yes, mostly. But so many emotions go into every situation, so it is not easy to say an absolute yes or no. It depends on the willingness of the offending party to show remorse and a determination to change. It also depends on the willingness of a wronged party to show compassion, to try to understand and forgive. I think how deeply hurt one is by the incident also matters. Ballantry's lies could never destroy me because I care nothing for him. Had we married and I found him in bed with another woman, I would have felt relief that it was not me having to endure his touch. But, to get back to your hypothetical about our being married, had it been you in bed with another woman, you taking those marriage vows of faithfulness and honor, and then breaking them? Camborne, that would have destroyed me."

He leaned forward and gave her hand a light squeeze. "But that is no' me, lass. Once I pledge myself to be faithful, then I shall be faithful to my dying day."

"This is why knowing you were with another woman would break my heart, because the complete trust I had in you would be broken. But I would also ask myself what I did to chase you away to the point you felt willing to break those vows you took so seriously."

"Ye would blame yerself?"

"Not blame, exactly. But I would try to look at the entire situation and determine whether it was something I did that contributed to the unhappy outcome. Perhaps this is also important, not merely to cast blame and ignore all that led up to the situation, or simply condemn the other spouse. Yes, one party may be mostly at fault, and I am not suggesting the wounded party ignore their hurt feelings or that they are not justified. But how does tossing hurtful insults at each other help anything? And where is one left if the only thing one has to hold on to is bitterness and anger?"

"I would not cheat," he insisted, trying to take in what Jocelyn said. In truth, he could not imagine himself ever wanting to cheat on someone like her. She was known as a harpy, but he had never met a more compassionate, sensible lady in all his days. Few people, whether men or women, were as fine or could ever measure up to her. He had known her for less than a day and already felt a strong attachment to her.

Why did he feel so roiled when this was not even a real situation and they were merely discussing possibilities?

But truly, the thought of ever betraying someone as kind as Jocelyn sat like a festering lump in his craw.

She sighed. "I am not suggesting you *would* cheat. All I am saying is that if you did—that if someone I considered to be as honorable and trustworthy as you are ever did something like that—it would be devastating to me because of my expectations and the fact that I would probably be in love with you. Because of that strong love, the hurt and betrayal would run very deep."

"So, ye are saying that the deeper one loves, the deeper the hurt, and the less chance of a mistake ever being forgiven?"

"I don't know. That is the truth. I honestly do not know what I would do because my response has to be so sensitive to the facts of the situation. I might forgive, but perhaps never forget that a wrong was done. I might forgive because there was so much good to otherwise counterbalance that mistake, and it would be worth it for me to fight to regain what was lost. Or that wound might be so cutting and painful that I could never forgive."

He raked a hand through his hair. "Lass, ye are only adding to my confusion."

"Because you think there has to be a factual right or wrong answer, but who is to say something is wrong for one married couple and yet right for another? Or that a serious transgression can never be forgiven?"

He groaned. "This is why I will no' marry. Taking on a wife would only addle my brain."

"Not so, Camborne. There is nothing wrong with having one's brain addled from time to time." She cast him a smile, one that made him forget what he was about to tell her. Well, he was going to disagree with her, but it suddenly did not seem important.

If Jocelyn thought it was a good idea to lose one's wits on occasion, then so be it. After all, she had done several rash things and he still liked her very much. Was he not glad she had run away from Ballantry? And wound up in his guest chamber at the Arbroth Inn because she hadn't thought ahead to do something as simple as tuck a coin purse in her gown? It could not cost very much to take a mail coach from Granby to Aberdeen.

He never would have met her except for her mistakes.

He considered her lack of planning as something in her favor, since it showed she did not have a manipulative, scheming nature.

The proprietress interrupted their conversation by bustling over to them and asking if they required anything else.

"Och, no," Malcolm said, patting his stomach. "It was all delicious."

He settled his account and then led Jocelyn back to the inn. The time had flown by, and it was nearing the three o'clock hour. He had no doubt Miss Farrell would be punctual and make it her mission to have all of Jocelyn's gowns ready by teatime in order to collect double her already-extravagant fee.

"Jocelyn! Jocelyn MacRaine, is that you?" a big man with a loud mouth who appeared mildly tipsy called out to her as they passed by the registration desk and were about to head upstairs.

Malcolm recognized the lout as an old schoolboy nemesis of his, one who obviously knew Jocelyn, too. "Bloody hell, what's that boil on the arse of humanity doing here?"

"You know Lord Burling?" she asked with a nervous edge to her voice, tensing noticeably as the gentleman approached. "Oh dear. What am I to say to him? He knows I was to marry Ballantry."

Malcolm took Jocelyn's hand and gave it a reassuring squeeze. "Let me handle it."

She groaned. "Should I be afraid of that?"

"No, lass. Never be afraid when ye're with me."

"Lord Burling," she said with forced merriment as the man slobbered over her hand while attempting to kiss it politely. "What a surprise to encounter you here."

Malcolm knew the pompous lord was not so drunk as to ever mistake him for Jocelyn's intended bridegroom. Nor was he surprised when the lout's blurry gaze fixed on him. "Camborne?" he queried with a hiccup. "Is that you? Ye're not Ballantry. Where's Ballantry?"

When neither of them responded, Burling released an ale-soaked breath and began to leer at Jocelyn. "Has he abandoned the fair maiden already? And Camborne has swooped in to comfort the unhappy bride? I can offer ye comfort, too."

Malcolm drew Jocelyn closer to him. "I see that ye haven't changed, Burling. Ye're still a crass sot."

"And ye're still a womanizing prick," Burling drunkenly shot back. "What are ye doing with Ballantry's wife?"

Jocelyn's eyes were so wide, they looked about ready to tumble from their sockets. She was obviously in panic, and no doubt disgusted by the baseness of the insults exchanged.

Malcolm, however, remained ridiculously calm, as he was about to take a leap across an abyss he had avoided for all of his adult years. "Ye're mistaken, Burling. Jocelyn is *my* wife."

She erupted in a fit of coughing.

"There, there, love," he said, gently patting her back. "I feared ye were coming down with a chill. Yer frock's too light for the Scottish weather. Did I not warn ye it was so?"

She cast him a desperate look. "Camborne…"

"Aye, love? Ye had better run upstairs and tuck yerself into bed. I'll have one of the maids bring up a pot of tea to warm ye, and honey to soothe yer irritated throat."

She did not need more prompting to dart upstairs.

He was now left alone with Burling. "Insult her again and I'll knock out all yer teeth."

"Ye don't scare me, Camborne," Burling retorted. "What happened? Did ye steal her out from under Ballantry's nose? Before or after the wedding? I believe I shall make a detour and pay Ballantry a call. Come on, Camborne. I'm no fool. Ye never married the girl. Ye're a Silver Duke and everyone knows they dinna marry. So, ye just took her, and Ballantry's probably hunting for ye both right now. Hot on yer trail, I expect. Was she worth it? Are ye tired of her yet? Let me know and I'll gladly take her off yer hands. She has an angel's body, but I'll wager she's a hellion in bed. Clawing and scratching yer back, writhing—"

Malcolm punched Burling in the jaw.

Aye, he ought to have restrained himself. But how could he allow the cur to speak of Jocelyn in that disrespectful manner?

"She's my wife," he said with a barely leashed anger. *"My wife.* Till death us do part and all those vows that go along with it."

He glared down at Burling as the arse fell to his knees, wanting to punch him again but knowing it would only draw more notice. He should not have punched him this first time, either. Now the common room was clearing out and its occupants were elbowing each other in order to draw closer and witness their fight.

This was the last thing he and Jocelyn needed, for his constant declaration that they were husband and wife would only draw them deeper into a quagmire.

"Ye'll pay for this, Camborne. Ye think being a duke will protect ye from retribution? Well, it won't." Burling wobbled as he attempted to get back up. "I'll get ye! I swear, I'll get ye."

"Show yer face here again and ye will no' walk out of this inn alive. Get out," Malcolm said, wanting to wring the man's neck. But he held himself back because the oaf was not worth this much trouble.

Malcolm was already nursing bruised knuckles on a hand that had been broken during the war. In truth, his hand was throbbing painfully and a weakened bone could very well have been broken again when he hit Burling, even though he had not struck him all that hard.

Indeed, he had used disciplined restraint. Burling would have been lying unconscious at his feet if he'd unleashed the full impact of the blow.

Well, Malcolm probably would have broken his hand for sure if he had gone at him with full strength. Not that it mattered when Jocelyn's honor was in question.

There was pure venom in Burling's expression as he staggered upright, the two of them now drawing an even larger crowd as they faced off like two raging bulls.

Oh, hell. Jocelyn was not going to like this.

Despite declaring her to be his wife—and oddly, he still felt not a qualm about the consequences of shouting it aloud so everyone would hear—Burling still did not believe him.

This was his blasted Silver Duke reputation to blame.

The Arbroth locals were not aware that Jocelyn was to marry Ballantry or that their wedding should have taken place a few days ago. But the gossip was going to spread like wildfire now. Burling had just referred to him as Camborne and mentioned his title, so all of Arbroth would soon realize he was a duke and not merely a well-to-do but inconsequential merchant by the name of Mr. MacRae. Most had likely put it together already.

Och, the speculation about him and Jocelyn would be rampant. Questions would abound. Why hide his identity unless he wished to hide his affair with Jocelyn? Were they married? Or had she married Ballantry and then abandoned him within hours of the wedding?

What an unholy mess.

"Ballantry will pay good money for this information," Burling muttered, nursing his jaw. "He canno' be pleased that ye've already turned his wife into a—"

He never got out the words, for this time Malcolm knocked the oaf unconscious.

And possibly broke his hand this time.

He felt a searing jolt of pain shoot from his hand straight into his brain. But as the momentary jolt subsided, he carefully felt along his flesh from fingers to wrist and found no bones awry. *Thank goodness.* It was just a bruise and the pain would soon pass.

He turned to the innkeeper, who stood amid the crowd gawking at him. "Is Burling staying here?" Malcolm asked.

"No, Mr. Mac—er, Yer Grace. Um, he's just passing through and stopped in for a meal and a pint of ale."

"Seems he drank the entire barrel," Malcolm muttered. "Get him to his coach and have his driver keep him out of my sight before I have a change of heart and kill him."

Several in the crowd gasped.

Malcolm merely glowered back, for he owed no one any explanations.

But it galled him that Burling would believe Malcolm had despoiled the virgin daughter of the Earl of Granby, stolen her away from her betrothed on a lark, and intended to dump her like rotting rubbish before the week was out.

Who else in the crowd believed it?

Bollocks.

Because of his blasted reputation, they would all think like Burling and wager he had not married Jocelyn.

Well, he *wasn't* married to her…not officially.

Whose business was it other than his and Jocelyn's?

Granted, Ballantry, as well as her parents, might have something to say about it. But Burling had no business in meddling at all, other than to purposely cause trouble.

And could not Malcolm and Jocelyn rightly be considered married, since they had both publicly declared they were husband and wife? These declarations alone should be sufficient even if it fell short of a formal ceremony. What did it matter if their hands were not bound in ribbons as they declared themselves husband and wife? Having made the declarations, would this not mean they would be deemed married under Scottish civil law?

Having punched Burling not once but twice, he knew firmer action had to be taken to protect Jocelyn's reputation. He was a duke of significant stature, and nothing short of a church wedding would quell all rumors and secure Jocelyn's status as his duchess.

Oh, Lord.

His duchess? Was he ready to take on a wife?

Burling regained consciousness as he was being led out by the innkeeper's boys. "What will ye pay me to keep quiet about yer whereabouts, Camborne?" he shouted as Malcolm was about to climb the stairs to return to his guest chamber. Burling was a pig and had always been one even as a boy.

"Tell Ballantry whatever ye wish, but let him know I'll shoot him dead if he dares touch my wife."

Och, he was sinking himself deeper into the quagmire.

My wife. My duchess.

Gad, he'd thought it again.

He had taken this giant leap and would probably die an inglorious death falling into this abyss of his own making. What chance did he have of successfully maintaining a marriage to Jocelyn?

He did rather like the idea of having her permanently in his life...assuming she did not kill him first.

He had assured her that he would take care of matters. Deepening the lie about their marriage was not what she'd had in mind. Nor was punching Burling and causing a scene. And now their true identities were revealed to one and all.

His gut began to churn.

Was his entire mishandling of the Burling situation a mistake she would never forgive?

A Scottish annulment could be obtained quietly upon agreement of the parties, especially since the marriage had not been consummated. They could take care of the matter once he got her safely to

Aberdeen. But he was no churl and knew he also had to offer her a true marriage, if this was what she preferred.

He would honor her wishes, even if it meant being shackled to her for life, for a marriage validly performed under the eyes of the church could not be so easily broken.

"Farewell, Burling. Here's hoping our paths never cross again," Malcolm said, detesting the beady, calculating look in Burling's eyes as well as the man himself.

"Here's hoping ye choke on yer own bile, Camborne!"

"Arse," Malcolm muttered.

The innkeeper hurried to catch up to Malcolm as soon as Burling was hauled away. "Yer Grace," he said in an urgent whisper, "I run a respectable establishment. I... That is... Oh, dear heaven. The lady..."

"Is my *wife*," Malcolm insisted. "I'll flatten the first person who dares repeat that bastard's lie. Duchess Jocelyn is my wife, and that's an end to it."

He stormed upstairs, knowing he had to make things right before the seamstresses came for Jocelyn's final fitting.

He opened the door without bothering to knock, for he was incensed by what had just transpired and wanted to punch his fist through a wall. Of course, that blow would certainly break a bone in his hand that was already sore and throbbing.

Jocelyn was standing in the center of the room, but looked up suddenly as he strode in. She had been crying.

"Blast," he muttered, shutting the door and coming to her side because she appeared so vulnerable and undone. He had to tell her the truth, which would now make matters worse. "Jocelyn, ye know how I told ye that I would take care of Burling?"

She nodded, and then surprised him by wrapping her arms around his waist and hugging him fiercely. "Thank you, Camborne. I knew you were the most wonderful man I had ever met in all my life."

Bollocks. That was a mighty high pedestal from which he was about to topple.

"Och, lass." He wrapped his arms around her, loving the soft give of her body as he held her in his embrace. "Ye may not wish to thank me just yet."

"Oh?" She sniffled and looked up at him. "I shouldn't? Dear heaven. The look on your face. What did you say to him?"

"First, let me assure ye that I did the only thing an honorable man could do to protect ye under the given circumstances." He did not know whether he ought to ease her out of his embrace now or hold on to her for fear she might storm out after he revealed what he had done.

He did not want to let her go because she had a truly exquisite body, and he liked the feel of her against him. Her skin was warm and her scent was that of the sweet apples he adored as a lad, those he would pick at their perfect ripeness and revel in the taste of as he took a bite.

But he chose to ease her out of his arms because they needed to discuss this matter seriously, and he wanted to look at her to judge her reaction.

He was not afraid of what she might do, but how hurt she might feel. Jocelyn was all about feelings, those dreaded little gremlins he always tried his best to avoid.

She was no harpy, either. Despite her reputation, there was little risk she would grab a fire implement and hit him with it. The gossip about her being an evil-tempered hag was cruel and untrue.

"Ye see, Jocelyn…" he said to the beautiful lass who had a kind and loving heart—or so he hoped, because this discussion would not go well otherwise.

"Yes?" She held her breath and continued to gaze at him with her dazzling blue orbs.

"That cur was threatening ye, trying to bribe me to pay him off or he would report yer whereabouts to Ballantry."

She let out the breath she had been holding. "Did you curse at him? Did you buckle under to his threat?"

"Me? Buckle under?"

"No, you would never give in to blackmail," she said with a nod. "I'm proud of you. He's another horrid toad, just like Ballantry."

"Och, lass." He raked a hand through his hair. "Ye will no' be proud of me when I tell ye what I did."

She groaned lightly and stared up at him. "What did you do?"

"Something I'm not sure ye're going to like."

"Camborne, out with it," she said. "What did you do?"

Malcolm released a heavy breath. "I hit him…and then I hit him again."

She gasped. "Did you kill him?"

"No, but only because I held back."

"Thank goodness," she muttered.

"He was conscious and swearing at me as he left."

The obvious tension in her body eased. "Oh, but that's all right, then. Isn't it? No maiming and no murder?"

"Aye, lass. He'll live into his dotage, no doubt. Scum like that often do. I'm not sorry I hit him." But he winced as he curled his hand into a fist.

Jocelyn had been looking at him and noticed that wince. "Did you break your hand?"

She reached out to take it, but he drew it away. "No, it's merely bruised. It'll heal fast. I'd do it again, if I had to. The cur deserved a beating to shut his foul mouth. But…"

"But?" Her frowning gaze fixed on him once more. "Oh, Camborne. What else did you do that you are reluctant to tell me?"

He raked a hand through his hair again. "I told him we were married. I shouted it loud enough for everyone to hear because we had drawn quite a crowd after I punched him. We exchanged curses and insults. But the point I am trying to make is that everyone now knows

I am the Duke of Camborne because Burling yelled it out in response to my bellowing he was a piece of offal."

She slapped her forehead, then dropped her hand to her side with a lengthy sigh. "Go on. Tell me the rest of it."

"So, this is no longer a mere incident where a wealthy commoner had an altercation with a lord of little consequence. Now everyone knows who I am and…"

"Oh, no. And what?"

"What choice did I have once my identity was no longer a secret shared with just the local innkeeper? Burling was about to make offensive comments about ye, elevating the scandalous consequences because of who I was. I had to declare ye were my wife. I shouted it for everyone in the common room to hear. What else could I do? I was no' going to let him shame ye, Jocelyn."

She looked like a pretty fish, for her lips were pursed and her mouth was opening and closing, but nothing was coming out.

"This leaves us with little choice," he continued. "If I dinna marry ye, then ye will indeed be shamed forever, because word has now gotten out and will soon spread throughout Scotland. This is no longer some little incident to titillate Arbroth residents. This is a scandal of monumental proportions that will likely reach as far as London."

She said nothing, just continued to stare at him.

Was she in shock?

"Och, will you no' say something? After my roaring at Burling—and I will accept full blame for that—we've lost all chance of keeping this deception strictly to ourselves. Well, the innkeeper was told we were married and now suspects I lied to him. But I assured him it was no lie. So, there ye have it. I'm thinking we'll need a quick marriage, a real ceremony, to protect ye. No harm done."

"No harm done?" she repeated with a dismayed laugh.

"Och, lass. I know I disappointed ye." But how was this any worse than the lies they both were already telling? Had she not herself declared they were married when she took over his room? Nor had either of them corrected the innkeeper or his staff when they had the chance. *Then* they'd both lied about being husband and wife to the seamstress and her ladies.

"Oh, Camborne. Only a handful of people in Arbroth had any interest in us, and most of them had no idea who you really were. And now we've leaped to every man, woman, and sheep in Scotland and possibly England knowing you are the Duke of Camborne? Every gossip rag will sell out within minutes when they carry the headline story of the Earl of Granby's daughter—the very harpy who ran off on her wedding day, no less—found cavorting with a Silver Duke."

"Aye, lass. That's it in a nutshell." He caught himself as he was about to rake a hand through his hair again. He would go bald if he did not stop doing this. "I have no doubt Burling will go out of his way to report this scandal to Ballantry."

"Or the gossip rags if Ballantry refuses to pay up. What do you really suggest as a solution?"

He released a breath, not quite daring to feel relief yet, but hopeful she would remain calm and not come at him like a shrieking banshee. "I'm *really* suggesting that I need to marry ye properly. I believe I have already suggested it as a means to avoid any scandal and protect yer honor. But now I must insist on it."

Jocelyn regarded him in disbelief. "Are you seriously willing to leap into the fire and marry me?"

"Aye, without question. There is no other choice. It *needs* to be done."

Lord, she was a pretty thing. Had he already ruined any chance he might have had with her?

"You? Are seriously offering to marry me?"

"Aye. Do ye think ye can look a little more pleased by the suggestion?"

Why was she making this so difficult? He was proposing to her, wasn't he? A *Silver Duke* proposing to her. All she had to do was accept and the scandal would go away.

Not only would it go away, but she would be married to a duke, the Holy Grail of every marriage-minded mama and daughter of marriageable age. Problem solved.

"Why should I feel pleased that our lies have trapped us in this situation?" she asked. "Or that your proposal is an offer made out of necessity due to reasons of shame and obligation? I know you feel obligated to protect my reputation."

"Aye, I do. Only a cur would leave ye dishonored. It is generous of ye to call it *our* lies when I was the one who lost my temper at Burling and turned this into a greater fiasco than necessary. Having done so, I dinna see any way out of this for ye but to become my duchess. It is very possible we are already considered to be married because of our declarations."

"Like a handfasting of a sort? It is not valid in England."

"But we are in Scotland, Jocelyn. Whether people accept that we are handfasted or have legally declared ourselves married, or whether they think I've seduced ye into running off with me and have now ruined ye…it makes no difference. The damage has been done. With the intensity of the scandal that is about to break, we cannot rely on half measures. Ye need to marry me under the eyes of the church. It is the only way I know how to properly protect ye."

"Do you not see the problem, Camborne? You keep saying you feel a *need* to marry me. But do you *want* to marry me?"

"Do not give me a hard time about this. I refuse to turn this into a discussion about feelings, because ye know mine are jumbled and I'm going to say the wrong thing. I *want* to marry ye, lass. It would be my greatest shame to see ye hurt because of me."

She stared at him for another long moment. These long pauses and contemplative looks of hers were putting him further on edge.

"Do you think you could be happy with me?" she finally asked, her voice so gentle and sweet in its hopefulness that it pained him.

He raked a hand through his hair yet again. Aye, he was certain he would go bald if he kept doing this. But she was asking him about feelings, and he was obviously the wrong man to ask about those perplexing emotions because he had spent a lifetime avoiding and suppressing them. "I dinna know. That's the honest answer. But I do know that I have never felt this protective of anyone before. Nor have I ever enjoyed a lady's company as much as I have enjoyed yours."

She was staring at him again. Was she going to hit him?

But she threw her arms around his waist and leaned her head against his chest. "Thank you."

"What?"

"I said thank you." She looked up at him and smiled.

"Then ye're not angry with me?" *Oh, Lord*. He had not a clue what was going on, but she had a beautiful smile for him, and that was good enough.

She nodded. "I am not angry, only sorry that I have caught you up in a mess of my own making. However, I would never recommend you for the diplomatic corps."

He laughed and hugged her. "Lass, dare I ask? What did I do right?"

"Is it not obvious? Well, I suppose it isn't if you are asking me this question. You were *honest* with me. You were honest about all of it, the blowing up at Burling and your determination to make it right. Most of all, knowing how averse you are to marriage, you stepped up to do whatever you felt was needed to protect me."

He smiled back at her. "Aye, I did do that. I will always do whatever is needed to protect ye, lass."

"Another brilliant answer. Thank you. But do you understand why I needed to ask you these questions?"

"No, lass. Care to explain?"

"The only reason I questioned your proposal of marriage was out of concern for *you*."

"For me?" When had anyone given a fig about his feelings? Certainly not his uncles when he was a child. They were not cruel, just inept. Anyway, they had long since passed on. Nor had the ladies he escorted around London ever cared beyond the trinkets he could give them.

But Jocelyn was expressing concern for *him*?

He shook his head, not quite believing what he was hearing.

"Camborne, it was never my intention to burden you with an unwanted wife. No one is going to marry me anyway, so I am not worried about the damage to my reputation. It isn't going to chase away any gentlemen callers that I never had in the first place. This is why I asked about how you felt. You've given me shelter, food, and clothes that include silk unmentionables," she said with a light laugh. "I was not going to force you to give your *life* over to me as well."

He placed his hands gently upon her shoulders and stared at her for a long moment. "Jocelyn, am I permitted to change my answer?"

"Are you rescinding your offer of marriage?"

"No, lass. If anything, I want to marry ye more than ever."

"You do? Oh, then thank you again." She let out a soft breath and cast him another radiant smile. "What answer are you seeking to change? And to what question?"

"Ye asked whether I *wanted* to marry ye or *needed* to marry ye," he said with a soft growl.

"And?"

"Lass, I do want to marry ye. I want to marry ye something fierce, because I dinna think I could ever be as happy being without ye as I am being with ye. Therefore, it is not only a need for my sense of honor to protect ye, but a *want* from the very depths of my heart because this past day with ye has been the most enjoyable one I have ever spent. Will ye have me?"

Her response was interrupted by a knock at their door.

"That will be Miss Farrell and her seamstresses," Jocelyn said, easing out of his arms and laughing softly as he released a string of invective.

"Lass, will ye?" He held her back when she started for the door. "Dinna torture me by making me wait until yer fittings are over."

She stood on tiptoes and kissed him along the scar on his cheek. "Yes, Camborne. My heart is soaring because I have never met a finer man than you. Three days ago, I felt doomed and miserable. Today, I feel relieved and happy. I will gladly marry you."

She squealed as he picked her up and twirled her around. "This very afternoon, lass?"

"No, you big ape. I doubt any minister will conduct a ceremony at this late hour."

"Have ye learned nothing yet about the power of wealth? Everyone has their price." He set her down, since she was trying to wriggle out of his arms to respond to the knock at their door, and he did not want her tumbling to the floor.

"I don't have a price," she insisted, standing before him with her hands on her hips and a frown on her lovely face.

"Lass, ye do." He gave her cheek a light caress. "Yer price is love and respect. It just isn't anything with an easily determined monetary value."

The knock came a little harder.

Malcolm strode to the door and allowed Miss Farrell and her ladies in. They scampered in like a herd of squirrels. He knew it was best to remain out of the way. Besides, he had a marriage license to obtain.

"I have a few errands to run that shouldn't take long. I'll be having an ale in the common room upon my return. There's where I'll be if ye have need of me."

Miss Farrell gave him a curt nod. "I'm sure we shall have no need to disturb ye. We have it all in hand, Yer Grace."

He paused as he was about to stride out the door. "Ye know I am

Camborne?"

She winced as she nodded again. "There was a horrible man shouting it through the streets as his carriage drove out of town, and…" She turned in dismay toward Jocelyn. "Casting vile aspersions about yer lovely wife. I'm so sorry," she said. "We know not a word of it is true."

"Thank you, Miss Farrell," Jocelyn said, obviously relieved and quite appreciative.

Malcolm was not quite as overjoyed. He understood the power of money. Miss Farrell was never going to say anything to put her fat fee at risk. But did anyone in Arbroth truly believe he and Jocelyn were married?

And what was it about Jocelyn that made him care so much about protecting her reputation?

But he did care, and this was another concern for him.

Why did everything about her feel so *right*?

Chapter Five

Jocelyn's tension eased when the seamstress and her staff immediately set to work on the final alterations and did not ask questions about her marriage to Camborne that had never taken place. She prayed he had the sense to keep quiet about their nonexistent wedding, too.

These dukes sometimes had too much confidence in their power and did not always see a problem so clearly. Not only was Camborne a duke, but a Silver Duke. This meant he had gained an overblown confidence because he was adored and pampered by everyone, especially the ladies, everywhere he went.

She breathed a sigh of relief when the final fittings were completed and the seamstresses set about making the small adjustments needed to deliver the finished product. It was almost teatime. Miss Farrell and her ladies had five minutes to hand over the gowns and claim double their outrageous fee.

For this reason, not one of them wasted a moment in idle chatter or even looked up when Camborne strolled back into their quarters to escort Jocelyn down to tea. "Ready?" he asked.

She hesitated to take his offered arm. "Um…almost. I…ah…"

He grinned. "Ye are truly softhearted. Ye're no' going to walk out of here until the last minute because ye want to be sure the gowns are turned over to ye and Miss Farrell gets her reward."

She nodded. "Are you angry?"

"Och, no. Do ye think I would have ye as my wife if ye did no' have this kindness in yer heart?" He drew out his fob watch and noted the time. "Will ye look at that—there's still fifteen minutes to spare before the inn's tea service starts. The clocks downstairs must all be wrong."

Miss Farrell, who had been listening in on their conversation, glanced up in surprise and smiled at him.

Jocelyn, taking full advantage of being his imaginary wife, kissed him on the cheek. "You are a wonderful man."

Twelve minutes later, the gowns were completed and handed over to Jocelyn. The workmanship was excellent despite the breakneck speed at which they were made. "Thank you, Miss Farrell. These are truly beautiful. I shall wear them with great pleasure."

Camborne looked on, not at all bothered by the fact that he was about to turn over an outrageous sum to the seamstress, which he did on the spot. "I am a man of my word," he said, also expressing his gratitude for her taking such good care of his wife.

"An honor serving ye," Miss Farrell responded. She and her staff bustled out.

Jocelyn heard them giggling with glee as they scurried down the stairs and raced out of the inn. No doubt they were heading straight to her shop to divide their earnings. She hoped Miss Farrell had the wherewithal to hide her share in a secure location. The seamstress was a thrifty businesswoman, and the windfall was going to be applied somewhere useful once she decided what to do with it.

Camborne had his arms folded across his chest and looked wickedly handsome as he reclaimed Jocelyn's attention with a deliciously engaging smile. "Shall we go down to tea now?"

She nodded. "Thank you for being so generous to these ladies. When we get to Aberdeen, I think I ought to reim—"

"Lass, ye're not going to reimburse me. Put it out of your lovely, stubborn head. Ye know the cost is meaningless to me. But what matters is that ye will no' freeze to death now that ye have suitably warm clothes."

"Freeze in August? There is little chance of that."

He shook his head. "Ye haven't spent much time in these Highlands, have ye?"

"No," she admitted. "My parents thought it more important for me to gain *ton* polish, so I spent most of my life in England training to be a proper wifely consort to a nobleman. But it is beautiful here. I've enjoyed everything you've shown me. Those abbey ruins were hauntingly magnificent. Well, I suppose magnificent is not a proper description, since this hallowed ground holds so much tragedy."

"Aye," he said thoughtfully. "The damage and destruction wreaked in the name of piety is a disgrace. All those innocent lives lost, murdered in the name of righteousness." He shook his head. "Bah! Men will always find idiotic reasons to fight. I'm sure jealousy, greed, and envy have existed since the beginning of time."

"You fought in the war against Napoleon," she remarked, glancing at the prominent scar that had been absorbed into his rugged facial features.

His eyes held the wisdom of the ages. They were a passage into his soul and filled with depth, but they were also sharp and beautiful, though tinged with a hint of sadness. His mouth was broad and his lips nicely shaped. His nose was prominent but sleek and solid, and his cheekbones gave his face that hard-as-rock, chiseled look.

However, every feature fell into place with natural splendor, even the dusting of silver threaded through his chestnut hair, creating the striking handsomeness of his appearance.

She shook out of the thought as he began to speak.

"This war, as all wars are, was harsh and futile. Napoleon ought to have known he would never win, but his thirst for power would not be quenched." He appeared ready to say more, then shook his head and held out his arm to her. "Do ye mind if we end this conversation?

I'm feeling a thirst for tea. Let's take seats in the common room and figure out the rest of our trip."

She placed her hand in the crook of his arm, which felt muscled and solid. "All right."

"But first, are we agreed that we need to properly marry as soon as possible, lass?"

"Yes, as soon as possible," she said, and began to walk out of the bedchamber, but he held her back another moment. "Is there something more?"

"Aye, lass. I have something else to tell ye."

"Oh, no. What else did you do?"

He held up his hands in mock surrender and cast her an appealing grin. Well, *everything* about him appealed to her. "Nothing bad, I promise. While the ladies were fussing about yer gowns, I sought out the local minister."

"Oh?"

"I've made arrangements for our wedding ceremony. It's to take place first thing tomorrow morning. I could no' in my heart allow even tonight to pass with ye unmarried and sharing my bed. But he insisted that he could not marry us today. So ye'll now be spending two nights outside of wedlock in my bed. I'm sorry, lass."

She wasn't in the least. Two nights with this duke? She could not wait until they retired for the evening. Was this sinful of her?

"I could sleep on the fl—" he began, but she cut him short.

"No. We'll share the bed as we did last night." She would rather be sleeping beside him while married, of course. But simply being beside him, even without sacred vows exchanged, was better than not being with him at all.

He gave a curt nod. "I promised the minister a fat donation to keep him quiet about our situation. I told him I would pay off the witnesses, too. Aye, it was an outright offer of a bribe. But ye'd be proud of me, Jocelyn."

"I would?" she asked with the arch of her brow, struggling to contain the urge to laugh. There was something quite charming about Camborne. For all his good looks, wealth, and power, he was remarkably uncertain of himself when dealing with ladies in matters outside of seduction. Yet he was endearingly earnest in his desire to do right by her.

"Aye, lass. I was tactful and called the witness bribe a gratuity. Either way, it was a price paid for their silence. Dinna condemn me for it. Ye must agree that we have to marry under the eyes of the Lord to protect ye. But it also has to be done discreetly, or else everyone in Arbroth will know we've been lying to them. To suspect is one thing, but to know it for a certainty…"

"I agree." Jocelyn stared up at him. She could easily fall in love with this man. He had the most honorable instincts she had ever encountered, for he had yet to cast any blame on her when she was clearly the one who had incited this entire mess. "I truly feel wretched about my dishonesty, because these residents of Arbroth are such lovely people."

"We were both dishonest with them."

"But your motives were more valiant," she said, casting him a wan smile. "I was just trying to take advantage of you."

He returned her smile with an affectionate one. "Am I complaining? I could have turned ye out last night. Instead, I went along with yer ruse. And before ye absolve me of any wrongdoing, I knew the consequences of being caught with ye in my bed. Dinna ask me why I was willing to take the risk, for I dinna quite understand it myself. I just knew I could no' turn ye out."

"And now you are stepping up to marry me," she said, feeling quite a bit of remorse for forcing him to it.

For herself, she was elated. She could not have made a better choice for herself than Camborne. Her fear was in disappointing him. Was it possible for a love match to blossom from such frail beginnings?

"We are not going to confess the truth, Jocelyn. I know it is not a wise thing to start off a marriage with dishonesty, but it is not quite the same. We have been honest with each other. Mutually dishonest with others. So, do not think ye are being noble minded by taking the brunt of the censure upon yer shoulders. I'll never allow it."

"I must thank you again."

"No, lass. None required. I'm just sorry ye will no' have the elegant wedding ye were probably dreaming about ever since ye were a wee lass. I considered having us wait until Aberdeen so I could marry ye in a grander church—the city is big enough to provide us a measure of anonymity. But considering Burling's reprehensible character, and the possibility that Ballantry is already closing in on ye…"

"I know. There is not a moment to lose. As for that elegant wedding," she said, grimacing at the thought, "I was in the midst of it when I ran away from Ballantry. I left him and over one hundred guests wondering what had happened to me. So, no more fancy weddings for me. A quiet one here in Arbroth is perfect."

"Then we are of the same mind? Marriage in Arbroth it is."

She nodded. "Yes, without question this is best. We would then arrive in Aberdeen as husband and wife, and no banker is going to deny me access to my funds while my husband, the Duke of Camborne, is standing by my side. Anyway, Aberdeen is likely where Ballantry and my parents will be waiting for me, since it is one of the few places where I can access my funds. You suggested as much, and I agree with you. However, I hope we can get in and out without incident."

"No reason why this cannot happen. No one will look twice at a carriage that does no' bear my ducal crest. I travel in an unmarked carriage for the purpose of attracting as little attention as possible," Camborne said.

"That did not work out too well for you in Arbroth, did it?" she remarked with a gentle laugh. "I stumbled into your bed and created this uproar."

"My life was becoming too dull," he said with a smile. "Perhaps ye were just what I needed to liven it up. If yer family and former betrothed are in Aberdeen ahead of us and watching for ye, I can go into yer bank alone and make whatever arrangements are necessary. They'll not spot ye until ye are ready to be seen."

"Unless Burling has found them first and told them about us. Then they will be on the lookout for you, too."

"Aye, that could be a problem. We'll deal with it when the time comes," he said with a shrug. "Yer father isn't going to remain angry once he realizes ye've married a duke instead of that rat-faced earl."

"Camborne, if all goes smoothly and we are married by tomorrow morning..."

He arched an eyebrow. "What is it, lass?"

"You were heading up to your lodge in order to hide away and fish. Would you consider allowing me to join you?"

The notion appeared to surprise him. "We go there together?"

She nodded. "We could even head straight up there instead of stopping in Aberdeen first, if you prefer. I mean, once we are married, what is the urgency of getting hold of my funds? We could always stop there on the way home."

"Home?" He stared at her for an uncomfortably long moment.

She gasped, suddenly realizing the reason for his apparent concern. "Oh! I'm so sorry for presuming... I got ahead of myself. We did not discuss anything about what is to happen to us after the wedding. Do you even want me with you? Are we to part ways in Aberdeen as soon as we get hold of my accounts? I would not blame you if you wanted me out of your life as soon as possible. I just thought... Well, I haven't really been thinking, have I? Not about my marriage to Ballantry. Not about my running away. Not about—"

"Lass, there's no reason for ye to get all wound up," he said, giving her shoulder a gentle stroke. "Let's just go downstairs and enjoy a cup of tea. All right?"

"Yes, all right." She took his arm and he led her downstairs into the common room, where sweets and savories had been laid out in a decorative display upon a long table against the wall.

Camborne led her to an empty table in the corner, away from most of the crowd. Everyone was surreptitiously eyeing them, but he did not appear to be affected by everyone's stares. He was used to having all eyes on him the moment he strode into a room, she guessed.

After escorting her to her seat, he strode to the long table and prepared plates for both of them. In the meanwhile, one of the inn's maids came around and poured tea into their cups.

Camborne returned and continued to appear quite relaxed as he settled in the chair beside her, still not troubled at all by the looks cast their way. This was a good thing, she supposed. The more naturally he behaved, the more likely the patrons were to believe they truly were married and not lying through their teeth.

"Jocelyn," he said in that delicious brogue that never failed to warm her insides.

"Yes?"

"Ye mentioned making plans for after we are wed."

"It is important. We need to know where we stand with each other. What each of us expects from the marriage. We really should talk about this."

"I dinna know if it is wise to do it here and now, lass. Ye're going to make me think about that discussion we had earlier, the one about expectations and sacrifice."

She blushed, recalling what she had told him. She had spoken to him as though she were an expert on such matters when she really had no experience at all. How could she expect anything more from him than what he had already given her?

"And what is wrong with getting to the heart of what our marriage is to be? Should we not be thinking about these things? Not necessarily to make any immediate decisions, but shouldn't we know what the other is thinking?"

He stared at her with a terribly serious expression on his face. "I want yer promise, lass."

"About what?"

"No matter what comes from this conversation, ye'll marry me tomorrow."

"Even if what I wish from the marriage is completely opposite to what you want?"

He nodded. "Aye. There's nothing ye can tell me that would be worse than my leaving ye unmarried to fend for yerself against yer family, yer friends and acquaintances, a vicious *ton*, and malicious strangers who think to lift themselves by treading on ye. I'll never let that happen to ye."

"You do realize this is completely to my advantage and all to your disadvantage."

"I am not disadvantaged by it. Do I have yer promise?"

"Yes, with my gratitude."

"So, now that we are going to talk about our marriage... What would ye care to do once we are lawfully wed?" He shook his head. "Dinna tell me what ye think I wish to hear. And dinna give me a *forever* answer right away."

She frowned, not certain what this meant. "What is a *forever* answer?"

"One that binds ye to me forever. Our plans need only be for a month in the future, or however long it takes for us to get ye free of Ballantry and secure yer funds. As for longer term, this is something we both need to think about as we get to know each other better, isn't it?"

She nodded, realizing she had not given the matter proper thought and had just gone with her heart. One might say she had fallen in love with Camborne at first sight because he was that perfect combination of handsome, smart, and wonderfully irreverent that proved irresistible to her.

Of course, it was ridiculous to believe an immediate attraction could be so strong and genuine as to be called love. But to call it mere infatuation did not give her feelings their proper due. She was no silly schoolgirl to giggle over a handsome boy. No, her feelings for Camborne were much more than childish attraction.

He melted her heart. She wanted to remain by his side for always and make this a real marriage, if he would allow it.

But what if he did not want this? What could she say if he chose to return to his Silver Duke life and tuck her away somewhere out of sight? She could not blame him, nor could she expect him to give up everything to tie himself to her when none of this was his fault.

And yet he was so unlike Ballantry. It was quite possible Camborne would desire a true marriage. This lightened her worries and gave her a glimmer of hope.

"Do you want children?" she asked abruptly.

He set his teacup down with a clatter and his face paled. "Children?"

"Yes," she said with a light laugh, hoping to keep the conversation casual. Perhaps she should not have led with that question.

Good grief. What was she thinking to hit him over the head with that hammer? Who leaped ahead to asking questions about offspring upon a day's acquaintance? It was a bit much, wasn't it? She did not even understand why this was the first question she had blurted. However, now that she had asked it, she did not want him to avoid a response.

"You know, those little creatures with sticky hands and constantly runny noses," she continued.

He chuckled. "Aye, I was one of those once. Eons ago."

"I would like to have children," she said quietly.

And yet this was such a huge demand of him. He had never married. What if he did not want them? More important, what if he did not want them with *her*? After all, her every action from the day of her wedding up to now had been witless. She could not blame him if he cut this conversation short and begged off their marriage.

However, she pressed on because she wanted to know whether it was even a possibility. Not that his answer was going to change their situation. She had to marry him or her life would be a disaster. In truth, she would have no life, since everyone down to the village ratcatcher would shun the shameless harpy who had jilted an earl on their wedding day to cavort in the bed of a Silver Duke.

Her choice was to marry Camborne and immediately become a respected and powerful duchess, or not marry him and be reviled, subjected to names much worse than harpy.

But to pursue this matter of children?

She tried to keep her expression as unreadable as his own, but she was not good at this, and he had to be seeing straight into her heart. "It is something I desire, although I would understand if you felt the opposite. Who is to say I am even able to have children at my age?"

He placed his hand gently atop hers. "Twenty-seven is hardly decrepit. Jocelyn, ye look like an angel."

"Hardly, but thank you. I'm sorry I shoved this at you. In truth, I'm not sure why it was the first thing out of my mouth. Had I felt more maternal, I would have accepted the best offer received in my debut Season and started working on getting those children. But I could not even think about it when none of those men who came forward interested me. I would not have been able to bear their touch."

"And ye think ye can bear mine?" he asked, still holding on to her hand.

She let out a long breath. "Yes. I think I might even grow to crave it, to be honest. But I'm sure other ladies have told you the same thing.

I'm just one among many."

"No, lass. Those others were merely pandering to me. Ye're different."

"Well, I thought I should be truthful with you before we take the leap and marry. You made me promise to marry you, but I have not insisted you do the same. I could release you from—"

"Absolutely not. It will change nothing about our need to wed. I'll be marrying ye no matter what future marital arrangements are decided upon. This is not up for discussion. That matter is resolved."

"All right." She made no further protest because this situation truly was to her advantage. More important, she sensed he was not the sort to marry and then abandon his bride.

Not that she knew him so well, but he appeared to be a man who would take his vows seriously. Despite all this talk of not deciding on their future just yet, she knew that if he promised to be faithful to her in their marriage vows, then he was going to keep to his word. He was going to do all in his power to be a good husband to her and make this marriage work.

She hoped.

"My thinking, lass," he said, "is that we ought to stay together at least for the rest of this month."

She was ready to stay with him for a lifetime. "I agree." If he wished to take it a month at a time, that was fine with her.

"I say this because Burling might incite Ballantry to take revenge beyond a mere financial settlement. I will not have ye insulted or demeaned, or have him attempt worse if I am not around to protect ye."

"Why are you mentioning a financial settlement? I will never give Ballantry a ha'penny. He's a lying, cheating wastrel."

"Jocelyn, sometimes these things are easiest resolved with a bit of coin exchanging hands. So what if he gets a little out of it? You'd be gaining yer freedom by cutting all ties to him."

"Are you suggesting I ought to *bribe* Ballantry to keep him quiet?" She tipped her head up in indignation. "Or should I politely call it a gratuity? And what of Burling? I won't give in to that oaf, either. Those funds are mine, and Ballantry will never get his greedy paws on any of it because he is the cur who broke our betrothal contract first, and I'll go to my death proclaiming he is an undeserving wretch."

Camborne grinned. "Are ye through being incensed?"

She cast him a wry smile. "Yes. Spleen vented. I know I have to be practical about this, even if it is the most galling thing imaginable."

"Will ye leave the matter up to me, lass? I'll have it settled as quietly as possible."

She tried to suppress her laughter, but it came out in little snorts. "Sorry. You handled Burling so…so…"

"Poorly?"

"Your words. I doubt I would have handled him any better. But you must admit to a few missteps. If not for the scene you caused, I would not be getting married now."

Camborne grinned. "Who knows? Ye still might have gotten that proposal out of me, but it would have taken a bit longer than a day."

"Right," she said with a roll of her eyes.

If the most beautiful women in England and Scotland could not have snared this Silver Duke, she was not likely to have caught him either.

Which made her think of the unfairness of what she was doing to him, and this sent a pang through her heart. However, she was not going to say anything to him, because he truly did not appear heartsick over their situation.

Why was he so accepting of his fate?

"He'll get nothing of yours," Camborne said, regaining her attention as he emitted a low growl. "However, I'll pay Ballantry whatever it takes to make this betrothal problem go away. As for Burling, if he opens his mouth, I'll knock out all his teeth."

"Then you'll wind up with a broken hand."

He glanced at his still-swollen knuckles. "It is a small sacrifice."

She let out a resigned breath. "No, you needn't hit him. If he approaches us, then I will pay him to silence him."

"No, lass. Let me handle the matter."

She arched an eyebrow. "As you did earlier?"

"Maybe," he said with a wincing grin, appearing to completely lack remorse for dropping the cur to his knees in front of all the occupants of the inn. "Never underestimate the power of greed, lass. Burling has malice in his heart and thinks ye'll pay dearly for it. But he knows I will kill him if provoked. So, I do the negotiating with Burling and Ballantry. Ye'll stay out of it because yer heart's too soft and they will trample it."

"I'm not a very good harpy, am I?"

He cast her an affectionate smile. "No, lass."

"Camborne, I am so very grateful for your assistance and protection."

"Ye've already said so, lass. Ye dinna need to thank me again when I've made a fair bollocks of the situation."

"No more than I have." She emitted a light laugh. "But I'll keep that in mind next time you assure me that you have matters under control and allow me to walk away."

Mr. Farrell approached them to ask if all was to their satisfaction.

Jocelyn nodded. "It is all excellent. And thank you for the recommendation of your niece. She is truly talented, and I love my new gowns."

The man beamed as he expressed his gratitude and then walked away.

"Oh, now everyone is looking at us again," she remarked as Mr. Farrell engaged his other patrons in conversation. These conversations had to be about her and Camborne, since everyone kept glancing their way. "What do you think he is saying about us?"

"Oh, probably taking bets on whether or not we are married."

"Camborne! No, that's awful."

He cast her a jaunty smile. "Och, love. Just jesting. I doubt they are talking about us at all."

But she knew he was only saying this to spare her the humiliation.

Did anyone in Arbroth believe they were married? And what would they think when she spent a second night sharing a bedchamber with this Silver Duke?

Chapter Six

"Ignore the stares, Jocelyn," Malcolm said, wishing he could ease her distress as they sat together in the common room pretending to enjoy their afternoon tea under everyone's scrutiny.

Jocelyn, it turned out, was surprisingly gentle of heart, despite her reputation. Harpies were supposed to be full of spit and fire, but she merely looked fretful.

Her fretting was due to her worries about *his* feelings and *his* being insulted, when she needn't have been concerned about him at all. His heart had an iron cloak of protection around it. Nothing was going to penetrate that secure barrier.

But her heart was incredibly soft and vulnerable as it lay bare for anyone to hurt.

This was why he was so determined to look after her and keep her safe.

"We are a happily married couple and that is all we need to convey," he reassured her. "Although dinna ask me exactly how that is done, since I've managed to avoid the parson's mousetrap all these years. I'll take my cues from ye, lass. Can ye pretend to be happy with me in a wifely way?"

"It isn't difficult," she replied. "As I've told you, my parents had a good marriage. I learned much from watching them. It is about our feeling at ease with each other, making small gestures of consideration to each other."

"Such as?"

"Knowing I like a lot of sugar in my tea—which I do, by the way. It is an extravagance, but one my family can afford. So, you ask for a sugar cone and then scrape some into my tea. What sweets are your favorite?"

He shrugged. "I'll eat pretty much whatever is put before me. Is that not clear from the food I piled on my plate?"

She smiled as she stared at his now-empty dish. "A wife would know if her husband had a hearty appetite. So, being as I *am* your wife…I might cut my slice of ginger cake in half and offer some to you. Just subtle gestures are all that is necessary."

"Comfortable companionship," he muttered.

"Yes, this is what will convince them we are truly married. Not heated looks between us."

He arched an eyebrow. "Shouldn't a little heat be necessary for two lovebirds such as ourselves?"

"Hot looks will only convince them we are having a torrid affair. Can you gaze upon me lovingly, as one might look upon one's favorite aunt?"

"Lass, ye're too beautiful for that. I dinna think I could pull it off."

She blushed. "Thank you, Camborne. All right, a little heat, but restrain yourself."

"And what about *you*, lass?"

She cast him a look of confusion. "What about me?"

"Ye need to gaze at me worshipfully."

She laughed and shook her head.

"What?"

"Have I not been doing just that?" She gazed at him with adoring eyes. "You are my knight in shining armor, Camborne. You are *every* lady's shining knight. But I have never been referred to as beautiful. Sharp tongued, yes. Cold and dismissive, also yes. Certainly never someone alluring enough to entice a Silver Duke."

He placed a hand over hers. "There's something I'd like ye to consider."

"Oh? What is it?"

"I know I said that I did no' want to discuss marital arrangements yet, but I'd like ye to give this some thought..." He worried that sitting in the inn's common room was a poor place to begin this sort of serious discussion, but no one sat close enough to overhear them.

"What is it?" she asked.

Did he dare tell her what was really in his heart?

Did he dare ask her to stay with him forever?

No.

What was he thinking? It was ridiculous to consider anything permanent, for they had known each other less than a day.

"Never mind. It was a foolish supposition. It isn't important."

"Obviously, this is something very important to you. Just tell me, Camborne. Is it about your fishing trip? Should I not go with you to your lodge?"

He nodded, allowing her to believe this was his thought when it had not even occurred to him to leave her behind. But now that it had been brought to his attention, how was she going to manage being out in the wild? "Aye, lass. It is a rugged place and will no' have all the comforts ye are used to having."

"I see," she said with obvious disappointment.

"But I dinna mind having ye with me. If ye choose to stay, I can teach ye to fish, and take ye on hikes. There's no better place to gaze at the stars. Still..."

She leaned toward him. "In truth, it sounds wonderfully romantic. Why are you so perplexed?"

"I am not perplexed."

"Yes, you are. You are doing that thing again...staring at me with all expression hidden so that I must guess what you are thinking."

"Are my concerns not obvious? It will be just the two of us at the lodge. No servants. We cook our own meals. Clean up after ourselves. And we'll be thrown together the entire time. I just want to be honest about what ye'll face."

She pursed her pretty lips. "Will I have to clean the fish we catch?"

He let out a breath and chuckled. "No, lass. I'll take care of that. And washing up the pans, too."

"While I watch and do nothing?"

"Well, it isn't as though I was counting on someone to do those chores for me, since I planned to go up there alone. But I would no' mind having ye with me. In truth, I would no' mind having ye there at all."

Her eyes took on a crystal-blue shimmer as they widened. "Truly?"

"Unless ye do not have a liking for the suggestion. I will no' force ye to join me. It will no' be easy living, but I think ye might enjoy it."

"I have never taken care of myself before," she said softly. "It was probably obvious from all my mistakes when planning my escape from Ballantry. But I would not mind learning how to fend for myself. Are we not agreed on our plan for this month? Well, perhaps we did not finalize it. But since there is no haste to get to Aberdeen once you and I are married, we can head straight to your lodge first, and later take care of my outstanding business. I'll leave it up to you whether we go to Aberdeen first or last. The point is, I am glad we shall be together for the month."

"Ye are? That warms my heart, lass." He raked a hand through his hair, for he was thrilled she wanted to be with him under these hard conditions, but also worried that she would not take it well and then want nothing more to do with him afterward. "Well, the thing of it is...I dinna think ye understand quite what ye are getting into. The lodge is isolated. And it has *no* comforts."

"Camborne, if you do not want me with you, then just say so."

"I do want ye with me," he insisted. "I just dinna want ye disappointed. However, I can think of no place better if we wish to get to know each other and work out how to move forward. Our impending marriage is a bit of a patched-up affair, hastily concocted and given practically no thought. Certainly nothing either of us was ever prepared for."

"I certainly wasn't," she quietly admitted. "It must be even more shocking for you. But you are taking it awfully well."

"No, lass. I just hide my feelings better. However, ye make me feel at ease when I'm around ye."

This was the truth, he realized. When had he ever enjoyed a woman's company this much? He had spent the entire day with Jocelyn and never once felt bored. This was saying a lot, because he detested shopping and had just spent hours in a ladies' shop with her. Had it been anyone other than Jocelyn dragging him around, he would have made up an excuse to run out within five minutes of stepping inside.

Just as important, he'd missed her in those few moments they were apart.

"There's quite a bit we'll need to work out before we reach your lodge. Will there be enough food for the both of us? Blankets? How are we to wash? I'll need soap, a proper scented soap with a womanly scent." Her eyes rounded. "Am I to bathe in an icy stream? I hate being cold. But you adore the cold."

He cast her a wicked smile. "I'll warm ye, lass."

"I'll bet you will," she responded with a smirk.

He paused to study her expression as it began to grow serious once more. "Och, what's wrong now? Ye dinna like the suggestion? Would ye rather return to yer family after we wed? Perhaps we should go straight to Aberdeen, get matters settled with Ballantry and yer family, then I'll head to the lodge alone, as originally intended."

"No, it's just..."

"What is it?"

She frowned.

"Jocelyn?"

She looked at him as though he ought to understand her thoughts.

Blast and botheration, was it starting already? Had he insulted her? Because she suddenly did not look pleased with him at all.

"I know you do not want to discuss this yet, but it is important to me, and shouldn't you know my feelings?"

"More feelings?" He groaned. "All right, what is it?"

"I do not want to be apart from you, Camborne. I just assumed we would be together once we married. For *always*. Husband and wife. A team. Bonded in matrimony. No invitation required. By extending an invitation to me, it implies we must part ways once the fishing trip and Aberdeen are over. Is this what you want?"

"No, lass." He scratched his head. "That is… I dinna know. Must we decide on it now? We hardly know each other."

"Doesn't this scare you? We are about to leap into marriage. That is a bond that cannot be broken without agonizing consequences, especially when one is a duke."

"Nor do I wish it undone," he said with a growl. "Jocelyn, I will no' leave ye shamed. I've already told ye that I'll do whatever I must to protect ye."

"Are we fooling ourselves? Are we both too set in our ways ever to make this work?"

"Never say this. Were ye not the one telling me about compassion. Forgiveness. Understanding. Sacrifice?"

She cast him a wry smile. "That's true. But I never said I was any *good* at it."

He laughed as he gave her cheek a light caress. "Ah, Jocelyn. Ye are very good at it. I'm the one likely to make a bollocks of our marriage. Not intentionally, for I would never want to hurt ye. But the simple fact is, I dinna stand a chance of making this work with anyone but yerself. And another fact is that I dinna *want* to make it work with anyone but yerself."

She nodded. "That eases my mind greatly. Well, we shall have the night to mull things over."

"There's nothing to mull over about *getting* married, lass." He did not intend to sound harsh, but there was no way out for her. She was a runaway bride—and that alone was a difficulty to overcome, but she might have done it in time. However, running into the arms of a Silver Duke, even if that Silver Duke had yet to touch her, had destroyed her standing in Society forever. No family would ever allow her into their home unless the scandal disappeared. In all likelihood, her own family would disown her.

"Lass, if ye think to run away from me as ye did from Ballantry, then think again. I may not be perfect. Indeed, I am far from it. But ye'll be destroyed unless ye reclaim yer respectability, and the only way to do this is to marry me."

"I know," she said. "I am not under any delusions that my family will welcome me back with open arms or that I will be treated any better than a leper by my friends and acquaintances. In truth, most barely tolerated me when I was respectable. Without marriage, I am exactly what Burling insinuated."

He tucked her chin in the palm of his hand and tipped her gaze upward to meet his. "Never. Ye are a lady. Burling is an arse. Unfortunately, too many people think like he does. But once ye're married to me, no one can touch ye."

"I know, and I am grateful for it. I am not going to run away from you. I'm looking forward to spending time alone with you. I hope it will be for longer than the month we spend at your Highlands lodge and Aberdeen." She eased out of his grasp. "Would you mind if I went upstairs to rest a while? I'll be fine for supper tonight."

"We can dine in our bedchamber, if ye're not feeling well."

"No, it seems shameful and decadent to do that. Besides, everyone will think we are hiding in shame and start talking about us if we fail to dine down here. I'm fine. Just a little washed out. I've developed a bit of a headache."

"All right, lass. If this is what ye wish." He tucked a curl behind her ear. "Burling really upset ye, didn't he?"

She nodded. "I know he is an insignificant gnat and I should not care what he says or does. You've come forward like a dazzling knight and defended me. But I cannot believe how stupid I've been, and how I've dragged you into my mess."

"Ye have a tendency to latch on to things and fret about them, don't ye?"

She nodded again. "Sometimes. I know this isn't a perfect start for us."

He laughed. "Aye, it could have gone a little better. But I hope we shall make the best of it."

"Do you think we might ever have a love match? This is what I would like. So, you may as well know my thoughts before you get deeper into this. Is this ever possible?"

He hoped so. Lord, he *ached* for it.

Was this not the very reason he had felt the need to get away and think? He had become so uncomfortable in his own skin that he could not tolerate it. Coming home after the war had left him aimless and bereft of purpose.

How better to reclaim that sense of purpose than to be needed again?

He escorted her back to their bedchamber, knowing he was disappointing her by leaving the question unanswered. In his own defense, was this not a lot to think about? He decided to return downstairs and have himself a pint of ale. He kissed Jocelyn softly on the mouth before leaving her side, a whisper-soft nothing of a kiss. Even so, fire roared through him the moment his lips touched hers.

It was the oddest feeling.

He'd felt passion before and understood it, but had never felt passion with quite this strength before because it was coupled with a sense of permanence.

Aye, he knew what this feeling was that had overcome him.

He was falling in love with Jocelyn.

And it scared the hell out of him.

Chapter Seven

Jocelyn stared at the bed she was about to share with Camborne for a second night.

The two of them had just come up from the common room after a late supper and a little dancing that she had quite enjoyed despite his still not having answered her question. In truth, it seemed he was purposely avoiding it.

Could he ever grow to love her? It hung between them once again as thick as a morning mist.

She had shaken off her disappointment earlier and accepted his reluctance to respond as merely a sign of his natural caution. Was it so surprising that he would be the last person in all of Scotland who would fall in love at first sight? Would it be so terrible if he took it slowly and fell in love with her day by day?

Having accepted that he was not going to answer her question had allowed her to enjoy their evening, which had turned into an unexpected and most pleasant surprise. The inn had brought in a couple of musicians, something they did with regularity, for a bit of midweek entertainment. It was a popular treat for the local patrons.

She had never danced with Camborne before, but one would never know it by the skillful way he led her about the makeshift dance floor. The mere touch of his hand to the small of her back had set her body tingling. Then he'd taken her in his arms and made her feel as though he wished to hold her forever.

Goodness, she enjoyed being in his embrace. Would he take her in his arms with similar warmth as they lay in bed tonight?

As she watched him begin to undress, her thoughts shifted back to the present and the one bed they would share. She understood his allure, for there was something quite masculine and exciting about the way he removed his jacket, cravat, and waistcoat, and then tossed them over a chair with casual precision.

Butterflies fluttered in her stomach, growing frenzied when he drew off his shirt to reveal his broad shoulders and honed, lean torso.

She watched the wondrous, undulating ripple of muscles along her arms as he sat upon the mattress to tug at his boots and remove them. "Lass, we have a big day ahead of us. Ye ought to ready yerself for bed."

His taut stomach muscles rippled, too.

"Lass?" he repeated with a knowing grin. "Should ye not ready yerself for bed?"

Instead of stand here gawping at him?

She nodded, but could not draw her gaze from the arms that she found so fascinating. Most men in their forties had turned soft, but not Camborne. There was a hardness to him imbued in his body and in his soul. The wall of protection he had built over the years was not only meant to guard his heart, but it surrounded his entire being and controlled his every action. What other reason could there be for his never getting close to a woman other than to bed her? He chose the ones he could safely bed, and kept a distance from those suitable for marriage.

And yet he was determined to marry her.

He had joked that he might have proposed to her even if not forced to. Sadly, she did not think so. They would have parted ways, perhaps each regretful of what might have been. Well, *she* would have been regretful. He would have resumed his Silver Duke entertainments and eventually forgotten about her.

For her part, she would remember him to her dying breath.

Tingles shot through her as he returned to her side, his big, shirtless body achingly close as he placed a hand lightly on her shoulder. "Jocelyn, are ye all right?"

She glanced at their bed, and then smiled up at him. "I enjoyed our dances."

His eyes crinkled at the corners as he returned her smile with a tender one of his own. "So did I, lass."

The air between them felt as intense as a bolt of lightning about to strike.

It had sizzled between them all night. She had felt spark after exciting spark as he twirled her around the dance floor, his hands confident as they slipped around her waist, or her shoulders, or entwined with her slender fingers as he guided her through the intricate steps.

All these years, she'd believed there was something wrong with her because she had never responded to any of the men who came forward to court her. Not a flutter. Not a tingle. Not a single butterfly flitting in her stomach.

Nothing at all.

It was not from lack of *trying* to like these men who had once wooed her. In those first years out, she had wanted to make a love match. As her family grew more impatient, she'd resolved to settle for something less than love. Kindness. Caring.

By year three, her standards had fallen to merely "tolerable."

But how much less could she accept? As one Season turned into another, and everyone began to believe there was something wrong with her, her standards had lowered to the point of her accepting the next suitor who asked.

This was exactly what she had done to escape her situation. Unmarried. A spinster. The disappointment on the faces of her parents had become unbearable. But after halfheartedly accepting Ballantry's proposal, she realized he was unbearable, too.

Hence the whispers confirming that she was a cold-hearted harpy. She had started to believe them, too.

Then it had all changed in the blink of an eye. This big Scot with his deep, growling brogue and those lovely threads of silver in his hair had startled her awake last night.

After all these years, she felt vindicated. She wasn't cold and she wasn't heartless. Was it not obvious that her heart had merely been waiting for Camborne to find her?

How different things would have been had she met him during her first Season. He might have offered for her. She would have accepted him with breathless anticipation. Mission accomplished. Married in her first year out. A love match, no less. Happily dreaming of building a life and a family with him in the ensuing years.

But fate had not been kind to her or Camborne, making them wait until now to find each other.

Well, *she* had found *him*. She was not certain what he thought of her.

Oh, he liked her. He even appeared inclined toward their having a more permanent arrangement after they married. But would he change his mind as he got to know her better? What if she disappointed him? There were no assurances he would commit to longer than a month in her company, or ever want to spend a lifetime with her, or sire children.

Still, she held out hope that he would make the effort to be a good husband.

"Jocelyn, shall I help ye out of yer gown?"

"What?" It took her a moment to shake out of her thoughts. "Oh, yes. Please."

He moved to stand behind her to get at the tapes and lacings that ran along her spine.

Was this not a perfect ritual to experience every night? She felt the gentle strength in his touch as he intimately worked the fastenings, and then sighed as his warm breath blew against her neck when he leaned closer to access the last of them.

Was this what love felt like? This wonderful ache to have him touch her, hold her, and be near her? Yes, it had to be so.

Was there a doubt she was falling in love with this big, handsome Scot?

"There ye go. I'll turn my back while ye slip it off."

"Don't." She blushed and turned to look up at him. "I mean…you needn't turn away. It isn't necessary."

Her voice was shaking and so were her hands.

He noticed and took them in his. "I noticed ye staring at the bed. I'll no' take ye before ye are my lawful wife, if that is what has ye trembling."

Tingles shot through her as Camborne smiled at her.

Yes, she felt *everything* with him. Weakness in the legs. Tingles. Shivers of pleasure. Her heart fluttering. Butterflies flapping about in her stomach.

All this after only one night, about to become two nights, in his bed.

"You mistake my meaning. I do not need to wait until tomorrow to give myself to you. I can hardly manage waiting another minute." She gasped. "Oh, I just said that aloud, didn't I?"

He chuckled. "Aye."

She gave a determined nod. "I meant it. I've never felt safer with anyone than I have with you. Nor have I ever felt *anything* in the way of passion or desire until I met you. This attraction is something I've only read about in those books with wicked titles that unmarried ladies are warned never to read. Of course, I could not wait to get my hands on them and devour them. The naughtier the hero, the better. These books are like eating grapes, popping them into my mouth, one after the other, until the entire bunch is consumed."

He chuckled again.

"Have you ever taken a woman against a wall, Camborne?"

He choked on his laughter. "Lass! That is not a proper question to ask me."

"You *have* done it! I knew it!" Her heart melted a little more because he was blushing and genuinely seemed appalled. But this intrigued her all the more. So, it was a naughty thing to do, and he had done it. She wanted to try it, too. Only with him, of course. "I wasn't certain how it would work. How are we each positioned? Would it be awkward? Oh, you are laughing at me now. Do not laugh at me, Camborne."

"I'm not laughing, lass," he said with a broad grin and a rakish gleam in his eyes as he drew her closer. "Ye're serious?"

She nodded.

"I dinna think ye understand what ye are getting into, especially untried as ye are." He gave her a featherlight kiss on the forehead that felt like a dismissal of her request.

She held him back when he started to draw away, and then led him to the wall. "Do I lean against it like this?" she asked, staring up at him.

He groaned. "Och, lass. Ye're torturing me."

"Camborne, you are torturing yourself. I am right here, curious and willing. Show me what is so special about it, because I do not see what all the fuss is about. It is just a wall, and I'm merely leaning against it."

But her heart fluttered as he suddenly placed his hands on either side of her, trapping her between his arms. "All right, but ye'll tell me if ye change yer mind."

She was not going to change her mind.

He was standing close, leaning into her so that she could feel his body heat. Her own smoldering body caught fire. Absolute, torches-blazing heat.

"I love the shape of your mouth," she whispered, her voice trembling slightly as he ran his hands along her body and ignited more of those lightning sparks she had been feeling all evening. There was a confidence in his touch and a promise of thrills that had her heart pounding rapidly.

The look in his eyes was exciting and dangerous. Did he mean to claim her tonight?

Please. Yes.

She could not wait for it to happen. Not merely a few kisses against the wall. She wanted *everything*.

He eyed her as though he were a ravenous lion about to subdue his tender prey. She was so ready to surrender to his soft touches and tender kisses. He even moved with a predatory grace. She *felt* his feral desire.

"I love the shape of yers, too." He tucked a finger under her chin and tilted her head up to meet his gaze. He had the most seductive eyes, turned slightly downward at the corners and holding the promise of pleasure. "Such lovely lips, lass."

"Will you kiss me, Camborne?"

"Aye, I'll kiss ye, my sweet lass. I'll kiss ye hard and I'll kiss ye breathless, and then I'll kiss ye some more." He crushed his mouth to hers and soon had her wrapped in scorching heat, an inferno that melted her bones and had her heart beating wildly through her ears, beating just for him.

He must have known this would happen.

Of course he had. He had all this knowledge and so much confidence from his years of experience.

Yet he made her feel desired, as though this moment was as new and exquisite for him as it was for her.

He had earlier loosened her gown and now gave it a light tug to slide it down her body. The delicate fabric pooled at her feet, leaving her wearing only her chemise. While the thrifty part of her meant to carefully set the gown aside, the hungry part of her tossed all logical thought aside while Camborne plundered her mouth and skillfully set her ablaze.

Would he fully undress her now?

She felt the heat of his hands as he stroked along the bare skin of her shoulders, waiting for him to remove this final garment. *Aching* for it to happen. But she realized he would not do it all at once. No doubt, he thought she needed to be slowly introduced to intimacy.

She wriggled against him, thinking to take it off herself, but he stopped her. "No, lass. Let me show ye," he said, then suddenly lifted her up against him so that her thinly draped bosom met the hard wall of his bare chest.

She gasped. Her fire intensified.

"Ye're so soft and glorious," he whispered raggedly, pressing up against her so that she was shockingly caught between him and the wall.

Deliciously trapped, for their bodies were intimately positioned, and nothing of their responses to each other could be overlooked. His skin felt hot and his eyes were fiery embers.

"What's next?" she asked.

"Hush, lass. Be patient. This is for yer pleasure." He wrapped an arm around her waist and held her more securely to the wall with the weight of his muscled body pressed against her. It was a light crush, meant to make her feel him but not inhibit her movements in response.

Oh, this was so exciting. To actually have this lovely ravishment happening to her, to no longer wonder what all the fuss was about… Oh, the delicious delight.

She gasped as his roughened fingers slid up her thigh. Camborne knew just how to inflame her senses.

Her brain was in a frenzy of new sensations. She took in every detail of his magnificent form, the tenderness of his touch, and the sensuality of his voice.

His skin held the scent of musk, an irresistible essence that had her mindless and wanting to lick her tongue along his neck because she needed to taste him as well as breathe him in.

But now he was licking hers, starting with a light suckle…and now untying the sweet little bow at the front of her chemise to loosen it and—

She almost shot up the wall as his mouth closed over the bud of her breast and he began to suckle it. "Camborne!" She grabbed his hair and twisted its soft waves within her fingers. "Camborne," she repeated, straining to manage a complete sentence because he had her panting. Actually *panting*. How long had it taken him to get her into this aroused state? A minute? Even less?

"Is this not better done in bed?"

He gave her breast a soft lick before easing away to glance up at her. "No, lass. I'll take ye completely if we're in bed."

Was that a bad thing?

Please, please, please.

"I am not afraid of your touching me." She sighed. "In fact, I thought I made it clear that I would not mind, um…"

He grinned. "Mind what, lass?"

"Do not be cruel and tease me. You know…doing *that*. All of *that*. Because I've never done any of *that* before, and you already have me half naked. And we will be married tomorrow, so it really should not count as sinful, should it?"

"We'll see, lass."

"We'll see?"

"Aye, Jocelyn."

"Oh, I understand. You first want to give me a sample of what I read in my book, of having your way with me against the wall. I am *most* grateful. And then are we to move on to doing more? But first, the wall…since I mentioned it…and I wouldn't have mentioned it if I wasn't curious."

"Do ye want me to carry ye to the bed, lass?"

"No, I'm content right here. I just do not want it to be the *only* thing you teach me tonight. But wanting to…*you know*. Is it too brazen of me? Do you disapprove? After all, I've only known you for two days."

"I dinna disapprove. I am ever yer servant."

"Ready to attend to my every need?"

His gaze turned steamy. "Aye, lass. Even the needs ye never knew ye had."

Her eyes rounded in surprise. "Such as?"

"I'll show ye. Will ye let me get back to what I was doing before ye distracted me with yer comments?"

She nodded.

He lifted her so that she was once again pinned against the wall but now had her arms gripping his shoulders and her legs positioned around his hips. She felt *him* against her and wasn't certain whether to move as he took the tip of her breast into his mouth once more and slid his hand up her thigh to seek her most intimate spot.

She shot up the wall again, but he took no mercy on her this time, holding her about the waist and bracing her against the wall in such a recklessly erotic fashion that she could never, *ever* look at another wall again without blushing. His fingers delved inside her in gentle strokes and she was soon liquid, all of her awash in sensation.

She did not know how he managed to hold her up while at the same time arousing her with the magical strokes of his fingers and soft licks of his tongue, but he had her braced securely as he completely engulfed her in fiery passion.

A powerful surge built up inside of her, a storm of emotion about to unleash, but her thoughts were of him and how he was pleasuring *her* and not taking this same pleasure for himself.

Did he mean to wait until they were married to fully claim her? That was the honorable sort of thing this big Scot would do. She hardly knew him, and yet she *understood* him and adored him.

But she thought no more about it, for his touch was exquisitely scorching and she felt an inferno surround her, swallow her whole. She cried out softly, unable to stop herself from coming undone.

He sensed it and knew it, too. "Och, love. Dinna hold back."

She cried out again as he intensified his onslaught, his tongue and fingers working her body without mercy.

"That's it," he whispered, his voice ragged as he sought to control his own body's response to their intimacy. "Let yerself go, Jocelyn. Dinna fight the feeling, my sweet, sweet lass."

She tried to assure him that she wasn't holding back a thing, but her breaths were coming too quickly now and she could not speak a word as stars exploded all around her and she felt herself soaring among them.

He covered her mouth with his as she yielded completely, his kiss fiercely tender while he absorbed her soft purrs and shudders of ecstasy. She understood it now, this power of intimacy when coupled with caring…and perhaps the incipient seeds of love.

He kissed her until her breathless moans subsided.

And then kissed her some more.

Only once she had recovered did he carry her over to the bed and collapse half atop her with a grunt. Laughing, he rolled onto his back beside her. "That was spectacular, lass. I think I threw my back out."

"Oh, no!" She propped herself on one elbow to study him. "You should have told me."

"Och, never. I'm only jesting, sweetheart. Even if I weren't, it would no' have stopped me. Men are *idjits* that way. How do ye feel?"

She glanced at the wall as though there ought to be a mark to commemorate the historic event, but there was nothing but a lovely floral wallpaper adorning it. However, the encounter would live on in her memory, his every touch vivid in its sensuality and seared into her heart. "I feel wonderful. Thank you for the experience. But you made it all about me and nothing for you."

"Ye gave me plenty, lass. Believe me when I say the pleasure was all mine." He arched an eyebrow and cast her a rakish smile. "Was it better than in yer books?"

She returned his conquering smile with a gentle one of her own. "Much, much better. I had no idea this wantonness was inside me all along. But I do not think anyone else could have brought it out in me," she said in all seriousness.

He took her hand and drew it to his lips to press a kiss upon her palm. "Ye know it was meaningful for me, too."

"Truly? Even with all your experience?"

"Aye, lass. There's a difference between satisfying one's needs and satisfying one's heart."

She sat up and rolled to her knees on the mattress so that she now sat beside him and could look upon him as he lay contentedly stretched crosswise atop the bed. "Then it wasn't merely a *need* for you?"

He gave a hearty chortle. "If I was only thinking of my needs, I would have taken ye here on the soft mattress and not heaved ye up against the wall. I'm sure I pulled a tendon or two while attempting to satisfy ye."

"Oh, you really did hurt yourself," she said, now distressed that her pleasure had caused him this discomfort.

"Och, no. Jocelyn, I would no' have traded this moment for the world."

"Nor I," she admitted. "The passages in those books I read did not do the act justice. I was not certain what to expect and was obviously unprepared for the thrill you provided."

"Words are important and have their place in learning, but nothing teaches better than life experience. Ye are obviously book smart, but lacking in any real experiences."

She nodded. "Woefully lacking, it seems. But I am eager to learn, if you will teach me."

"Aye, once we are married I'll teach ye all I know. Not only about the bedchamber, for I think ye've been a bit sheltered about many things. Not yer fault, lass. Yer parents wanted to protect ye from the difficulties of life. Ye need to be more aware, but I'm not going to tell ye everything."

"Why not?"

"Because ye're compassionate and some of what exists out there will break yer heart. Ye're to be my wife. Will I not be taking a vow to love and protect ye? I'll no' do anything disrespectful to ye or to ever cause ye pain."

Her eyes widened. "Such as what?"

"It does no' matter. My point is, ye're in good hands with me. Ye're in *safe* hands with me. I'll teach ye whatever ye wish, but for one exception. I'll never teach ye anything that might hurt ye."

Her heart beat faster. "Does this refer to general knowledge of the world or knowledge of the bedchamber?"

He drew her down atop him and wrapped his arms around her. "Both, lass."

"Will you kiss me again, Camborne? Or are you too sore now?"

"For kisses? Never too sore for those." His expression softened as he traced his thumb gently along her lower lip. "Kissing ye is a pleasure."

He pressed his lips softly to hers as he rolled her under him and lifted onto his elbows so that he did not press the full weight of himself atop her. Not that she would have minded, for there was something wonderfully stirring about his big, muscled body, and the way the two of them fit perfectly to each other despite their obvious differences.

His shoulders were broad, while hers were small. He was lean and hard, while she was not very big at all, although she was amply bosomed and had typical womanly curves. His legs were long, muscled, and powerful. Hers were well proportioned and firm, since she was active and tended to do a lot of walking daily, but they were more slender than muscled.

Still, they were perfectly suited to each other.

"Camborne..."

"Aye, Jocelyn?" He gave her a whisper-soft kiss. "What is it, my lovely lass?"

Her heart pounded as she worked up the courage to reveal her aching wish. "Make me your wife tonight."

He inhaled lightly and then his sharp, assessing gaze fixed upon her face. "Ye know I ache for it, but are ye certain?"

"Never more certain of anything in my life," she said softly. "If things go horribly wrong tomorrow, then I will always have the recollection of us as we are tonight."

He frowned. "I am marrying ye in the morning, Jocelyn. Nothing will stop me from protecting ye."

"I know, and you will accuse me of needlessly fretting again. But I'm not... Well, I'm not fretting very much. I ask this because it is pointless to wait another night when my heart has already accepted you. It has, Camborne. I am not going to pretend otherwise."

He appeared troubled by her admission.

Was it because he wanted to remain respectful of her innocence, since she was a lady? How could he still think of her as a lady after her brazen behavior against the wall? Not quite the gentle, coaxing way he intended to initiate her into intimacy, was it?

But she was well beyond any shyness now. She had wished for this day to arrive for years already. Perhaps gentleness and a slow approach were necessary when she had been a shy girl making her Society debut. But now that she was all of twenty-seven and still untried? She wanted it all with Camborne and had no intention of waiting another hour, much less an entire day.

Or had his own pleasure merely been a pretense? Did he not find her attractive?

She did not think he was feigning his own desire, but how was she to know? He had gained his reputation as a Silver Duke because he knew how to make love to a woman. By natural extension, he could easily make that woman feel adored by him, even if he did not feel all that passionately about her.

"Camborne, am I pleasing to look at?"

He laughed. "Are ye jesting? Ye're so lovely, ye make my heart sing every time I look at ye. Why ask me that?"

"Because you seem reluctant to claim me. I thought you would leap at the chance, but it does not appear to delight you at all."

Perhaps he was not ready to allow their hearts to be involved yet. He had told her that she was not like the other women he had seduced, for none of them had been virgins. To him, this meant he could not bed her and afterward walk away. Was this the reason for his reluctance? In his mind, he had committed to be her husband. But in his heart...he had not made that commitment yet.

The knowledge hurt, for her heart had accepted him already.

She began to fashion the ribbon at the front of her chemise in a bow, but he sat up and stopped her. "Leave it, lass," he said, his voice a deep rumble and his brogue as thick as the air that surrounded them. "I'll have the garment off ye in a minute anyway, so dinna bother to tie it."

She had worried that she did not have any of his heart.

But she had never felt more loved than when he blew out the candle that softly illuminated the room in a golden glow and reached out for her in the darkness to take her in his arms. The gentleness of his touch had her almost in tears.

However, it was not long before all thought fled and he had her mindless and surrendering to passion as he made her body thrum and throb, as her insides melted and she turned boneless...as he entered her and claimed her for his own.

She came undone again, the stars exploding with even greater force than before.

Only then did he take his release.

It was thrilling, exciting beyond words, but also messier than she realized it would be. He had withdrawn just as he reached the heights of his arousal.

She understood what this meant…he would marry her, but he had not yet decided about having children with her.

She did not let this sadden her, for the moment was exquisite in every other way.

"Stay in my arms, my lovely lass," he said with tenderness once they were both sated and he had cleaned her off with gentle care. He had even taken a moment to pick her gown up off the floor and carefully drape it over a chair before returning to their bed and drawing her close. "Sleep in my arms tonight, Jocelyn."

He said this for her sake, somehow knowing she needed to hold on to the wonder of their connection this first night when she had given all of herself to him.

This was how she fell asleep, lost in the warmth and strength of his arms.

This was what she hoped her future would be.

How could anything be more perfect?

But would Camborne feel the same? Or would he tire of her before the month was out?

Chapter Eight

THE MORNING LIGHT shone down on Jocelyn's face as Malcolm stood beside the bed they shared and stared down at her. He had quietly gotten up at sunrise, washed and dressed, and meant to walk over to the wheelwright's shop in a few minutes to see how the repairs were coming along. The shop was not far from the inn and he would be back within the hour, but he did not want Jocelyn to think he had run off if she awoke and did not find him asleep beside her.

Lord, she was beautiful. A dark-haired angel of his very own.

Their coupling last night had been incredible, as though her body had been made to fit his, and her skin was just the right softness beneath his roughened palms.

But it was not merely that their bodies matched so well. He dared not think about the fit to his heart or the way she filled his empty soul.

Too soon.

Too soon to hope this could be real.

He knelt beside her and shook her gently, smiling when she responded with a snuffle.

The lass was also a sound sleeper. Perhaps because she felt safe with him.

"Jocelyn," he whispered, giving her bare shoulder a light caress. "I'm going to check on the carriage wheel. All right?"

She mumbled something unintelligible and swatted his hand away.

"The carriage, lass. I'm going to see if the repairs are done." He intended for them to leave the village as soon as they had their proof of marriage in hand, for he could not risk that sneaky rat Burling finding the Earl of Ballantry and sending him here for a confrontation.

Jocelyn grumbled and finally sat up. "What time is it?"

He smiled, for she had not donned her chemise after their coupling, and he now caught glimpses of her warm skin and the lovely swell of her breasts that peeked out above the blanket. "Early yet, lass. But I dared not leave ye without yer knowing where I've gone."

"The wheelwright," she said with a lazy yawn, then noticed her state of undress and hurriedly drew the blanket to her chin. "How much did you see?"

"All of ye, Jocelyn. Did ye forget what we did last night?"

She blushed. "I remember it well."

"I should hope so. Ye seemed well pleased."

"I was," she said with a light groan. "But I'm sure this does not surprise you."

"It *pleases* me. I liked waking up next to ye."

She nodded and emitted a trill of laughter. "Mutual, Camborne. Two nights beside you and I am not tired of you yet."

"Nor I ye. Shall I have them send up a bath for ye, lass?"

"Oh, yes. A bath and a breakfast. I'm famished."

He kissed her on the nose and then handed her the chemise he had removed from her luscious body last night. "That's because ye exerted yerself something fierce," he said, casting her a roguish smile.

She hastily donned the garment and gave him an impish grin in return. "Speaking of exertion, how does your back feel?"

"Perfectly fine. But I fear we've made a dent in the wall while going at it like a pair of wild monkeys."

She laughingly gasped and smacked his shoulder. "Do not tease me."

"Very well, sweetheart. Here, wrap this robe around ye, too." He handed her one of the new garments purchased at Miss Farrell's shop yesterday. "Latch the door once I'm gone. I won't be long."

He strode to the door and was about to walk out when she called to him with a voice so sweet, it wrapped around his heart. "Camborne…"

"What is it?"

"Last night was the best night of my life."

He could not suppress his smile as he said, "Mine too, Jocelyn. Mine too."

It was true.

He walked out before she saw how much her words had affected him. As he descended the stairs, he noticed Mr. Farrell coming out of the common room that appeared to be empty at this early hour but would soon fill up as travelers prepared for the day's journeys. "Could ye send up a bath and a breakfast for my wife, Mr. Farrell? I'm going to check on my carriage repairs. We'll be heading out today if the wheelwright has fixed the damage."

"At once, Yer Grace," the innkeeper said, and summoned one of his maids to give her the instructions.

The village was just starting to stir as Malcolm walked with a purposeful stride along the high street toward the wheelwright's shop. This was a seacoast village, so there was always a light wind off the sea that carried the scent of salty water, seaweed, and fish. Gulls soared above the water, and some circled the dockside for discarded scraps.

The sun shone with the intense brightness of morning light, but there were storm clouds gathering on the horizon and slowly rolling toward land. The sea was also beginning to roil, for he could hear the light crash of waves upon the coastal rocks and noticed more whitecaps than usual as the menacing weather approached landfall.

He felt a few drops of rain begin to fall as he climbed the hill toward the shop. "Botheration," he muttered, hoping to be done with the wedding ceremony and put some distance between them and Arbroth before the rain struck with full force. A soft mist or a few droplets would not slow them down, but a full-on storm was another thing altogether.

One could only hope those clouds would break up once they reached land.

He heard the clang of a hammer striking metal as he approached the wooden structure bearing the wheelwright's sign. "Good morning, Mr. MacInerney. Any news for me?"

The burly man set down his hammer and wiped his hands upon his apron as he gave Malcolm a respectful nod. "Aye, Yer Grace. Happy to report yer carriage was repaired last night and ye're all set. I was about to have one of my boys deliver it to the inn's carriage house this morning."

"Excellent. Have him do it at once." Malcolm was not surprised the man was now referring to him with a deference accorded because of his title. Everyone in the village must have heard of his run-in with Burling and what had been said.

Malcolm settled up with the beefy Scot whose cheeks were already ruddy from working over his fiery kiln. He next stopped at the church to make certain the minister was prepared for the wedding ceremony.

Not that there was much to do in preparation of a rite he hoped would take no more than ten minutes to complete. But he wanted to be sure the witnesses would arrive at the appointed hour because every moment was precious. With a storm almost upon them and Ballantry hot on the heels of Jocelyn, he wanted no delays. "They will be here on time, Your Grace." The minister checked his timepiece. "These witnesses are most dependable."

"Get them here sooner."

The minister regarded him with some surprise. "Sooner?"

"Aye, the weather is about to turn foul, and we have a long journey ahead of us."

Malcolm thanked him and made his way back to the inn, an uneasy feeling in his gut that had nothing to do with the gathering rain clouds or the darkness over the sea. "Bah," he muttered, silently berating himself for behaving like an old woman.

But as he turned the corner toward the inn, he saw a fancy carriage draw up in front and recognized the crest emblazoned on the door as that of the Earl of Ballantry. Climbing out was not only Ballantry, but that rat, Burling, and an older man and woman.

Jocelyn's parents, perhaps?

He ran into the inn through the kitchen door and hurried up the servants' stairs. A maid was just leaving the room he shared with Jocelyn. He waited a heartbeat for her to disappear down the main stairs before rushing into their shared quarters without bothering to knock. "Jocelyn! We have to get out of here right now."

She had just gotten out of the tub and was standing naked in the center of the room with towel in hand. She gasped and hastily wrapped it around herself.

"No, lass," he said, taking a moment to bolt the door. "No time for bashfulness. Dry yerself off and get dressed straightaway."

But how he ached to toss her back in bed now that he had caught her in that state of undress. Gad, she had the most exquisite body.

He shook out of his improper thoughts, for there was not a moment to lose. "I'll help ye with the laces. Here are yer shoes. Hurry, love. We haven't any time."

She paled as she rushed to dry herself off and immediately scrambled to don her new undergarments. She then grabbed one of her new gowns while he took the rest of her belongings and stuffed them into the travel bag he had purchased for her yesterday. "I need your help," she said. "But don't bother doing up every lace. Just help me tie a couple. I'll throw a shawl over my shoulders to hide the gap. Are we all packed? Have we forgotten anything?"

"Dinna fret. I'll buy us anything we leave behind." He'd bought her a soft valise for ease of travel to his Highlands lodge and was glad he had thought of it yesterday and not left it for today. He had not expected them to be fleeing like hunted outlaws this very morning.

"Rotten luck," he muttered, angry and frustrated that Burling had come upon Ballantry so soon and led him straight back here. What were the odds?

Well, it did not matter. Burling had found Ballantry and the older companions who could only be Jocelyn's parents.

Jocelyn's hair was wet from its fresh washing, but there was no time to properly brush it out or pin it up. He grabbed a fistful of her pins and stuck them in his pockets. In the meanwhile, she hastily dragged her hairbrush through her lush curls. A few droplets struck his face while he next stood behind her to lace up more of her gown.

But he left most of it undone, as she had suggested, because the voices were getting louder on the stairs. "We have to go. *Now.*"

"Wait! Where are my hairpins?"

"I have them, love. I think I have everything. Here's yer shawl. Toss it on and let's go."

Fortunately, his own bag was already packed—he had never bothered to unpack it, since he found it easier to take items out as he needed them. He had gotten into the habit of moving fast during his war years, and this had never left him.

He stuffed her hairbrush in his pocket, then grabbed both bags. "Follow me, sweetheart."

They tore down the servants' stairs and raced to the inn's stable. "Ready the carriage and put our bags in there right now," Malcolm told the surprised ostler, thrusting both bags in his hands. "Send a boy to wake my driver and have him drive the carriage to the church. The boy should tell him it is urgent and he must meet us there right away. *Right away.* Got that?" He reached into the breast pocket of his jacket and withdrew a few pound notes. "If anyone asks ye about us, ye're to tell them the Duke of Camborne and his wife left fifteen minutes ago in his carriage—describe it as a ducal carriage with the Camborne crest on the door."

"Yer crest, Yer Grace?"

He nodded. "A lion with his teeth buried in the neck of a wounded hart, and two swords dripping blood crossed over their heads."

Jocelyn's eyes rounded in horror.

"Aye, lass. The Cambornes were a bloodthirsty clan." He turned back to the ostler. "Ye're to tell anyone asking that we headed south."

"South. Och, aye." The man tucked the notes into his pocket and nodded. "Yer Grace, ye have no need to worry. I'll no' give ye and the lovely lass away."

"The lovely lass is my wife," Malcolm growled.

"Of course, Yer Grace."

Obviously, no one was ever going to believe him. Besides, he had no time to argue with the ostler. He grabbed Jocelyn's hand and stealthily led her from the inn. He hoped against hope that the ostler would lie for them. Jocelyn's parents and Ballantry only needed to be distracted long enough for the wedding ceremony to take place.

Jocelyn was out of breath and in tears by the time they reached the church and rushed in. The minister came forward to greet them, but his smile immediately faded when he noticed she was crying. "Lass, are ye being forced to wed?" he asked, casting Malcolm a righteous look of disapproval.

Jocelyn glanced at him and then at the minister. "No! This man is my salvation. There is no one in the world I wish to wed more. I love him," she said with such sincerity that Malcolm almost believed her.

Why should he *not* believe her? Jocelyn gave herself to him last night. For all her reputation of being a harpy, this lass was sweet and true. She could not have given her body to him without his also having won her heart.

This filled him with contentment, but he dared not dwell on it just yet. He took her hand in his as he spoke to the minister. "There are some evil people trying to keep us apart. The lady is of age. Obviously, so am I. We both wish for this wedding to take place immediately.

Where are the witnesses? There is no time to waste."

The minister glanced once more at Jocelyn, no doubt worried Malcolm was the evildoer and she was his innocent captive. At her nod of reassurance, he hurried off to summon the witnesses, which he advised were already here and waiting in his office.

"It will be all right, love," Malcolm said, trying to calm Jocelyn, who was shaking and could not seem to stop. "Let me do up yer gown properly while we have a moment."

She nodded and removed her shawl. He worked nimbly, hoping to finish the task before the witnesses returned and she was further embarrassed.

"There, love. Done. I might have missed a few eyelets, but no one will notice."

She ran her fingers through her hair. "Oh, Camborne. My hair's a mess."

"It looks beautiful. Here, let me help ye brush it out a little better." He fished her hairbrush out of his pocket. "Close yer eyes and take a deep breath. Everything will be all right. Ye're with me now. I'll keep ye safe."

She nodded, but her hands were still shaking. He continued to brush back her hair, loving the softness of her dark curls.

"It is not even properly done up," she said in a strained whisper as the minister returned with the two witnesses in tow. "What will they think of me?"

"Is it not customary for a bride to leave her hair unbound on her wedding day?" he replied, hoping to make her feel better as the three gentlemen approached. "If not, we'll start our own tradition."

The minister summoned them to the altar, and the witnesses took their positions immediately behind them. Jocelyn appeared so tense that she probably heard nothing of the introductions the minister made and had not a clue who these two men were. But Malcolm took note of their names and would make certain all was properly entered in the marriage papers.

The ceremony was quick, the prayers recited with blasphemous speed at Malcolm's command, and then he and Jocelyn signed the parchments certifying their union.

The witnesses then did the same. The minister's signature came last. "There, all done. Felicitations to ye both. May ye have a long and happy married life."

Malcolm took Jocelyn in his arms and hugged her fiercely. "Ye're safe now, lass. Ye're my wife, truly and forever. No one can ever take ye from me."

She hugged him back just as fiercely, once again shedding tears. "Thank you. Thank you, Camborne. I—"

"Stop the wedding!"

Whatever else she meant to say was interrupted by Ballantry's bellowing. Malcolm thought she was going to say that she loved him, but he could not know for certain. The elderly gentleman and lady who had stepped out of Ballantry's carriage along with him earlier were close on his heels. Burling ran in last, his face red as he gasped for breath because he was a sot and a wastrel, and the slightest exertion had him wheezing and panting.

Malcolm and Burling had been in school together. They were of similar age. However, the years had not been kind to Burling. He looked dissipated and worn out, but remained as nasty and spiteful as ever.

Malcolm drew Jocelyn safely behind him. "Ye're too late, Ballantry. Jocelyn is married to me and I will no' let ye touch her."

"She is my betrothed! Ye had no right!" Ballantry snarled, attempting to reach around him to grab Jocelyn.

Malcolm blocked his path, for he was not letting her *former* betrothed anywhere near her. He gently nudged her behind him when she tried to step forward to confront the cur. But he would not allow it, not while the man was enraged and might strike her. "Leave him to me, lass," he said.

"Try to calm the situation," she muttered, no doubt concerned there would be blood spilled in this sacred place.

He had no intention of being the first to spill blood or even toss a punch. However, if Ballantry wanted a fight, then Malcolm was not going to back down from the challenge. He was no gentleman and would not pretend to be one. The only option he would offer Ballantry was to walk away and never approach Jocelyn again. She was now his wife, and the sooner Ballantry accepted it, the better off they would all be.

"Ye broke yer betrothal when ye broke faith with Jocelyn," Malcolm said with the calm and reason of a diplomat. "Do ye dare deny it? She saw ye with her own eyes, betraying her not an hour before the wedding was to take place."

"Ha! So what? Will ye pretend ye're any better, Camborne? Yer reputation precedes ye. Is the lady so foolish as to believe ye'll ever be faithful to her?"

"She has my vow. I will not break it. Now, back away before I run ye through with my blade. Think twice before ye tangle with me, Ballantry. As ye said, ye know my reputation." He turned to Burling. "As for ye, ye little rat…"

Burling squealed and ran out of the church.

"Did ye pay him, Ballantry? Ye wasted yer money. Jocelyn will never be yers."

"Now see here!" the older gentleman roared.

Jocelyn stepped to Malcolm's side. "No, Papa. It is done. I am now the Duchess of Camborne. So choose your side carefully, for my loyalty is to Camborne now, and I shall never break faith with him."

Her father glowered at Malcolm and then turned his anger on his daughter. "Ye've pledged yerself to this *infamous* Silver Duke? My child, I did not take ye for a fool. Do ye not understand what this man is? Married or not, he will abandon ye before the week is out."

"That is a risk I am willing to take," she said, her chin raised proudly. "Ballantry did not even give me the courtesy of an hour before cheating. As for Camborne, he will never cheat. He married me and gave me his sacred promise. I *trust* him always to honor that vow."

"Jocelyn, how can ye be so blind?" her mother said with a sob, approaching. "Do ye even know the man? No one in Scotland has a worse reputation."

"It is completely undeserved," she said, looking up at Malcolm with such adoration, his heart melted a little. "Everyone calls me a harpy, do they not? Yet that is not who I am at all."

"Lass, I'll not give ye cause to doubt me." Malcolm gave her hand a light squeeze.

Their exchange did nothing to lessen her father's worry. "Jocelyn, child, ye dinna understand the problem. Ye have a betrothal contract."

"That he broke!" she exclaimed, pointing an accusing finger at Ballantry.

The old man was not in the least swayed. "Dinna be foolish. We are bound by the terms, whether ye like it or not."

"And so was he bound by these same terms, one of which was an oath to honor and respect me. I read the contract. I know what it said. Was I not the one who insisted on that language being included? All he had to do was be discreet, and he could not even accomplish that. He violated his oath of honor numerous times, including the very morning of the wedding."

"I did not violate that oath, since we weren't married yet," Ballantry retorted.

"Your promise commenced upon your signing of the contract, as was clearly stated in the terms. And what did you do? The ink was not yet dry before you began to work your way through my cousins, my maids, and even the—" She glowered at him. "I shall not say who else I caught you with, but you know what I saw. Am I supposed to believe you would have behaved respectfully toward me for the rest of your life when you could not even honor our betrothal contract for all of five minutes? You cannot stand me. All you ever wanted was my dowry."

"That's right," Ballantry said with a smug sneer. "And I'll take ye, yer parents, and Camborne for all ye're worth because ye are the ones who broke faith with me. I'll drag the lot of ye through the mud. I'll shame ye and then I'll shame ye some more. Most of all, I'll laugh hardest when Camborne tires of ye and tosses ye aside, as he will do before the week is out."

"Cur!" Jocelyn curled her hands into fists and appeared ready to punch her former betrothed. "I'll laugh hardest when my noble Camborne kicks you into the mud to wallow among the pigs, because that is what you are, Ballantry! A pig!"

"And ye are a harpy! Ye're right, I canno' stand ye. But I'll have yer dowry, mark my words. What will ye think of her then, Camborne? She'll come to ye with nothing, for I'll have all of it and ye'll be left with a sharp-tongued pauper."

Malcolm had noticed her father and mother exchange frightened glances every time Ballantry mentioned Jocelyn's dowry. What was going on? Jocelyn had confided some of her concerns to him yesterday.

Was it possible her parents had dipped into Jocelyn's funds? How much had they taken?

And when did they think to tell Ballantry that her dowry was less than they had represented? Were they not concerned what he might do to her when he found out he had not gotten what he bargained for?

Had they lost it all?

Dear heaven, what would Ballantry have done to Jocelyn upon learning all of it was gone? Malcolm shuddered to think.

He gave a silent prayer that she had married him instead of that wretched fiend who only wanted her for her dowry. Ballantry, that fortune-hunting rat, would not have waited until the ink was dry on their proof of marriage before demanding her accounts be handed over to him.

The cur would have physically beaten Jocelyn when her parents admitted the funds were gone. How could they not have realized this? Or did they think she was too stubborn and independent, and deserved to be put in her place? Perhaps they thought she was clever enough to handle Ballantry.

He did not have the heart to mention it to Jocelyn, certainly not here and now. Perhaps he would bring up the subject delicately at a later time and confess his suspicions. After all, Jocelyn had brought it up herself, although she did not wish to believe it of her parents.

But he would have a private word with her father and get to the truth. They did not appear to be cruel people. By the distress on her mother's face, he saw there was much motherly concern for her daughter. But he had yet to make out their characters.

The doors to the church had been thrown open when Ballantry and the others burst in, but the light spilling in was now darkened by a large, hulking shadow in the doorway.

"Ah, Terrence. Ye've arrived. What delayed ye?" Malcolm asked his driver, who was a giant of a man and had been a loyal soldier under his command in the years on the peninsula fighting Napoleon's army.

"Sorry, Yer Grace. I stopped to have a word with Lord Ballantry's driver. Had to tell him what was what so there would be no misunderstandings."

"Ah, that was clever of ye." Malcolm turned to Ballantry who was reaching into his boot, likely to withdraw a pistol. "Dinna try it. Ye will notice that Terrence already has his firearm drawn. I need only give him a nod and he'll blow yer head off."

Jocelyn's parents gasped, as did the minister and witnesses.

Ballantry merely cursed as he straightened and held out his hands to show he was unarmed. "Call him off me, Camborne."

"No."

Jocelyn had been standing beside him, her hands still curled into fists, but she now looked pale as she glanced up at him. "No one needs to get hurt."

"I agree, lass. And no one will now that Ballantry knows better than to ever draw a weapon on you or me. Isn't that right, Ballantry? Because I will no' hesitate to kill ye myself if ye ever do it."

Ballantry growled. "This isn't over, Camborne. I will be coming after ye. Ye stole Jocelyn from me and ye know it. Ye'll pay for making a fool of me!"

"Ye did it to yerself, Ballantry." Malcolm shook his head. "Ye'll only get yerself killed if ye ever attempt to come at me. And I'll kill ye slow and bloody if ye ever lay a hand on Jocelyn. But here's my proposal to ye, since ye seem to be feeling aggrieved. My wife and I, and I hope her parents," he said, nodding toward her mother and father, "shall meet ye in Aberdeen in a fortnight to settle matters. Ye want Jocelyn's money and I want Jocelyn. I'm sure we can come to amicable terms without any blood being spilled…for it shall be yer blood, not mine, that pours onto the floor."

"Now see here!" Jocelyn's father cried. "In a fortnight? What's to become of my daughter in the meanwhile? As her father, I have a right to know."

"He's taking me fishing," Jocelyn said before Malcolm could stop her from giving anything of their plans away.

"Where I'm taking her is none of anyone's business," he interjected. "But I'll have her safely back in Aberdeen at the appointed time, Lord Granby. Dinna fret about yer daughter. She is perfectly safe with me. Join us in Aberdeen in a fortnight. Ye'll find us staying at the Balgownie Arms. Are ye familiar with it? It's a lovely inn with a glorious view of the sea. Never ye worry—I'll have my clerk secure rooms for all of us there."

He turned to Jocelyn's former betrothed. "This is where ye'll find me if ye wish to talk settlement. I strongly suggest ye accept this gesture of peace I've offered ye, for I will never offer it to ye again."

Ballantry cursed him. "I'll see ye rot in hell for this, Camborne."

"No, ye won't. Ye'll see reason once ye calm down and realize there is more profit to be had in settling rather than fighting with me. I dinna lose my battles. I *never* lose, as ye know from my reputation." Malcolm turned to Jocelyn. "Love, we had better be on our way."

But he knew by her expression that this confrontation had distressed her. Despite everything, she cared for her parents, and it would not be so easy to pull her away from them.

She held him back when he took her gently by the arm. "Camborne, may I have a moment with my mother and father?"

It wasn't a good idea, not with Ballantry still fuming and itching to withdraw that pistol from his boot. But Terrence was now beside them and still had his weapon trained on the man. "All right," he said with a sigh, hoping she would be quick about it.

Jocelyn drew her parents aside. He could not hear their conversation, for they were off in a corner and speaking softly. But he did hear her father's outburst in response to something Jocelyn had said. "Ye mean to tell me ye've only known him two days? Lass, have ye gone mad? Two days!"

And two glorious nights, Malcolm thought.

Bollocks.

"Then he had nothing to do with yer running off?" her mother asked incredulously. "Ye were complete strangers until two days ago?"

"I had no idea who he was, but..." Jocelyn wasn't going to confide what they had done last night, was she? He smothered a smile of relief when he heard her next words. "He's been a complete gentleman, and...and I love him," she declared, tipping her chin up as though daring anyone to take issue with her statement. "He's wonderful."

He and Terrence exchanged glances, for the driver had been with him for years and knew he was not anywhere near as wonderful as Jocelyn seemed to believe. Nor did Ballantry think he was anything other than a hound who stole other men's wives and ruined their daughters.

He had never actually *ruined* anyone, for he was always careful to steer clear of virgins. In fact, Jocelyn had been his first—his first, and now the only woman he would ever touch from this moment on. Nor had he ever broken up a good marriage, only engaging in affairs with married women when both husband and wife were already unhappy with each other and had made no secret about it. Where was the harm when the spouses did not like each other and were never going to touch each other again?

But that last part Jocelyn had said about him, about his being wonderful...that stuck in his craw and troubled him, because it was not really true. He had spent most of his life keeping others at a distance. Indeed, who besides Bromleigh or Lynton, his fellow Silver Dukes, had he ever trusted or confided his worries to? Even with them, he often held back.

How could he ever be considered worthy when he took advantage of unfortunate situations and walked away without a second thought once he was no longer amused? Absolving himself of blame because he had not actually created the unfortunate situation was simply a convenient lie he had told himself to condone his bad behavior.

It could not be denied that he had taken advantage of unhappy situations and never felt an ounce of remorse for it. Was this not the very reason he was reevaluating the course of his life? Yet Jocelyn's faith in him truly affected and heartened him. He *wanted* to be this better man she thought he was.

Well, she probably did not believe he really was all that good. She had just blurted those words in his defense because she did not wish herself to look like a fool.

Her parents had rightly accused him of the wretched things he had done. However, this was his chance to live up to Jocelyn's hopes and prove he could be a husband to adore and look upon with pride.

"Tell yer baboon to drop his weapon and let me leave, Camborne," Ballantry said, sounding deflated although his expression remained one of fury and disgust. "I'll wait until Aberdeen to hear from ye, but ye'd better have a good offer on the table for me or ye'll regret it."

Malcolm nodded. Terrence lowered his pistol, but did not take his eyes off the untrustworthy Ballantry.

"Are ye coming?" Ballantry called to Jocelyn's parents. "I'll not be waiting any longer for ye to coddle yer viper of a daughter."

Her father shook his head at Jocelyn and turned to leave. But her mother had taken only a step before she suddenly clutched her heart and fell against Jocelyn.

"Oh, no! Camborne, help me! Mama, what's wrong?"

Her father immediately rushed to his wife's side. "Love! Is it yer heart?"

His wife managed a nod.

Jocelyn's father shot her a scathing glower. "Ye know she is no' well. And yet ye did not think twice before putting her through this ordeal. Ye knew how delicate she was, and ye ran off anyway…and now ye're married to this…to this…*scoundrel* who'll abandon ye at the first opportunity."

Ballantry stormed out laughing.

Aye, the man was all heart.

Malcolm motioned for Terrence to follow him out and make certain he would not get up to any mischief while they were all distracted.

Malcolm and Jocelyn's father assisted the woman to a pew and helped her to lie down while Jocelyn fumbled through her mother's reticule for smelling salts or medicine. "Papa, what is she taking for her condition? I cannot find anything in here."

"It's in Ballantry's carriage."

Malcolm ran outside to catch up to Ballantry and make certain he would not order his driver to take off and leave Jocelyn's parents behind. Not that he cared if he stranded the pair here, since he and

Jocelyn would take care of them. But her mother needed her medicine.

He had just stepped outside when he saw Ballantry's driver toss their bags out with reckless disdain. Ballantry sneered as they landed in a muddy puddle. "The Granbys are yer concern now, Camborne. I dinna care what ye do with the lot of them, but I had better get my settlement. See ye in Aberdeen."

He hurled a few more insults and then ordered his driver to head to Edinburgh.

What was there for Ballantry in Edinburgh? The courts? A judge to bribe? Society friends to spread more gossip? Malcolm shrugged off the concerns, for he had powerful friends, too. Ballantry was an irritating gnat he would squash if the man did not cooperate and accept the settlement Malcolm was willing to offer.

In truth, he would pay a king's ransom to protect Jocelyn.

What was it about the lass…now his wife…that made him feel this way?

"Bloody bastard," Malcolm muttered while he tried to figure out which bag held the medicine.

"Can ye not find it?" Terrence knelt beside him and watched with concern as Malcolm hastily burrowed through her things and found nothing, to his frustration. "Best we get Lady Granby to the inn, Yer Grace."

"Aye." Malcolm looked up as rain began to patter on the ground. "Toss those bags onto our carriage. Give me a moment and I'll carry her out. But Terrence, I'll want ye to follow Ballantry to Edinburgh once I have Jocelyn's mother settled."

"Aye, with pleasure. What do ye need me to do?"

"I'll tell ye once we're back at the inn." Malcolm then hurried back inside.

Jocelyn's father, the minister, and their witnesses were all gathered around Lady Granby, whose head was cradled on Jocelyn's lap. Jocelyn must have found a vial of perfume in her mother's reticule, for Malcolm could smell it on the handkerchief now pressed to the woman's head. The men looked on helplessly while Jocelyn did her best to soothe her mother, but the poor woman was still struggling to breathe.

"Och, lass. I could no' find the medicine. I looked through yer bags, too," he said to her father. "Did she run out of it, perhaps? But she seems to have steadied."

Jocelyn nodded. "She has, although she is still having difficulty breathing. Papa, did she finish her medicine?"

Her father raked a hand through his thinning gray hair. "It is likely. She's been taking a lot of it these past few days."

Jocelyn's expression crumbled, for she surely blamed herself.

"Best we stay in Arbroth a few days longer and see that she recovers," Malcolm said. "I know ye want to take care of yer mother. We'll get her comfortably settled at the inn. All right?"

She nodded. "Yes, thank you."

"I'll have the innkeeper give them our room if there are no others available." He turned to the minister. "Who's the local doctor? Is he any good?"

"Och, aye," one of the witnesses said. "He's one of the Farrells. Samuel Farrell. He served in the Scots Greys, Yer Grace. Saved a lot of wounded men. He's who ye'll be wanting for Lady Granby. I'll summon him for ye and have him meet ye at the inn."

"Thank ye, Mr. Grampion," Malcolm said, noticing the slight widening of Jocelyn's eyes as he referred to the man by name. "That's kind of ye."

"Yes, Mr. Grampion," Jocelyn said, casting the man an achingly sweet smile. "My family and I are most grateful."

Malcolm carried Lady Granby out of the church and settled her in his carriage. Jocelyn once more held her cradled on her lap while he and her father sat opposite them. The ride was short, for this was not a large village and everything was close.

Malcolm hopped out as the carriage rolled to a stop and ran into the inn to find Mr. Farrell. "Plans have changed," he said as the innkeeper hurried toward him. "We'll need our room back for another few days, and a room for Lord and Lady Granby, my wife's parents. Lady Granby is not well. She needs to be put into bed right away. I understand the doctor is a relative of yers."

"Aye, Samuel Farrell is my cousin. And an excellent doctor, too. I'll send one of my lads to—"

"Not necessary. Mr. Grampion's already gone to fetch him."

Within a matter of minutes, Lady Granby was settled in the chamber next door to theirs. Fortunately, that room and the one he and Jocelyn had occupied were still available. Malcolm secured them for the next few days.

Jocelyn remained by her mother's side while her father helped Malcolm and Terrence look through the Granby belongings once more in the hope of finding his wife's medicine. "Och, it's all gone," he said with a sigh of resignation.

"The doctor will tell us what she needs. There's a local apothecary who will fill the order. I'll take care of it," Malcolm assured Lord Granby.

"Much appreciated, Camborne," the man said grudgingly, and left them to see to his wife.

Malcolm and Terrence brought in the rest of the bags and made certain they were cleaned of mud before they were brought upstairs.

Terrence had been sleeping in the rooms above the stable, but Malcolm suggested he take more comfortable quarters at the inn. "No, Yer Grace. I'm happy where I am. Ye needn't concern yerself with me. Ye'll want me following Ballantry to Edinburgh soon anyway."

Aye, he would. But having the driver wait in a stable in the meanwhile did not sit well with Malcolm. Terrence was more than a coachman to him. They had fought side by side in many battles, and the big, gentle man had always watched his back. In truth, Malcolm doubted he would have survived the war had Terrence not been protecting him. For this reason, he had offered Terrence employment after the war and always offered him better quarters than those above a stable.

It was almost a game by now. Terrence always declined the comfort, even when at the Camborne estates, claiming he was a simple man who liked being around horses and felt more at home among the stable grooms than other people.

In truth, Terrence wasn't simple at all. He was honest, brave, and loyal. But he did feel more at home around animals and the grooms who took care of them. "Animals dinna lie to ye," he always said.

Malcolm had to own that this was true, for one always knew when a dog was going to bite you or a snake was going to coil and strike a victim with its venom. The same could not be said about people.

"Then make certain ye get yerself a good meal," he said.

Terrence grinned. "That I will, Yer Grace. Ye needn't coax me for that. And ye get yerself a strong drink, for ye've not only acquired a wife but her entire family to look after."

Malcolm laughed. "Och, aye. I certainly fell into that, didn't I?"

"Ye dinna seem too upset about it," Terrence remarked.

"I'm not." Malcolm rubbed a hand across the nape of his neck as he gave it another moment's consideration. "Surprising, isn't it?"

Terrence shrugged. "Ye do what ye must for those ye love."

"I—" Malcolm was going to say that he was not in love with Jocelyn, but stopped himself. He certainly had strong feelings toward the lass that he could not deny. "I had better see to Lord and Lady Granby."

He stopped first in his chamber to wash the mud off his hands. The room had yet to be cleaned, but he knew Mr. Farrell would have his maids attend to it promptly. He was not going to fault the man, who could not have expected this morning's chaos. Indeed, the hour was still early, not even ten o'clock in the morning. Malcolm and Jocelyn hadn't been married half an hour yet.

He smiled as he scrubbed his hands.

Married.

How was he ever going to explain this to his fellow Silver Dukes?

The door had been left open, since he only meant to take a moment to wash up before looking in on Jocelyn and her parents, but he suddenly sensed someone watching him. He turned in a hurry, reaching into his boot for a weapon because he did not trust Ballantry and would not rest until the oaf had been bought off.

To his surprise, Jocelyn was the one standing at the threshold.

He quickly dried his hands and then set the cloth aside. "What is it, love? Is your mother still struggling?"

She nodded. "The doctor's just arrived. He's tending to her now. I left him talking to my father. I'll question him afterward. Will you stay with me while I speak to the doctor?"

"Of course, lass."

"Thank you. My father did not want me in there with them as they spoke now."

Malcolm frowned. "Why not? What have they got to hide?"

"I don't know. That's why I hope to speak to him once he finishes his examination." She stepped into their bedchamber and glanced around. "The tub's still here from my morning bath."

"The menservants are busy with the departing guests right now. They'll take it out soon."

She smiled. "Camborne, I enjoyed my sinful night with you."

He laughed. "There'll be plenty more of those, if ye wish."

She came to his side and hugged him. "I'm very grateful for all the help you are giving to my parents, but I'm so sorry about the mess I've made of your plans. Truly, I have completely upended your life."

"Ye haven't. If anything, ye've made it more…interesting."

She laughed as she stared at him, affection glistening in her eyes.

"That's a polite way of putting it. I think we broke the speed record on church weddings. I doubt the minister has ever gone through a service faster than we made him do it for our ceremony. He must think we are sacrilegious pagans."

"No, just eager lovebirds." He gave her a light kiss on the mouth. "Good thing we did hurry him along. Yer parents and Ballantry were very close on our heels. Had I realized just how close, I would have insisted on marrying ye last night. But ye're my wife now, Jocelyn. Whether or not we broke all speed records, the ceremony still counts."

"Then you don't hate me yet?"

"No, lass." He took her back in his arms. "I'm never going to hate ye."

"I wouldn't blame you if you did. What will you do about your fishing trip?"

"It isn't quite as important as it was before I met ye. The fish will be in the stream whenever I get there. Nor will they mind if I never get to catching them."

"You are remarkably forgiving, Camborne. I doubt my parents will ever forgive me, especially now that I have pushed my mother to the brink of... I dare not even suggest the worst. She has always had these heart flutters, suffered with them for as long as I can remember."

"Even in yer childhood?"

"Yes, even back then. But I thought she was faking. After all, I faked stomachaches to get out of having to take my piano lessons. She seemed to use her heart palpitations for similar reasons. What better excuse whenever confronted with something she did not wish to do?"

"Ye thought she was shirking her duties?"

She nodded. "Yes, because I surely was using my stomachaches as an excuse to shirk. As it turns out, I was wrong. They are real, and it is all my fault she is experiencing this latest difficulty."

He took her by the shoulders and looked straight into her lovely eyes. "Dinna blame yerself. Ye dinna know all the facts."

"What facts are there to know?"

He did not wish to confide his suspicions about her dowry and her father using it for himself.

"Camborne, what do you mean?"

His gut was telling him that her mother's stress had more to do with a missing dowry than Jocelyn's running off on the day of her marriage, which probably was a relief for her because the issue of the dowry would be delayed—if not forgotten altogether for months, or years—or possibly never come up if Jocelyn had remained a spinster. But rushing into the church behind Ballantry and realizing Jocelyn had married him, a reprehensible Silver Duke, must have put her in an apoplexy.

Jocelyn's father had to be worried, too. It was one thing for the Earl of Granby to be dealing with the Earl of Ballantry. They were two peers on equal footing, although Ballantry was petty and not above being cruel. He might have hurt Jocelyn in retaliation for not getting the funds expected under the terms of the betrothal contract.

Did her parents believe she was clever enough to fight him off?

But to now be dealing with the Duke of Camborne, perhaps the most powerful duke in all of Scotland, had to be scaring them quite badly.

Malcolm knew he had an awful reputation. One he fully deserved. He was known to be ruthless. In fact, he had been just that whenever he deemed it necessary.

However, Jocelyn was his wife now. That vow meant protecting her and also those she loved, even if they were foolish and had spent her dowry.

"Camborne, tell me. What are you unsure about? The facts are plain. I have behaved stupidly at every step."

"Ye haven't been stupid, lass."

She sighed. "You know I have been. And when I was not acting stupidly, I was acting selfishly."

"Are ye saying ye married me only for selfish reasons?"

"Well, no. I never would have married you if I did not care for you. I could never have done what we did last night with anyone other than you."

The admission warmed his heart. Perhaps this was why Jocelyn fascinated him so much. She spoke what was in *her* heart.

"Then where's the problem? Why are ye beating yerself up, lass? Stop blaming yerself for yer mother's ills. I saw the way ye were with her. Ye held her so lovingly. It was yer natural response. Ye care for yer parents. Just because ye dinna agree with them on whom to marry does not mean ye've been a disappointment to them."

"I do understand this in logical terms, but it is so hard for me to see them ailing and take no responsibility for their suffering when I know I have contributed to it. I was the idiot who chose Ballantry because I was so tired of the constant carping about my spinsterhood. Thinking upon it now, my father was not quite himself after I announced my acceptance of Ballantry's proposal. My mother was delighted, but he only grudgingly went along with my decision."

She pursed her lips as she gave it more thought. "The betrothal contract was severe, and I do not believe my father expected him to accept the terms. But the wretch did. However, I did not come in here to bemoan my actions."

"Ye came here to give yer father privacy while he spoke to the doctor."

She nodded. "That and…I came in here to tell you again how grateful I am to you for everything you've done for me and are now doing for my family. Truly, I think I must be walking in a dream. I don't wish to wake up from it and find you aren't real."

"Och, love. I'm real." He gave her a soft kiss on the lips, but broke it off when he heard someone clearing his throat. He turned to the doorway and saw it was Jocelyn's father. The man looked gaunt and broken.

Jocelyn gasped and ran to his side. "What did the doctor say about Mama?"

"It was a close call, but she will recover. She needs bed rest. She also needs things to remain calm around her. So, I need to know…are there any more surprises in store for us, Jocelyn?"

"No, Papa. That's everything."

He turned to Malcolm. "And yerself, Camborne? Let's hear yer surprises now."

Jocelyn stared at her father. "Papa, what are you talking about?"

But Malcolm understood the question. Her father wanted to know when he was going to abandon Jocelyn. Not *if*, but *when*. And whether it would be as early as this week.

He had questions for Granby, as well. "Granby, come downstairs with me. Ye look like ye're in need of an ale, and we need to talk."

Jocelyn cast him a warm smile, obviously thinking he was going to ingratiate himself with her father.

He wasn't. He meant to find out just how much of her dowry he had squandered.

But there she was, gazing up at him with so much trust and admiration that he began to wonder whether he ought to simply back off and let the matter rest for now.

However, this was not in his nature. He wanted the truth. What he would do with it afterward, he had not an inkling yet.

But Granby was not keen on talking just yet, so Malcolm did not press the matter. Instead, he let the man return to his wife's side.

When Dr. Farrell emerged from Lady Granby's bedside, Malcolm and Jocelyn took him aside and asked their questions. The doctor did not appear keen on speaking to them, but Malcolm insisted and the doctor was not about to ignore a duke's request. "Her heart is weak," he admitted.

Jocelyn's eyes began to tear.

"Och, Yer Grace, do not fret. Yer mother could live for another decade, if not longer. There is no telling with this sort of disease. I understand from yer father that she has suffered from palpitations of the heart ever since early in their marriage, perhaps longer. This leads me to believe it is a familial trait and she may have been born with this weakness. Keeping her free from strain will help, but there is no magic potion."

They asked the doctor several more questions before he left. Then Jocelyn excused herself to return to her mother's side. "I won't be long. Do you mind terribly?"

"No, love. Take all the time ye need." Malcolm needed to seek out Terrence, anyway. There was work to do in preparation for his meeting with Ballantry, and he needed Terrence's assistance. The first thing was to send him off to Edinburgh to keep watch on the untrustworthy earl.

He found Terrence enjoying a hearty meal in the common room. "Ye wish me to leave right now?"

"Not a rush," Malcolm assured him, settling at Terrence's table and watching him eat. "He's riding by carriage and ye'll be following him on horseback. There are plenty of horses available, since this is a coaching inn and their stables are full of good stock. I'll speak to the ostler. Select a horse and gather whatever ye'll need."

Terrence nodded.

"It should no' take ye too long to catch up to Ballantry. Even if ye dinna catch up to him, ye'll find him easily, since he maintains a townhouse in Edinburgh. Once there, ye're to discreetly follow him around. But I also want ye to engage investigators to dig up whatever information they can about him."

Terrence set aside his now-empty plate and nodded thoughtfully. "Secrets he wishes to hide?"

"Aye. The deeper and darker, the better. I dinna care if he tries to destroy me, but I'll no' be letting him humiliate Jocelyn."

Terrence smiled. "Ye really care for her, Yer Grace."

Malcolm chuckled. "Aye. Most inconvenient, don't ye think?"

"Not at all. Ye're now married to the lass, and I think she means to make ye happy. Dinna behave like an *idjit* and disappoint her."

There were only three men in the entire world who could talk to him this openly and honestly. His two Silver Duke friends, Lynton and Bromleigh, and Terrence. "Ye hardly know her," Malcolm remarked. "Why are ye so protective of her?"

Terrence's expression turned soft. "Amid all the fuss over her mother, she still found a moment to seek me out and apologize for the disruption she caused."

"She apologized to ye?"

"Aye, and then she asked me if I'd had the chance to have my breakfast yet." He cast Malcolm a broad grin. "When I said that I hadn't, she sought out Mr. Farrell and insisted I have the very best and advised him to charge it to yer account."

Malcolm laughed. "Ye're in my employ, so all yer expenses are on me."

Terrence shrugged. "Ye might want to assure her of that fact. She thinks ye're cheap and purposely had me sleeping in the stable."

Malcolm laughed again. "But ye're my coachman. Is this not the standard accommodation, rooms above the stable?"

"Aye, but she considers me yer friend and protector. I assured her it was my choice and my preference. She then thanked me for protecting ye at the church."

"Seems the two of ye had quite the conversation. Took me months to get that much talking out of ye when I first met ye. Why so gregarious with her?"

Terrence grinned again. "She's prettier than ye are, Yer Grace."

"Aye, she certainly is lovely," Malcolm said with some pride, for she was now his wife.

After seeing Terrence ride off for Edinburgh, Malcolm decided to take Jocelyn for a walk through the village to get her mind off her ailing mother. The rain had cleared and the sun was burning holes through the clouds to expose a deep blue sky.

She was reluctant at first. Malcolm insisted because there was nothing either of them could do for her mother other than let her sleep. "Is this what ye wish to do, lass? Just sit around and fret?"

"What else am I to do? It is such a helpless feeling."

He understood well about those helpless feelings, as he'd watched his entire family die off one by one. But the doctor had assured them that Jocelyn's mother would recover. Was this not the best news? "Come on, lass. Walk with me."

"All right."

It did not take long before she admitted to feeling better. "Thank you. I needed to get out in this clean air."

They strolled along the dockside and stopped by the various stalls to look at the wares on display. The sun bathed Jocelyn in its soft light, and Malcolm thought she looked more beautiful than ever. It was an odd feeling, for he was such a cynical clot and could not recall any other woman of his acquaintance growing more beautiful with the knowing.

Then again, he did not pursue nice women. In truth, most were horrid, greedy, scheming. Was it any surprise their beauty dimmed with the knowing? Even the most strikingly gorgeous ones had a worn look to them if one studied them closely. None of them had a sparkling inner light. He supposed it was because they felt so little joy in their lives despite having every luxury at their fingertips.

But this was the sort of woman he sought out. No love involved. No hearts. All he'd offered were casual dalliances.

Then Jocelyn had come along.

"Anything strike yer fancy?" he asked as she admired some lace fichus at one of the stalls.

"You've already bought me more than enough," she insisted.

He purchased a lace fichu for her. When her gaze lingered on another, he bought that one for her, too.

She smiled at him as they walked on. "Camborne, you cannot buy me everything I admire."

"Why not?"

She pursed her lips and frowned at him, but it was not a serious frown. She was smiling at him again in the next moment.

Lord, he loved her smile.

Would he have fallen in love with her if they had met in a London ballroom? Or at a musicale? Or house party? Would he have been drawn to her under any of those circumstances? Or behaved like an arse and ignored her to pursue the wrong sort of woman?

He had jested about it the other day, told her that he might have chosen to court her.

Perhaps it was not a jest.

Was it possible Jocelyn was the missing part his soul had been seeking?

Chapter Nine

Several hours later, while Jocelyn remained by her mother's bedside spooning broth into her mouth now that she was feeling a little better, Malcolm insisted her father join him for an ale in the common room. There was nothing either of them could do here, so he would not allow Lord Granby to come up with more excuses to delay their chat.

They walked downstairs together. It was early evening, and the sun was beginning its slow descent upon the horizon. Mr. Farrell was standing on a chair, busily lighting the candles on the wall sconces as Malcolm and Lord Granby entered and took an open table in a far corner. The tables of golden oak took on a reddish hue as candlelight illuminated them.

Mr. Farrell moved on to light a blaze in the fireplace that took up most of one wall, and had a massive wooden mantel that stretched across the entire length of it.

Jocelyn's father tossed out the first question the moment they settled at their table in the busy room. "Camborne, whatever possessed ye to marry my daughter?"

"Haven't quite figured that one out yet," Malcolm admitted, knowing her father would never believe he had fallen in love with his daughter at first sight when *he* did not even believe it. But that was mostly his being stubborn and unwilling to admit anyone could ever gain such control over his heart. "But I like her, Granby. My intention is to make this marriage real."

Granby shook his head. "I wish I could believe ye."

"Jocelyn is the one who needs to believe me. In truth, I dinna care what anyone else thinks of our marriage or of me."

"She likes ye, Camborne. I'll give ye that. She said ye've been honorable and protective of her. So I'll have to thank ye for taking care of my lass."

Malcolm nodded. They remained quiet a moment to enjoy the ales one of the maids set before them.

As silence extended between them, Malcolm decided now was the time to get to the heart of the matter. "How much of Jocelyn's dowry did ye take for yer own use?"

Her father set down his mug with a thunk, almost spilling it. "Are ye accusing me of stealing from my own daughter?"

"No, I would simply call it appropriating…or borrowing. The funds were yers to do with as ye wished before ye had them set aside for Jocelyn's dowry. But having set that goodly amount aside and then letting it be known she was to receive this upon her marriage… What I dinna understand is why ye failed to say anything to her or Ballantry when ye knew that ye no longer had it to give to her?"

"It is none of yer business, Camborne."

"On the contrary, it is *entirely* my business now that I am her husband. Ye stayed silent and let her enter into that misbegotten betrothal. Did ye have no care for what Ballantry would do to Jocelyn once he found out she had come to him penniless?"

"I would have taken care of the situation," Granby mumbled.

"How? He only wanted her for her money, and ye were about to send her to him without so much as a ha'penny. Once married, there would have been nothing ye could do to protect her from his wrath."

"What will *you* do to her, Camborne? Isn't this the more important question, since ye're the one who married her?"

Malcolm frowned. "Me? Nothing. I dinna have a care for her

wealth. Or rather, her lack of it. I married her because…"

Bollocks.

He was about to say he married her because he loved her, but that was absurd. He liked her and had rapidly grown used to having her around. It could not be denied that he had formed an attachment to her, but he could not and would not admit to having developed feelings for her beyond this.

"I married her because she needed me to do it."

Granby shook his head. "That makes no sense. If ye never met her until she arrived here, then what cause would ye have to care what happened to her at all? Or have ye known each other longer and had this planned all along?"

"Planned?" Malcolm swallowed his ire. "Ye think I planned for her to attach herself to that toad, Ballantry? And then was I supposed to leave her at his mercy once she went through with the ceremony?"

"But she dinna go through with it," Granby pointed out. "And to answer yer earlier question… Ye have no idea how stubborn Jocelyn can be. Once she had set her mind to marrying Ballantry, nothing was going to dissuade her. I had hoped including those terms about his moral behavior in the contract would end matters, but it didn't. Nor did I believe Ballantry would do her serious harm, although my opinion of him has changed, as we've been thrown together chasing my daughter these past few days. Turns out he is not the man I thought he was."

He sighed. "I was glad she ran off, because the bounder would have made her unhappy whether or not she came to him with a proper dowry."

"Ye should have been honest with her from the start. Lucky for her that she did run off, though her timing was not the best." Indeed, Ballantry got exactly what he deserved, but it had been a dangerous thing for Jocelyn to run off on the very morning of her wedding.

Her father frowned. "Are ye going to blame me for her reckless escape?"

"Ye contributed to it, so dinna bother to deny it. She might have been accosted or murdered while making her way to Aberdeen without sufficient funds for travel or a decent meal—and dressed in her wedding gown, no less. She was forced to endure cold nights without heat or food. Do ye still believe I helped her plan this? Och, aye. That surely was a brilliant plan on my part, to make her suffer through all that. Do ye really think I would put the woman I love through this ordeal? Er, assuming we had a relationship?" Malcolm took a sip of his ale to calm himself down, because he was unreasonably riled by the thought of Jocelyn coming to harm.

And more riled by the fact she had already found her way into his heart.

Her father was trying to deflect attention from her lost dowry by blaming Jocelyn for the misbegotten betrothal and then running away. But this was only inflaming Malcolm's ire. "Granby, had I set eyes on yer daughter earlier, rest assured I would not have let Ballantry win her hand. I would have stepped forward to marry her myself."

Granby guffawed. "Right, ye expect me to believe ye would have seriously courted my daughter?"

Malcolm shrugged. "Believe what ye will. I married her, didn't I?" He leaned forward and regarded Lord Granby with all solemnity. "What did ye do with her dowry? And how were ye going to deal with Ballantry so that he did not beat Jocelyn senseless when he learned he had been deceived? Or are ye still in denial that he would have treated her so brutally?"

"Ye dinna know the dowry's all gone," Granby said with a growl. "In fact, I've a mind not to give it over to ye at all. Why should I when ye likely ruined my daughter before ye wed her? Ye and Jocelyn have caused me harm, and ye've caused me and her mother a mountain of grief. I owe ye nothing."

"Are ye that eager to break yer daughter's heart? Ye'll break it for certain when she realizes ye consider her no better than a common harlot. That's what she'll believe, and all because ye refuse to admit ye've cheated her out of her dowry. Granby, stop blowing hot air at me and just tell me the truth. I'll not be harming Jocelyn no matter what ye tell me. But if ye wish to keep yer daughter's respect, then let me help ye."

"Help me?" Granby's ears perked. "What are ye suggesting?"

"She doesn't need to know ye touched any of it. How much of her dowry did ye take?"

"Are ye offering to replace it?" He stared at Malcolm in confusion. "By heaven, ye are! Why would ye do such an absurd thing? Ye dinna know me. Ye owe me nothing. And yet ye would allow my daughter to keep her love and respect for me? Why, Camborne? I dinna understand it."

Nor did Malcolm, if truth be told.

But it did not take great perception to see how much Jocelyn loved her parents. He was doing this for her and the sake of their family unity. Having lost his own, he fully understood how precious it was.

"Tell me what the shortfall is and I'll see it replaced, but I will do this only on the condition that ye then hand it straight over to Jocelyn. She can do with it as she wishes. I'll make the arrangements as soon as I deal with Ballantry and get his claim out of the way. Until then, simply tell Jocelyn the dowry stays where it is until there is a settlement with Ballantry."

"Och, what are ye planning to do about his settlement?" Granby asked before downing the last of his ale. "I'll contribute whatever I can. In truth, ye've made me even more ashamed of my behavior. But ye dinna understand how it is between me and my daughter. She's always looked up to me, thought I was the wisest man alive."

He wiped his eyes as tears began to form. "It was my pride, my stupid pride that held me back from admitting I had made a bollocks of our finances. I kept it from my wife, too. But I had to tell her the situation once Jocelyn ran off. This is why her heart's been acting up, having to worry not only about Jocelyn's safety but what's to become of us now that we are teetering on the brink. I'll get it sorted out in time, for not all the investments were bad. Several are still profitable, although barely."

"Then ye're not completely wiped out?" Malcolm did not know if he could believe the man.

"No, not wiped out…yet. Hopefully, I can salvage some assets. So, there it is. I have little available to contribute toward buying off Ballantry at the moment. It's all in the bloody bad timing of it. As I've said, I've made a string of unwise investments and am presently strapped. Dinna tell Jocelyn, please. These were deals she advised me against taking. Turned out she was right. But I was a stubborn dolt and would no' take advice from the lass. She's smart, ye know."

"Glad to hear it." Malcolm did not doubt that Jocelyn was book smart and perhaps had good financial instincts, but she was unwise as to the harsher ways of the world. Perhaps this was why he felt such an overwhelming need to protect her.

"Ah, speaking of my daughter," Granby said, staring at the doorway, "here she is now. Ye canno' breathe a word of this to her."

"I won't. Is this not the entire point of our discussion?" Malcolm's heart shot into his throat as he spied her lovely form approaching. Her smile was dazzling as she started toward his table.

Her father slapped his hands to his thighs. "We've had a good talk, Camborne. I'm thinking perhaps I misjudged ye. Well, take care of my lass. Now that she's down here, I had better go upstairs and tend to my wife."

Everyone in the common room was staring at them—not surprising, since gossip was rampant and they were trying to make out what was really going on. Malcolm was no longer concerned about Jocelyn's reputation, since it was plain to see that her parents had joined them and were referring to the lass as his wife. In any event, this morning's hasty marriage ceremony had protected her from the worst of the gossip. However, everyone had to be wondering about Ballantry's role in this affair.

Malcolm did not really care what they thought of him or the jilted bridegroom. But he would not countenance any insults whispered about Jocelyn.

She walked toward him with the sweetest smile on her face and took the seat he offered as he rose to greet her. "How is yer mother faring, lass?"

"Better, thank you. She is sleeping for the moment. Her breathing's less strained."

He settled down beside her. "And what about yerself?"

She shook her head and sighed. "I'm fine now that I know she is out of danger. But what a terrible wedding day it has turned out to be for you. I'm so sorry for all of this."

"No, sweetheart. Never ye worry about me."

She took his hand when he held it out for her. Hers felt soft and delicate as he wrapped it in his. This seemed to please her, for her eyes lit up like silvery moons at this small gesture of affection. "But I *want* to worry about you. May I not do this? You are my husband now, and this day has been nothing like a wedding day ought to have been." She cast him another sweet smile that touched his heart with its sincerity. "Do not be angry with me."

"Jocelyn, I assure you that I am not."

"Then you are a finer man than I already believe you are. I'm very happy I married you. Do you mind that I am admitting this? However, I am truly sorry that I have upended your fishing plans." She cleared her throat. "What shall we do? I know you intended to go to your lodge for several weeks of peaceful contemplation, and then we considered stopping in Aberdeen first. But my mother is in no fit shape to travel just yet. Nor do my parents have transportation, since Ballantry has stranded them here with us."

"What do ye care to do?"

She glanced down at their hands, for he was still holding hers. "I want to stay with you, if you will allow it. Wherever you choose to go and no matter how long you decide to stay there. I would like my place to be with you."

"Then so it shall be. We stay together, whether here or in Aberdeen or in the wilds of Northern Scotland."

Her eyes widened. "Truly?"

"Aye. This seems to surprise ye. Had we not decided upon this already?"

She nodded. "Yes, but that was before my parents showed up, and we were never looking further ahead than one month. I was afraid this morning's turmoil had changed everything. But I am relieved. I thought I would have difficulty convincing you to keep me with you."

"Blame it on my protective instincts. Ballantry's a rogue, and I dinna trust him not to hurt ye."

"I doubt he will try anything now. But I was afraid you'd had enough of me and the theatrics that seem to follow me around."

"Ye thought I would give up on ye after less than a day of marriage? Why? Because ye're believing what yer father and Ballantry said? That I am a womanizing hound and will have no regard for the woman I take as my wife? So ye're believing what the others are saying about me and waiting for me to abandon ye at the slightest hint things are not going as I expected?"

"No! Of course not. Well…something like that," she admitted, blushing. "But also because this marriage was not freely made. You cannot deny it, Camborne. For whatever odd reason, you decided I needed protecting and that you were the man to do it. Ours is not a love match, or even a business arrangement, nor was there ever a contemplated family alliance. Which leaves me at a loss to understand your continued indulgence of all I have put you through."

"Dinna think too hard about it."

She laughed softly. "I know you believe I am not a planner, but that is not really true. I think and fret over everything…other than my botched escape from my own wedding to Ballantry, which was accomplished without any forethought whatsoever. Why are you so calm about all of this? Our situation has me fretting endlessly. Not only do you have an unwanted wife, but you now have her parents as an added burden."

"Jocelyn, there's yer mistake."

She looked at him once again, her lovely, big eyes questioning. "What do you mean?"

Perhaps this was not the best place to talk about his reasons, for they were deeply personal, and the wounds he had been carrying since childhood had yet to heal. "Take a walk with me."

She nodded and immediately rose, taking his arm as they walked out. There was something in the little things she did that pleased him, even something so small as placing her arm in his, that seemed to be done on natural instinct.

She did it because she liked him and felt close to him. She was not thinking of flaunting their connection or putting herself above others. She was not pretending to claim him as her property, or attempting to demean others with her superior status, or attempting to ingratiate herself with him.

There was no guile, no scheming involved.

There was simply Jocelyn.

And she liked him.

He did not know if this was the reason he felt he could confide in her. Gaining his trust should not have been this easy for her to do. Was she even aware how much he already trusted her? Perhaps there was something in the way she looked at him that brought out something in his heart that he had believed lost for all time. She admired him and considered him to be heroic, which he decidedly was not.

But it was nice to be looked upon kindly.

And would he ever tire of her sweet smile?

The night breeze had a little bite to it, so they hadn't walked far before he and Jocelyn returned to the inn. He waited downstairs while she ran upstairs to fetch her shawl. His heart seemed to turn lighter when he saw her hurrying down a moment later. She looked so happy to be in his company. Yes, most ladies felt this way, but only because they expected expensive trinkets out of him.

Jocelyn had yet to even ask him about the financial terms of their marriage. Not a thought about the allowance he would provide for her clothes, jewels, a carriage, a London townhouse, servants, and general spending money.

None of it. These questions did not appear to be on her mind at all.

Perhaps this was inconsequential to her because she believed she had ample funds of her own to use for those purposes. Still, marriage to him meant he now had control of her assets. She knew this, and yet she was not questioning him about his intentions.

Did she trust him that much?

She was ridiculously appreciative of all he had given her these past few days, and perhaps assumed his generosity would continue. After all, he had made quite a fool of himself in spending on her wardrobe. She knew he was rich.

Still, he doubted that she cared. Despite having been raised an earl's daughter, she did not have expensive tastes and seemed remarkably appreciative of the simpler things life had to offer.

They strolled toward the harbor, their path illuminated by the village lights and a silvery moon now visible as twilight settled over the harbor. He wrapped her in his arms as they stood by the dockside, for even her shawl was not sufficient to keep her warm against the cooling wind.

"Explain it to me," she said as they stood side by side looking out upon the shimmering water. "Why are you so solicitous of me, especially considering the demands I've placed on you?"

He tucked a finger under her chin to turn her face toward him and kiss her lightly on the mouth. "Ye've made no demands on me," he reminded her. "What I've done has been of my own accord."

She wanted to disagree, but he kissed her again.

Perhaps it was not something he should have done so openly, but there were few people out here now, for the fishermen tended to rise early and retire early. The market stalls that thrived in the daylight hours were all shuttered now.

There were a few taverns close by that seemed to be busy, but Malcolm was not worried about the patrons of these establishments. The hour was still early and most would not be drunk yet. Still, he did not intend to keep Jocelyn out for very long—just long enough to reveal a little of what was in his heart.

But where was he to start?

Start at the beginning, ye arse.

Yes, he had to tell her all of it. She would find out the truth eventually, and he did not want her leaving him once he was so deeply in love with her that his heart might never recover. He had to tell her the worst of it, and then deal with the consequences.

"Ye're curious to know why none of today's events have sent me running," he said, opening the conversation.

Jocelyn nodded. "You've been so kind to me and my family. No one else would have done this."

He laughed bitterly. "Lass, this is because no one else has suffered under the burden of..."

"Of what?"

She was looking up at him with such trust that he could not bear it.

"I killed my family." Having made the declaration, he let out a whoosh of air. If felt as though he had been punched in the gut. This was what had haunted him all these years. He never spoke about it, had not even dared to mention it to Bromleigh or Lynton, two men who were as close as brothers to him. "My parents. My siblings. All of them dead, and it was my fault."

She inhaled sharply. "How? Did they not die when you were a little boy? This is what you told me."

"Aye, I was a lad of six at the time. Do not ask me how it happened or why it happened, for I could no' tell ye. All I know is that I was the one who brought home the infection that killed them all."

He was surprised when she gave him a light shove. "Do not tell me you have been blaming yourself for this horrible thing all these years? You were six years old. *Six*. No child is ever to blame at that tender age. And how do you know that you were the one to bring it into the family?"

"I was the first to come down with it."

"So what? They might have been infected at the same time as you but took longer to develop symptoms because they were older and had acquired more resistance."

"No, I gave it to them. That's what the doctor told my uncles."

She looked appalled. "And they repeated this vile thing to you?"

"No," he said with a shake of his head. "I overheard them talking to the doctor about it. Months later, when I had fully recovered, I questioned my uncles. They admitted it had been my fault."

She shoved him lightly again and then hugged him. "They are such fools! It wasn't your fault. If your parents and siblings had any idea blame had been cast upon you—a child who had just experienced the loss of all his loved ones—they would have come back to haunt those silly men. The doctor, too! He could not know for certain how the disease had come to ravage your family. Even if it was obvious that you had succumbed first, so what? You were as defenseless as they were. The disease was to blame. *Not you.*"

He smiled at her, for she looked so fierce in her defense of him.

Perhaps this is what he had been missing all along, this complete and utter, loving support.

How odd it felt not to be fighting alone. How nice it felt to be defended by this mighty maiden with raven-dark hair and crystal-blue eyes, this lovely fae being who barely reached his shoulder and whose body was fashioned of soft curves instead of hard muscle.

He had married her because something within his soul had compelled him.

He'd thought it was his need to protect her. But his soul had recognized the true need. She was the one meant to protect *him*.

She stared up at him with watery eyes.

He groaned. "Are ye going to cry, lass?"

"No. I am merely feeling misty eyed because I now understand why you married me." She placed a hand against his scarred cheek. "You are finally ready to forgive yourself for this terrible thing that happened to your family all those years ago…a terrible thing that was never your fault."

"Is that so?"

"Yes, for this was the true purpose of your trip to your lodge. This malaise you were feeling was your heart telling you it was time to move on, to stop depriving yourself of the joy you deserve."

He tucked a finger under her chin and gave it a light tweak. "I did not realize I had married a philosopher."

"Oh, I have read many books on the topic." She smiled. "Along with books on having sex against a wall."

He laughed.

"Are you ready to stop punishing yourself?"

He desperately ached for it. But was he able to dust away years of torment and unburden himself just yet? He doubted it would be that simple.

"Jocelyn, I married ye because I made a bollocks of my confrontation with Burling, and this would have ruined ye unless I stepped forward and made ye my wife."

She nodded. "Yes, that is partly true. But think about it, Camborne. You were ready for a change, weren't you?"

He gave her chin another tweak. "Not that drastic a change."

She did not get irritated, and instead laughed softly along with him. "All right, perhaps not such an extreme move immediately. But this is in the direction you were headed. You wanted a family life again. You wanted loved ones around you, for this is what you've missed so badly. Camborne…"

"Aye, lass?"

"Is this why you did not mind marrying me? I'm sure it was, and I am glad of it. I want to be this for you. I had no desire to be this for anyone else who came before you."

"Which is how ye earned yer reputation as a harpy."

She nodded again. "Deserved, I suppose. I spurned every suitor and none of them took it well. Then you came along and…everything about you felt so right. I think I am falling in love with you. Oh, do not be angry with me. I cannot help what I am feeling. Nor do I expect you to feel the same way. It happened so quickly for me, in the blink of an eye."

"Lass, we've barely known each other two days."

"I know. It makes no sense. But I felt a stirring in my heart from the very first moment I saw you. I should have been scared, for you were drunk and growling as you woke me up. But even as I trembled, I wanted to kiss you to keep you from bellowing at me. Then I thought myself mad for even considering such a thing. But I still wanted to kiss you."

His insides warmed as she spilled her feelings. She truly was a refreshing breath of spring.

"Och, I will admit to being most surprised to find a lump in my bed. Did I frighten ye terribly with my growls?"

"A little, at first. You were quite big and daunting. And you had caught me trespassing." She sighed. "But then you sat at the foot of the bed and asked me why I was in hiding. My fear soon passed. You were impossibly handsome and so very kind. I could feel your protective concern and knew you would not harm me. Well, I hoped I was right in trusting you, because I really wanted to kiss you."

He laughed again. "And there I was, thinking the very same thing about ye."

"Camborne, I know you will think it is too early for me to say this because we cannot possibly know each other well enough yet…but I really am in grave danger of falling in love with you."

He cleared his throat.

She sighed again. "I do not expect you to feel the same way. You are not prone to rash judgments. I did not think I was either, but then I ran away from my wedding and stumbled my way to you. I have been in raptures over you since that first night. I did not plan it and I did not believe it could possibly be real at first."

"Jocelyn, ye canno' know for certain."

"Because it is too soon? Yes, this is true. I did not believe I would be so fortunate as to have a love match. Do you think you are capable of falling in love?"

"With ye? Or is this a general question? I have no' thought about it. More accurately put, I refused to think about it."

"But you would have thought about it while fishing at your lodge." She pursed her lips as she contemplated their situation. "I wonder what might have happened had you been looking for a wife when I made my Society debut."

"I dinna think ye would have liked me much back then. I purposely avoided the respectable *ton* parties where I might have found ye. Seems I found ye anyway. My destiny girl," he whispered, wrapping her in his arms.

"Yes, destined. That is a good way to describe us."

He agreed, although he was not yet ready to say more. So he kissed her instead, sinking his lips onto hers and loving the soft give of her mouth as she accepted him.

She could become a craving need.

How was it possible for her to make his heart sing?

He did not want to have these feelings for her yet. He was still such a mess inside. Perhaps it was as she had said—he was tormented and unsettled because he was aching to forgive himself and move on.

But what if he wasn't able to move on? What if he could not escape the blame that still had him in a stranglehold? What if opening his heart to love only led to more tragedy?

All it had taken was one mistake, and he'd lost his entire family. A contagion caught and brought home to attack his parents and siblings.

"Let's take it one day at a time, lass."

"All right." She tossed him the gentlest smile, but he saw the disappointment gleaming in her eyes. "This was a wonderful first step. I'm glad we had this meaningful conversation."

He wasn't.

On the one hand, he'd needed to tell her. On the other hand, his heart simply wasn't ready yet.

But this was one of the things he liked about Jocelyn, her compassion. Her honesty, too. She could not lie to him.

But he was not nearly as nice as she was.

Would he revert to his old ways and break her heart?

Chapter Ten

Later that evening, Jocelyn found herself once more staring at the bed she and Camborne shared. Her excitement mounted, for she would now be sharing it with him as his wife. Would it feel different? Perhaps even more wonderful because of the commitment behind the intimate act? She would find out soon, for he was eyeing her with heat and the hint of a rakish smile as he undressed.

"Jocelyn, ye're staring at the bed again."

"Only for happy reasons, Camborne. Do you mind that I call you that? It feels so formal. Would you prefer me to call you by something other than your title? By your given name, perhaps? Or an endearment? Or *husband*?" she said with a grin, for she could not deny the thrill of becoming his wife and was enjoying the newness of it.

He laughed softly. "No, lass. Camborne is fine. I happen to like the impudent way ye say it. Ye're a little thing, and yet I feel as though I ought to leap to attention whenever I hear it on yer lips."

She cast him a look of dismay. "Oh, no. Then I do sound like a harpy."

He moved behind Jocelyn and wrapped his arms around her. "No, lass. Ye sound as though ye can stand up to me and at the same time hold me in yer affection. It sounds good. Not at all cloying or demanding, and not subservient either. While we're on the topic, do ye have a preference for what I should call ye?"

She leaned back slightly to nestle against his bare chest, for he had slipped off most of his clothes and now wore only his trousers. "No," she said with a shake of her head, warmed by the heat of his skin. "Whatever you're comfortable with is fine with me."

The mere sound of his voice made her tingle. The deep, rich brogue was so delicious. It always got her heart racing.

He kissed her softly on the neck. "Would ye mind if I called ye 'sweetheart' whenever we are in private moments?"

She turned in his arms to look up at him in surprise. "I would not mind at all. This would please me immensely. Are you sure?"

"Not a doubt, *sweetheart*."

She could not contain her smile. "Thank you, *Camborne*."

Perhaps this was his compromise, since he was not ready to say that he loved her—not that she expected him to make any promises or admit any attraction at this early point in their marriage. Obviously, he did not want to make her feel unwanted. Settling on this endearment was a good compromise and assuaged her disappointment.

In truth, she was not really disappointed that he did not love her yet. This was too big a step for him to take, considering how guarded and cautious he was. She knew it would happen in time.

Well, she hoped it would.

She leaned back against him, loving the warmth of his skin against her cheek and his subtle, musky scent.

His heart beat strong and steady, while hers was rampant. "I'm glad I waited for you," she whispered, more to herself than to him.

But he heard her and kissed her lightly on the neck again. "So am I, sweetheart."

He then helped her out of her gown, leaving her only in her linen undergarments.

She moaned softly. "I should have worn the silk today."

"No, lass. It does no' matter. Ye look lovely just as ye are. Besides, ye had no time to think about it, as we were in a mad rush to reach the church."

"It feels like a lifetime ago." She was seriously considering wearing those silk unmentionables tomorrow, because she was beginning to understand the sensual power of a woman's body in silk. It was but a fabric, but somehow enhanced the sensation of touch and stirred one's desire.

She yearned to have him desire her. Would he respond at all to her plain linen undergarments?

He kissed her bare shoulders as he slipped the straps of her chemise off her.

"Jocelyn," he said, her name tearing from his lips with a heartfelt groan as he regarded her with smoldering eyes. He swept her in his arms and they fell onto the bed, clutching each other and eager to fulfill the duties of a wedding night. His kisses were hot and hungry, more so than last night, when, she realized, he had been gentle and determined to hold back.

But not tonight. He seemed ravenous for her, his lips searing as they crushed down on hers, devouring her and conquering her, demanding she surrender.

Was there a doubt she would? She was his wife, his to possess and love forever more.

But he was hers, too.

He kissed her breasts and then lower, his need to know her and memorize all of her almost primal. He inhaled her scent, tasted her skin with soft licks that set her on fire and sent her to new heights of pleasure.

Each hot kiss, each intimate touch of his roughened hands, had her tingling, and she was soon soaring.

This was his way of claiming her, of connecting their bodies and their hearts. Of binding their souls.

Of promising to always protect her.

She was his craving, and by this love act he was embedding her in his soul.

She was doing the same, feeling the same primal hunger.

Dear heaven. His big, muscled body was insanely hot.

He moved inside her with powerful grace, touched her and stroked her until she was mindless and breathless and wanted him so badly, she thought her heart would burst.

She tried to hold back as he took her, but she was on the verge of shattering and still hungry for more. She wanted *everything* of him.

"Ye're almost there, love," he murmured, and then smiled when she softly cried his name. "I have ye, Jocelyn. I have ye, my lovely lass."

She clung to him and took his deep thrusts as he filled her with pleasure.

He soon followed in his own release, emitting a lion's growl and rolling onto his back once he'd drained every drop of himself inside her. Breathing heavily and smiling rakishly, he drew her into the circle of his arms and settled her atop him so that her bosom pressed against his chest and her legs tangled with his.

Their bodies were hot and damp. Their breaths had yet to steady. Their bedcovers were in an impossible tangle around their bodies.

Naked bodies.

His was magnificent, hard and muscled and scarred in places other than merely his cheek. He had one scar at his hip and another along his upper arm. She traced her fingers along the dusting of hair on his chest to feel for more. "Did you get these during the war?"

He let out a breath. "Some of them. Others I got when falling down drunk after a night of…of doing things I should no' have been doing. But those days are over for me. I gave ye my vow."

She gave him a light kiss on his chest. "Camborne, I hope to make you happy."

"Ye will, lass. Ye will."

"You sound quite sure."

He smiled as he ran his fingers lightly through her unbound hair. "I am. Why should I stray when I have the prettiest girl in my arms? And the tastiest, too. I love yer scent. Ye're a sweet summer apple. Delicious."

"And just a bit tart?"

"Ye're perfect. I love the way ye respond to my touch."

"Camborne," she said with a roll of her eyes, "all women must respond to you in this fashion. I'm sure they do."

He shrugged. "Aye, could be. I never knew what was real and what was not. Mostly, it was a mere performance to gain my favor in the hope I would be generous afterward. It's different with ye, lass. Better. I will always get honesty from ye."

She nodded. "I love this. I will never mind falling asleep in your arms. In fact, I believe it is a requirement."

He arched an eyebrow. "That we share a bed?"

She cast him an impish smile. "I believe it is written in our marriage license."

He kissed her on the forehead. "This husband is happy to comply with the terms of said marriage license. My arms will always be open to ye, Jocelyn."

"Mutual, Camborne."

He ran his fingers lightly through her hair again, his touch as gentle as a caress. "How do ye feel, lass? Did I hurt ye?"

"No, it was wonderful. I think yesterday's initiation rite against the wall has turned me wanton. It was a lovely sampling of the thrills to come."

"Och, lass. That wall... It was nice. But it could no' have been comfortable for ye."

"Worse for you, although you did not seem to mind. I like this. You and me with our arms wrapped around each other. You make me feel cherished." She let out a shaky breath. "You make me feel glad I held out for you." She glanced up at him. "It is *you* I see, Camborne. Not your title. I hope you know this."

He rolled her under him so that he was atop her, but propped on his elbows so he would not crush her with the weight of his big body. "Ye've nothing to prove to me, Jocelyn. I know ye are sincere."

Did this mean he trusted her?

"Out of curiosity," she said, "what makes you so certain about me?"

He put his mouth to her neck and kissed her lightly. His breath was warm and the touch of his lips made her tingle. "Ye still haven't asked me for anything."

She frowned. "What did I need to ask you for when you've given me everything without my ever having to say a word? You've also insisted on paying for my parents, their room and meals at the inn, the doctor visits, and a carriage to take them back home once my mother is fit to travel. This is more than generous of you. I would not protest if you chose to take the expense out of my dowry. It is quite substantial, you know. Did my father tell you how much I bring to the marriage?"

He tensed. "Jocelyn, I dinna care. I dinna marry ye for yer dower fortune."

"But not even to ask about it? It is fifty thousand pounds."

An odd look came upon his face. "It does no' matter. I dinna care if it is nothing."

"But it matters to me. I did not come to you penniless," she insisted, wondering at his expression. It did not make sense for him to dismiss this bounty. He had just accused her of having no interest in his wealth. But was he not doing the same?

Why should she be asking for an accounting of his assets when he cared nothing for hers? How was her attitude any different from his?

Bringing something to the marriage was a source of pride for her, especially since she had trapped him into marrying her. Not on purpose, of course. And he did not seem to mind being caught or feel that he'd been tricked.

But he seemed determined to avoid this dowry conversation altogether.

Well, they would sort it out later. Why talk when his naked body was atop her and making her feel amorous again?

There was much to be said for men in their forties. Camborne's body was exquisite, a manly body—fully developed muscles and gloriously broad shoulders. Yet he was trim in the waist and firm in the legs.

His face was manly, as well. Solid jaw, well-defined angles, lips that had the power to possess her with their warmth and seductive strength.

He did not behave like a child, as many young bucks in their twenties did. Some behaved like spoiled children even into their thirties. But everything about Camborne spoke of honor and valor, intelligence and duty. He was experienced. No one was ever going to make a fool of him.

When she told him her thoughts, he rolled off her and fell onto his back laughing. "Lass, I am an *idjit* in so many ways, especially when it comes to women. Is it not obvious?"

"You've been wonderful to me," she insisted.

He turned serious. "Ye're going to hear a lot of scandalous things about me where women are involved, and they're probably all true. But ye're my wife, and the only one who will have to put up with me from now on. As for business affairs, I was never fleeced, and no one has ever made a fool of me. But I have made a fool of myself by purposely surrounding myself with the commoner element of Society. I consorted with ladies I knew would try to take advantage of me. I threw them bones—sometimes very nice bones. But no one ever got anything out of me that I dinna want to give."

She wanted examples.

He resisted, at first. Finally, he told her a story or two about stupid things he had done recently. One misguided affair that concerned an actress and another that concerned an unhappily married countess. He refused to name either of the ladies involved. "This is in my past, Jocelyn."

She understood this. She was not going to admonish him for actions taken when he was unattached.

In truth, she had stopped really listening the moment he said she was his wife and the only one who would have to put up with him.

Did this mean he was thinking of her as the only woman he would bed? Was he thinking of permanence?

She snuggled against him, embarrassed that she had yet to don her clothes. But she liked the warmth of his skin against hers, and loved the gentle way he touched her with his roughened hands.

He stopped talking and began to kiss his way down her body, her breasts, her stomach, and made his way lower.

This night was turning into something quite decadent. But there was something wonderful in the way he held her, as though he wanted her in his arms forever.

Yes, it was this feeling of forever that had her smiling. He made her feel safe and adored.

He also seemed to like her breasts very much. She liked the way he touched them and suckled them.

"Och, lass. Ye're the prettiest thing I've ever seen," he whispered after they had coupled again and both of them were tangled in each other's arms.

The air around them was hot and filled with the scent of their coupling. It was a scent unique to them as husband and wife.

Well, she hoped it was. She did not like to think Camborne had shared this experience with other women. But he had, of course. This was his reputation.

She tried not to dwell on this fact. This was her wedding night.

"It is no' the same, love," he said, cutting through the silence.

She looked up at him, meeting his sharp, assessing gaze. "What isn't the same? And how do you know what I am thinking?"

"Yer lips are puckered and yer brow is slightly furrowed. Yer expression is wistful and fretful, which means ye're thinking too hard about what we've been doing and now wondering if I've felt the same with those others before ye. I haven't. Ye canno' keep comparing yerself to them. What we have is completely different, Jocelyn."

"How is it different?"

She knew it was not the same thing because she was his wife. But was it different in a better way?

She was less experienced than his prior conquests. She had come to him as a stranger. He had been acquainted with those other ladies. Some of his casual liaisons had gone on over the course of years.

Did they *perform* the sexual act better than she did?

They must have, for she was a novice. Camborne had a lot to teach her.

"It is different in that none of them were mine to love and protect. Nor did I have any inclination to take them on as my responsibility. They belonged to others, and I preferred it that way. But ye...ye're mine, Jocelyn. I mean to keep ye in my heart. I mean to keep ye safe and look after ye."

"I do feel safe with you," she said.

"I'm glad of it, lass."

She fell asleep to the soothing strokes of his hand along her arm.

<hr>

JOCELYN AWOKE IN the morning to find herself alone in their bed.

Smothering her disappointment, she sat up and looked around. "There you are," she said, smiling as she watched Camborne standing by the room's small mirror hanging upon the wall, shaving. He must have quietly washed up, for his hair was wet and there were droplets of water on his arms.

She wanted to run her fingers through the thick chestnut curls that he'd brushed back to keep them off his face. He looked so handsome.

The air held the fresh scent of sandalwood and lather. He wore nothing but a towel wrapped around his hips.

He turned toward her, smiled, and then winked. "Morning, love. Did ye have a good sleep?"

She nodded, her heart already pounding because he looked so magnificent. "Yes. I slept quite soundly. What time is it?"

"Early still. Not quite seven o'clock. I dinna mean to wake ye."

She yawned. "You didn't. I'm usually an early riser too. But last night wore me out. Not that I am complaining, mind you. Last night was nice."

He'd finished shaving and wiped the last of the lather off his chin, then strode to her side and sat beside her on the bed. "It was better than nice, sweetheart," he said in a husky murmur, and kissed her softly on the lips. He smelled clean and male.

She had to wash up, too.

But he did not seem to care.

He gathered her in his arms and captured her mouth in a hungrier kiss. "Best ever," he whispered, drawing away and proceeding to dress for the day.

She was disappointed that he did not return to their bed. Perhaps she was not all that enticing.

But he came to her side and kissed her again. "I canno' get enough of ye, lass."

"Mutual, Camborne."

She had to be patient. They would enjoy each other again tonight.

"Lass, we'll never get out of this bedchamber today if ye dinna stop looking at me that way."

"How am I looking at you?" Which was a ridiculous question to ask, because they both knew she had been gawking at him, practically salivating as she watched him dress.

"The same way I'm feeling about ye, only I hide it better." He sighed. "Ye're the prettiest sight a man can look upon when he wakes for the day."

She blushed.

"Gad," he muttered. "I'm in danger of becoming a besotted husband. I had better head downstairs and have my coffee. Shall I order a bath for ye?"

She nodded. "Yes, please."

"I'll have breakfast sent up for ye, too. Once ye're ready, we can check on yer parents."

Dear heaven.

She had been mooning over Camborne and not thinking about them at all this morning. What a dreadful daughter she was! But she had left her mother's side yesterday knowing she was on the mend. Since her father had not come knocking at their door last night, she expected they had passed a quiet night and were likely still sleeping.

"Yes, that is a good plan," she said.

Mercy. Mercy. Mercy. How could she forget all about her parents? In truth, Camborne had her so mindless with desire that she was in danger of forgetting her own name.

"Do you realize that in two hours we shall be married one full day?"

"Is that so?" He laughed. "Are ye going to give me a marriage report each morning, lass? Like a weather report? *It is forecast to be raining and we have now been married three months and two days.* I'm not likely ever to forget the day I married ye. Besides, it only happened yesterday. I'd have to be hopelessly foggy not to recall."

Shaking his head and still laughing, he walked out and quietly shut the door behind him.

Jocelyn rubbed her hands along her face. "You are such a silly goose," she chided herself.

Had he meant to make a jest of their marriage? Was she the only one who considered it significant? Waking up to each other this morning was something special, but he was going about his routine as though the day was like any other.

Jocelyn shook off the thought. She was fretting over nothing. Had he not held her in his arms last night and made her feel cherished?

Well, he probably made all his partners feel cherished. She was the latest in a long line of women.

No, not the latest. She was the *last*.

Or was she?

Chapter Eleven

The sun shone brightly into Malcolm's carriage as he, Jocelyn, and her parents approached the Balgownie Arms in Aberdeen shortly before noon. It had been two weeks since his confrontation with Ballantry, and it was now time to meet Jocelyn's former betrothed head-on and dispense with any duty owed the cur.

"What a lovely place you've chosen for us," Jocelyn gushed, her eyes wide as she peered out of the carriage window in delight. "My parents and I have been to Aberdeen several times but never stayed anywhere nearly as lovely as this inn."

Malcolm followed her gaze. "Glad ye like it."

The inn had a magnificently sweeping view of the sea, and yet was conveniently located near many of the finer attractions in Aberdeen. The city itself had a bustling port and was one of Malcolm's favorite places for its quieter Society, as well as its proximity to the natural splendor of the Highlands. One did not have to step far to find anything one wanted.

As for him, he had all he wanted because Jocelyn was by his side. They'd been married two weeks now, and he was falling more deeply in love with her each day.

He was even growing to love her morning reports. "Good morning, Camborne," she would say, her beautiful mouth swollen by his kisses and cheeks pink from a heavenly night nestled in his arms. "It appears we are to have sunshine today, and we have been married for fourteen days."

This had been her report this morning, concluding with an "I love you" that she had decided he needed to hear daily, even though he was not encouraging this commitment. Jocelyn felt it was important to tell him anyway.

Of course, the lass hid nothing of her feelings. He would have easily noticed how she felt even if she had never spoken the words aloud.

Her smile as she gave him these morning reports elated him and wrapped around his heart. Yes, married two weeks now. An entire fortnight as husband and wife. Who would ever believe it? He had never been more content.

However, this feeling of contentment had a darker side to it, for it brought on a pain he dared not let her see. The cause of this pain was simple. Having now found her, he dreaded losing her.

This was what troubled him most.

He was a man who liked to be in control at all times, but how did one control destiny? Was there a higher power that played them like puppets? Jocelyn had been on the run with funds enough to get her to Arbroth. He had been forced to stop there overnight to repair a cracked carriage wheel.

What destiny gave, it could also take away.

He hated this helpless feeling, this worry that she would be snatched from him. What could he do to prevent it? Or would he remain unable to do anything to save her, just as he had been unable to save his parents and siblings?

He settled his gaze on Jocelyn, who always had the ability to make him smile. She was happy in their marriage, fairly radiated her joy like a bright sun. He knew she would never leave him willingly.

But was she not just as helpless as he was? She could be taken from him in the blink of an eye. If ever that were to happen, the heartache would swallow him up whole and drag him into a dark abyss from which he might never climb out.

This was the agonizing risk of opening one's heart to love. It left one aching and vulnerable. Love was happiness, but it was also the destroyer of souls.

For this reason, he had tried hard to avoid falling in love with Jocelyn. But it was a losing proposition from the start. She was embedded in his heart and digging in deeper with each passing day.

"Do ye think Ballantry will show?" Jocelyn's father asked, stirring him from his thoughts.

"I expect so," Malcolm replied. "He is in need of funds and will want this matter settled as expeditiously as possible. Whatever the source is of no concern to him. He wants the money. Whether from you, me, or Jocelyn is irrelevant to him. The only question is, what will it take to make him go away?"

Jocelyn's smile faded. "It is all my fault this is happening."

Her father stayed silent.

Her mother was frowning at her father, no doubt urging him to tell Jocelyn the truth about her dowry, a truth she herself had only learned of recently. But the old man clamped his lips shut tight and allowed Jocelyn to continue placing blame on herself.

"It is no' yer fault," Malcolm said with a soft growl. "Ye did the right thing in escaping him, Jocelyn."

"But I—"

"Ye were getting pressured by all around ye to marry, lass. Ye canno' be faulted for accepting his offer. Besides, it led ye to me. I'm no' complaining about it." He cast her an affectionate smile that he hoped would stir her from her unwarranted feelings of guilt.

He supposed they all carried their own demons, some small and some large. But these were the travails of life, the bad mixing in with the good.

Which was why one had to grab the good and appreciate it while it lasted. Was he not better off having Jocelyn for whatever time they were given? How empty his life had been until he met and married her.

She suddenly gasped and pointed to someone standing in the entryway of the inn. "Lord Burling's here. What a scurvy leech he is. This must mean Lord Ballantry is here and waiting for us, too."

Malcolm took her hand when she balled it into a fist, and kept it firmly in his against her mild protest. "Ye are not to hop out of the carriage and punch him."

"Indeed, Jocelyn," her father intoned, "I forbid ye to engage that lout!"

"I was not going to hit him," she grumbled. "Much as I would love to lay him low."

Malcolm raised her fist to his lips and kissed it, knowing it would soften her resistance. He did not want her anywhere near that toad, but she appeared stubbornly determined to confront Burling. "Stay clear of him, lass. Ballantry, too."

He did not want her near either of those men, not even after he had settled with them. Well, he wasn't about to give anything to Burling. The toad could put the touch on Ballantry once that wretch was flush with his settlement funds.

Malcolm's heart began to pump faster. He looked forward to dealing with Ballantry. The result would not turn out as the blackguard expected. Jocelyn's former betrothed was likely counting his money already, but he was about to have a rude awakening. Malcolm was going to offer him much less than the bounder expected.

Jocelyn wriggled in her seat, her lovely derriere suddenly in Malcolm's face as she stood up and then leaned half her body out the open window.

He laughed and put his hands around her waist to nudge her back onto the seat bench as she was about to shout at Burling. "Jocelyn, save that fire for the bedchamber," he said, not caring whether her parents heard him. They were married, after all.

She gasped. "Camborne!" Her cheeks burned a bright pink and her big eyes crackled with defiance as she stared back at him. "Why did you stop me? I was merely going to—"

"I know what ye were going to do. But ye're a duchess now, not a street fighter," he told her, although he hadn't minded almost getting a mouthful of her delicious arse between his teeth. "Ye need do nothing more than give him a freezing stare to put him in his place."

"But he is such a toad!"

The lass showed every range of emotion on her lovely face. He would have to teach her how to hide those, although he wasn't certain he would ever succeed...or ever wanted to succeed. Her honesty and openness were among the things that endeared her to him.

"All right," she muttered, still disgruntled as she resumed her seat beside him.

That she settled against him, her body pressed to his, revealed she was not really all that irritated with him. This was another thing he liked about Jocelyn, her inability to hold a grudge or maintain her annoyance.

In truth, she was a sensible lass. She was willing to admit when she was in the wrong and readily forgave him when it turned out he was in the wrong. The mistakes were small and hardly worth fighting over. Also, she was very gentle with him.

He could not have found a more perfect wife for himself if he'd searched for a thousand years. He considered it a small miracle she had tumbled into his bed that first night. Had the choice of a wife been left to him instead of being thrust upon him, he would have chosen badly, because he was a clueless arse.

Fate had intervened and saved him.

"What happens next?" Jocelyn asked as they drew up in the inn's courtyard, and Terrence drew the team to a halt in front of the white stone structure.

The very day of their Arbroth wedding, Malcolm had sent Terrence off to Edinburgh in the hope he might discover something to gain leverage over Ballantry in the upcoming settlement negotiation. The coachman had returned four days ago with information that could destroy Ballantry, if true.

Perhaps marriage to Jocelyn was making Malcolm soft, for he was not of a mind to grind Ballantry's guts to mincemeat. But nor was he going to allow the bounder to take advantage of Jocelyn.

She was staring at him, awaiting his answer to her question.

"Nothing is going to happen yet, lass. You and I will merely settle in our rooms, wash the dust off our clothes, and perhaps grab a bite to eat if ye are hungry. Yer parents, I expect, will do the same." Malcolm was eager to dispense with Ballantry, but he did not want Jocelyn involved. This settlement matter weighed too heavily on her heart.

Besides, she did not have it in her to be cold or calculating. He did not want her interfering in the nasty bit of business he was about to attend to. Indeed, it *was* nasty, and Ballantry would be enraged.

He had sent Terrence to Edinburgh to engage certain investigators of good reputation in the hope that they would dig up something on Ballantry. But the reports Terrence had brought back were startling. In truth, the information discovered was so damaging, Malcolm would not be surprised if Ballantry ran off with his tail tucked between his legs.

He now had all the leverage. He could offer Ballantry nothing, and even demand payment, if he had a mind to do so. The secret was so explosive, the bounder would be begging Malcolm to keep it from ever coming out.

However, he still intended to offer Ballantry a settlement because he wanted the oaf to leave Scotland and set up residence somewhere on the Continent, perhaps France or Italy. Those would be his terms. Not a shilling would exchange hands unless Ballantry left the country permanently.

The man's estates would be far better off handled by his nephew, a decent lad who was already tending to the properties while Ballantry lived his life of debauchery. The nephew would maintain them and turn them into something for him to eventually inherit once Ballantry passed.

Based on Ballantry's reckless womanizing, he was bound to die of the pox in a matter of years, or be shot by an angry husband.

Not that Malcolm thought himself much better. He had been a hound, too. But it was different. He'd carefully chosen his conquests and never grabbed just any pretty skirt. He'd maintained a code of honor of a sort, never bedding innocents or breaking up solid marriages.

But the point was not to dwell on his own misguided past. The point was for Jocelyn's former betrothed to keep his distance from her, never disparage her, and never cross paths with her again.

Burling scurried off like the rat he was upon spotting them alighting from their carriage. No doubt he had gone to warn Ballantry of their arrival.

Bastard.

The sooner Malcolm dealt with Ballantry, the sooner that unsavory pair would leave. He and Jocelyn could then enjoy their marriage without the threat of retribution from Ballantry hanging over their heads.

Not that he gave a fig about any threats against himself. He was a grown man and could defend himself. Protecting Jocelyn was his only concern.

He was also looking forward to spending time alone with her. Of course, the matter of her dowry also had to be put to rest. This was a delicate situation to resolve, but an easy one. The earl and his wife loved their daughter, and she loved them in return.

While he was going to help the earl maintain his pride by giving him the funds to replenish the dowry account, Malcolm hoped Jocelyn's father would come around on his own and admit what he had done.

He did not like keeping this secret from Jocelyn. In truth, he wanted nothing but honesty between him and his wife.

He briefly thought back to their first day together, when he'd taken her shopping to purchase clothes she lacked. It was a day of joy for him. He needed more days like that, just him and Jocelyn getting to know each other, and finding they liked each other.

"Let me help ye down, Lady Granby," he said, hopping out of the carriage when it rolled to a stop. He assisted the older pair out, and then took his sweet time assisting Jocelyn. He liked the feel of her body and was in no hurry to let her go.

She cast him an impudent smile. "I am in no danger of falling, Camborne. You may let go of me at any time."

"What makes ye think I am holding on to ye merely to hold ye steady? May a husband not enjoy holding his wife?"

She laughed, and then leaned into him to whisper, "I think our bodies are in danger of fusing if we continue to behave as shockingly as we do in bed each night."

"All right, lass," he said with a conquering grin. "I'll let ye go, but stay close to me. I dinna like ye to be out of my sight while Ballantry and his toady Burling are here."

She nodded. "I'll stay close."

He kissed her on the nose before escorting her inside and signing their names in the register. The proprietor, a genial man by the name of Wilbur Grant, knew Malcolm because he always stayed here when he came to Aberdeen, which was fairly often.

"Welcome, Yer Grace." He was effusive in his congratulations when Malcolm introduced Jocelyn as his bride, and then introduced her parents. Mr. Grant showed them to their rooms while his staff carried in their luggage.

Of course, none of them had much that needed to be brought in. Malcolm always traveled light, never having a reason to bring more than his minimal needs, since he had an entire wardrobe available to him in every house he owned.

Jocelyn had nothing more than the gowns and other articles purchased for her in Arbroth, while her parents, having taken off in a mad dash with Ballantry to track down Jocelyn, had merely crammed a few garments into their travel sacks, never thinking they would be gone from their home for this long.

Well, it did not matter. Malcolm would purchase whatever else any of them needed while in Aberdeen. In truth, it felt good to have a reason to spend on Jocelyn and her parents. Until now, his only spending on others was to acquire consolation gifts for women he'd bedded and then never thought of again.

"Lord and Lady Granby, I hope this chamber meets with yer approval," Mr. Grant said, his expression one of pride as he opened the door to the guest chamber Malcolm had requested for Jocelyn's parents.

"Quite lovely," Lady Granby said, sparing a smile for Malcolm.

"Yes, it'll do nicely," Lord Granby added with a nod, also casting a glance at Malcolm. But his regard was one of shame, Malcolm was distressed to realize. Granby was a prideful man, and it must have wounded him to know Malcolm was providing for them all. These were luxuries *he* should have been able to provide for his loved ones.

Of course, it was not possible, since Granby had squandered much of his wealth, along with Jocelyn's dowry, on those bad investments.

Malcolm and Jocelyn left her parents and followed Mr. Grant to their suite of rooms. The suite provided the finest quarters available at the inn. It had a splendid view of the sea from the bedroom and the small but elegant parlor. Since it was a corner suite, it also had a view of the city from its west-facing windows.

Jocelyn turned to Malcolm, her eyes wide and her smile endearing. "This is beautiful."

"I'm glad ye like it, Yer Grace," Mr. Grant said, bowing to her.

"We are at yer service."

Malcolm shut the door to afford them privacy once the proprietor left. "Nice, isn't it?"

She laughed warmly. "Fit for a queen, Camborne. You certainly know how to travel in style. I thought the inn at Arbroth was heavenly, but this is beyond description. Just look at this stunning view of the sea."

He came to stand behind her and wrapped his arms around her. "It'll be nicer once I've rid us of Ballantry and his rat-faced toady."

She nodded as she leaned against his chest. "I know I was incensed when he threatened us back in Arbroth, but I am past my ire now. Use as much of my dowry as you see fit to pay him off. Truly, I will feel better if you use what I've brought into the marriage rather than expend a shilling of your own funds."

"Jocelyn," he said, tensing as he always did whenever she brought up the topic, "whatever I have is meant to be shared with ye. I've told ye before, I dinna care what ye bring to the marriage. It was not the reason I married ye."

"Still, it was my mistake, and I would feel better if it did not cost *you*. Well, I suppose everything I have is now yours according to law. I must have been delirious when I agreed to marry Ballantry. The thought of that barbarian taking control of anything of mine just curls my stomach." She sighed and nestled closer to him. "He must be desperate for funds if he is already here. I'll wager he won't wait an hour before sending word to meet you. Will you allow me to sit in on your conversations?"

"No, lass. This is better left between me and Ballantry."

"And my father?"

"It is best if I handle Ballantry alone."

She turned to look up at him, her expression mildly admonishing. "Famous last words. Just do not punch him or shoot him unless he attacks you first. We do not want a repeat of the Burling incident."

He chuckled. "Will ye always hold that encounter against me, lass? It did not turn out so badly for ye, did it?"

"No," she admitted. "One might even say that I owe Burling a debt of gratitude for forcing us together. But watch out for Ballantry. He has no morals and will cheat without compunction. I do not want you to get hurt."

"Nor do I wish for ye to be hurt," he said in all seriousness. "I'd like ye to stay with yer parents while I'm downstairs talking to Ballantry. As ye said, neither man is to be trusted. In fact, I'm going to have Terrence guard ye while I'm conferring with Ballantry. I fully expect him to have planned something nefarious."

"Oh my. Camborne, do you really think he would be so foolish?"

"Aye, love. But no harm done if I am proved wrong."

"What if his plan is to harm *you*? Shouldn't Terrence be watching you?"

He shook his head. "I've been taking care of myself since I was a child. He'll not get the better of me."

She hugged him fiercely. "Promise me you will be careful. I do not want to lose you."

He had no intention of doing something foolish and risking the loss of all he had gained by marrying her. "Ye'll be the wealthiest widow in the land if they succeed in doing me in."

She gasped. "Do not even jest about this! Do you think I care about material possessions over you?"

"Lass, it was merely a harmless quip. Dinna get distressed," he said.

"Besides, how am I to inherit anything from you, since we haven't taken care of our betrothal matters yet? Not that I care. Let your fortune go to the next in line for the Camborne title. It is *you* I want by my side, not your treasure chests."

He had upset her, and now sought to smooth things over. This moment was as good as any to reveal a little of what he had already done. "Jocelyn, ye will never be left destitute. What did ye think I was doing while we were in Arbroth waiting for yer mother to return to health?"

"Taking care of Camborne estate matters," she replied.

"And did ye not think protecting my new wife was one of the most important matters? Much remains to be formalized, but I've made immediate arrangements with my bankers to establish an account for ye. It is in yer name alone, and I've placed one hundred thousand pounds in it."

"Camborne!" Her eyes popped wide. "That is ridiculous."

He grinned. "Too little?"

She huffed. "Too much, as you well know."

"It is not nearly enough. I'll be adding yer dowry to it once matters are resolved with Ballantry. Och, Jocelyn. Are ye going to cry?"

"No… Maybe. You leave me speechless with your generosity. You've only known me a fortnight."

"Ye're my wife."

"And happily so," she replied. "I know we will eventually need to discuss these terms, but can we not merely enjoy each other for now?"

"Aye, lass. We can do both, and we will finalize this outstanding matter of our marriage settlement once Parliament is back in session and I return to London. I'll have my solicitors there prepare the necessary documents."

He wasn't keen on returning, but he was one of the Scottish dukes nominated to sit in the House of Lords and could not shirk this duty. Nor did he wish to shirk it, for he'd always understood the importance of his role in protecting the interests of all Scotsmen.

This would also give him the opportunity to catch up with Bromleigh and Lynton. Those two confirmed bachelors would have a good laugh over his marriage. Perhaps the news would have reached them by the time he and Jocelyn arrived in London.

He would take their ribbing good-naturedly, for he certainly deserved to be given a hard time about his former views on marriage. He was considered the wildest of the three Silver Dukes, and that reputation was not exaggerated. He had done some questionable things he could not reveal to Jocelyn because she was still too innocent. Yes, they had enjoyed their nights of intimacy. But she was, at heart, too sweet and good to be told those other things.

She was also very sentimental. Tears formed in her eyes.

"Lass, what has ye about to cry?"

"When *you* return to London? Does this mean you will not be taking me with you?"

He frowned. What had he said to make her think he would leave her behind?

She swallowed hard and began to speak shakily. "I suppose I could return to Granby with my parents. Is this what you want?"

"No, Jocelyn. I want ye with me." He worried about her and wanted to protect her. How could he do it if she was not with him?

And he did not expect she would want to live with her parents once she learned the truth about what her father had done. He'd emptied her accounts, all of them. Even the ones held in her own name.

He'd left her with nothing.

Malcolm did not have the heart to tell her. But this was another matter that needed to be addressed while they were in Aberdeen. It was her father's secret to tell, his shameful behavior to confess.

That Granby had waited this long to admit the truth to Jocelyn did not sit well with Malcolm. But he had promised Granby he'd keep silent. He had also promised to replenish Jocelyn's lost funds, and he fully intended to do so. He never went back on his word.

However, it had been a mistake to give Lord Granby these assurances. He had wanted to protect Jocelyn from heartbreak. But hiding the truth from her would only postpone the inevitable and make matters worse.

At the time, it had seemed important to Malcolm to spare her feelings. She looked up to her father, this man who had doted on her for much of her life. It had been so important to Malcolm to keep that family unity alive. Of course, he had been thinking of his own family and how much he missed them to this day.

But keeping the truth from her was not wise. In fact, deceiving Jocelyn was a terrible idea, and he worried that it might blow up in his face. He could only hope her father would do the right thing and tell her what he had done.

A knock at their door shook Malcolm out of his thoughts. Jocelyn scampered out of his arms and stared up at him with concern. "Is it Ballantry come to claim his funds already?"

"I doubt he would tip his hand and show his desperation. It would reveal he held the weaker hand."

She nodded. "Perhaps my parents, then, or the staff delivering something for us."

"Aye," he said with a nod, moving toward the door.

But his neck was beginning to prickle. Something did not feel right.

"Step back, lass. I dinna want ye in their direct line of sight." Why did he suddenly feel as though something was about to go terribly wrong?

Chapter Twelve

Malcolm strode across the elegant suite and opened the door to his worst nightmare. Worse than coming face to face with Ballantry or Burling with their pistols drawn and ready to shoot him in the gut.

"Bollocks," he muttered under his breath.

Far worse.

He stared at Lady Bathurst and her sister, Lady Thurston, two utterly immoral and shameless sisters he had once bedded out of sheer boredom on one of his nights of drunken revelry at a *demimonde* house party that was better described as a week-long orgy.

Had he not just been thinking of his regretful actions and resolving never to reveal any of them to Jocelyn? Were demonic imps at work? For here stood two reminders of one of those regretful nights.

The ladies appeared more gleeful than surprised, which meant Ballantry must have summoned them for the sole purpose of humiliating Jocelyn, of letting her know that her husband was a womanizing dog who would discard her as soon as he tired of her.

The pair ate him up with their hungry eyes, their ravenous appetites bared as predatory smiles appeared on their faces. "Then it is true," Lady Bathurst said with a high-pitched laugh that grated on his ears. "Camborne, we could hardly believe it when the proprietor mentioned you had married our cousin."

His head began to spin. "Cousin?"

These are Jocelyn's cousins? The very cousins who had betrayed her with Ballantry?

Every vile Scottish curse he knew now ran through his head. This was bad.

In truth, *bad* did not begin to describe the pile of *shite* he had just fallen into.

Jocelyn had mentioned Ballantry's bedding her cousins while betrothed to her, a remark that had angered him at the time because Jocelyn did not deserve this shabby treatment. Ballantry's misbehavior was reprehensible, but the actions of her cousins were unforgivable. That Jocelyn was considered a harpy was no excuse for their shaming the lass. They were her blood kin.

He could not fathom a more complete betrayal.

Jocelyn did not appear pleased to see them, but came forward to greet them politely. "Cassandra, Millicent, do come in."

Malcolm silently groaned. He wanted to get away from these Scottish tarts but dared not leave for fear of what they might tell Jocelyn. Was there a doubt they would tell her everything and delight in her pain?

He decided to remain and do his best to repair the damage they were certain to inflict.

"Are you truly married to Camborne?" one of them asked.

He could not recall which was Cassandra and which was Millicent. All he remembered was that they had big breasts and his face had been in them much of the time.

Oh, Lord.

Jocelyn tipped her chin up and said proudly, "Yes, Millicent. I am."

Ah, the redhead was Millicent. The blonde had to be Cassandra.

The two of them were still eyeing him like he was their next meal.

"Last we saw you, you were fleeing your own wedding to Ballantry. What happened?" Cassandra asked, still eyeing him voraciously. "Were you and Camborne secretly lovers all along? How delicious."

She licked her lips and tossed him a look that said she would like to lick certain parts of him, if he were willing to drop his trousers. "Not that I blame you for succumbing to that silver tongue of his," she continued. "Or has he not pleasured you in that way yet?"

Dear heaven.

Now Millicent turned her wolfish gaze on him. "We thought Jocelyn was a virgin. She certainly had us fooled. Were you the one to pop her berry, Camborne? I'm not surprised she would choose you to be her first. You are irresistible."

He took a step back when Millicent reached out to put her hands on him.

Jocelyn was staring at him in stunned silence. He moved to her side and placed a possessive arm around her waist, praying she would not slap it away. This was already worse than any slap he might receive.

She turned to her lascivious cousins. "I did not realize you knew my husband."

Her cousins tittered. "Oh, we are *well* acquainted with him," Millicent said, her meaning as subtle as a hammer dropped atop Jocelyn's head.

"*Intimately* acquainted, one might say," Cassandra added with a catlike purr.

"*Intimately* acquainted?" Jocelyn turned to stare at him once more.

"It was well before I knew ye, lass," Malcolm said, wondering whether he should just shut up and find the biggest hole into which he could bury himself. Better yet, he ought to just magically disappear. Make some hasty excuse and clear out.

Perhaps it had been a mistake to stay, but would it not have been worse to leave her unprotected? What sort of family was this? A father who stole from his own daughter, and cousins who thought it was all in good fun to reveal they had slept with her husband.

No, he could not leave Jocelyn to these she-cats. He could not even *think* of that drunken night with these ladies—and he used the term "ladies" loosely, for there was not a shred of decency in them. Indeed, he could not think of the debauched things they had done without his stomach churning in revolt.

Lord. Lord. Lord.

Jocelyn held herself like a duchess, speaking to her cousins in a serenely polite manner while arranging to meet them later for tea as though absolutely nothing out of the ordinary had transpired.

She smiled and gave every appearance of remaining unaffected while escorting them to the door. But he could tell, despite the proud tip of her chin maintained throughout their conversation, that she was dying on the inside and would burst into tears as soon as that door closed.

All his fault.

Their suite was large, consisting of an elegant parlor, a balcony, private closet for their grooming and bathing needs, and a large bedchamber. It still was not large enough for him to hide away, to shrink to nothing and disappear.

He sank onto one of the plump parlor chairs, leaned his elbows on his thighs, and buried his face in his hands. "I'm so, so sorry, lass."

He heard her release a ragged breath, but was too ashamed to look her in the eye just yet.

"I assume these are the cousins ye were talking about when ye mentioned Ballantry had partaken…dallied…broken faith with ye."

She sniffled. "Yes."

He groaned as he looked up at her, and then rose to walk to her side. "Truly, Jocelyn. I'm so very sorry," he said, taking her in his arms to offer comfort and hoping she would not shove out of them in disgust. "I would no' have hurt ye for the world."

She buried her face against his chest and cried softly. "We weren't married. You had never met me. How could you know?"

But he felt her ache, for it seared as deeply in his bones as in hers.

"I am not blaming you, Camborne."

He was glad of it, but her forgiveness did not absolve him of his shameful behavior. "I know it still hurts ye. I regret my actions to the depths of my soul. I wish I could go back in time and take it all back."

"But you cannot. It is done and cannot be undone."

He sighed. "I was drunk and stupid. It is no excuse, nor am I trying to excuse myself. They meant nothing to me and I probably meant less than nothing to them. Not an ounce of feeling among us."

He ought to shut up now. Talking about it would only make her feel worse.

He wished he could wrap her in his heart and protect her from this stinging hurt. But it was too late. While he had built protective barriers around his heart, she had built none around hers. Indeed, he had been constructing his barriers ever since childhood, and they were now too thick and solid ever to be penetrated.

But Jocelyn had no defenses and deeply felt every attack.

"Lass, ye are the only one I'll ever take to my bed now that we are married. I gave ye this oath on our wedding day and I mean to keep it. I am never going to touch anyone else."

She shook her head against his chest. "It doesn't help me if it's a lie. You'll only hurt me worse."

"It isn't a lie," he insisted. "I'll keep faith with ye till the day I die. Please, Jocelyn. Ye have to believe me."

"Why?" She began to sob. "I've woken up every morning and told you that I love you. You've never said it back to me. But I am not berating you for this. What hurts is that I still do not know whether you'll want me with you at the end of the month."

"But I told ye that I'd take ye to London with me."

"I had to pry it out of you."

Gad, he'd been so stupid. "Jocelyn, I want ye with me."

"For how long?"

He let out a breath. "For as long as ye wish."

"Not good enough, Camborne. What is it *you* want?"

He wanted her.

Why could he not just say it?

Instead, he listened to her cry.

"I wanted so much to be special to you," she said between soft sobs. "How stupid of me to think I could ever stand out."

"Och, lass." He felt a resounding ache. "Ye are special to me. Are ye not the lass I married? Ye know me well enough by now to understand my nature. Ye could not have forced me into marrying ye if I weren't willing. No matter the circumstances. I *wanted* to marry ye. What can I do to prove it to ye?"

"Nothing," she replied between more sniffles. "There is nothing you can do."

This hurt him deeply, for he wanted very much to be the best husband to her. Did she not deserve the best? And yet he had not even given her a bride token to commemorate their wedding. It was not something he had forgotten about.

In truth, it had been on his mind since the day they married. He meant to select something beautiful when they returned to London. But were there not decent jewelry shops in Aberdeen, too? Why delay?

He knew of a fine one not far from the inn. He knew of it because this had been his way of dealing with ladies he'd bedded. This was how he bought off his tarts—whether commoner, or gentry, or of the nobility—delivering each a pretty bauble after a night of frolic.

Was there a single one of them who'd ever wanted just him? Had any of them ever refused the gift?

As though cheap jewels could absolve him of all wrongdoing.

But he was not moving on from Jocelyn and would never treat her so shabbily.

Did he dare offer her jewelry? What he wanted for her was something meaningful, something that came from his heart. This bride token had to be a gesture of affection and respect for her. But would she consider it as that when she knew his method of operation around women?

"What can I do for ye to stop this ache?" he asked. "There must be something ye'd like. Something I can—"

"Don't you dare think to buy me off, Camborne!" She angrily looked up at him through tearful eyes. "That is the *worst* thing you can do for me."

"All right, lass." He trailed his fingers lovingly along the nape of her neck. "Please, tell me what to do to make ye feel better."

But he knew.

He had to tell her that he loved her.

Why could he not say it?

"I'm not blaming you," she said.

"But ye are hurting so badly, I canno' bear to see ye in this pain. Worse, to know that I have been the cause of it."

"I'll be all right in a moment."

He did not think so. Her breaths were still ragged.

She had such a tender heart.

"I did not care when they amused themselves with Ballantry even knowing he and I were betrothed," she said into his chest. "He is a worthless man and I immediately regretted entering into the betrothal. But even as the dread built up inside me, I was still too prideful to admit my mistake. I would have eaten the contract, if I could. Just swallowed it up and chewed it to nothing but pulp in my stomach to make it go away."

He tipped her chin up so that their gazes met. "Lass, ye would have poisoned yerself."

"I really did not care at the time. I think I felt at my lowest point after finding out my betrothed and my cousins had betrayed me. Yet it was also a release, in a way. A warning that I had brought this disgrace upon myself."

"Dinna blame yerself and absolve their betrayal. They were the wrongdoers here, never ye."

"You were not in the wrong either, Camborne. You had never even met me. And did I not tell you my cousins had loose morals?"

"That ye did, lass. But their morals are not merely loose," he said with a groan. "They are completely nonexistent. They have no scruples whatsoever. How could they hurt ye like that and still come to yer door smiling? It is shameful. That I did no' know ye at the time does no' make it all right or make me feel any better. It reflects quite poorly on the life I have led up to now."

"You were in the midst of changing it," she reminded him.

"Still does no' make me feel any better for the hurt I've given ye." He kissed her softly on the lips, hoping she would not pull away in disgust.

"I'll be all right," she told him when he drew his mouth off hers. "It just galls me that my own cousins…" She emitted a sob.

"Och, lass." He held her in his embrace a moment longer, offering no resistance when she drew away after a short while and cast him a vulnerable smile that made him want to take her in his arms again.

But he was the offender and thought it better to allow her to take the lead in their interaction.

She drew out her handkerchief and wiped her tears. "Ugh, and now I have agreed to meet them for tea later. My stupid pride again. I could not allow them to think they had hurt me. But they are going to smirk at me the entire time. I'll die on the inside if they give me lurid details of your…prowess."

"Blessed saints," he muttered. "I was a pitiful drunk and probably made a complete arse of myself. In truth, I dinna remember half of what transpired. If they tell ye I was good, dinna believe them. No man that drunk can perform adequately. Ye could plead a headache and cancel."

"And give them the satisfaction of knowing they had upset me?"

"I'd offer to join ye, but I think this would make matters worse."

"It is a terrible idea. No, they'll climb all over you. I'm surprised they refrained while in our suite just now." She sighed. "I'll be all right, truly. You had best deal with Ballantry and Burling."

"All right, lass." He could only hope her cousins would ride off with Ballantry, since he was obviously the one who had brought the vicious duo here. One of them was a widow and the other had a husband with one foot in the grave. Malcolm forgot which was which—not that it mattered, since they would both be widows soon.

Jocelyn's cousins were two of the most mercenary women he had ever encountered in all his years of depravity and debauchery. However, he had to admire them in a perverse way. They were completely open about their immorality. They were selfish, hedonistic creatures who cared not a whit who they used or who they hurt.

They were also as sharp and ruthlessly determined as Napoleon when undertaking their objectives. The pair made him look like a pious saint in comparison.

He could not call them out for liars because they were honest in their utter lack of remorse. They never hid their intentions, and made no secret of using their sexual talents to gain rich husbands for themselves. Elderly, sick husbands who were quite generous in their marriage settlements. One was already a wealthy widow and the other would soon be one. It was only a matter of a months before the poor sod took his last breath.

He gave thanks that Jocelyn was nothing like this pair.

With a shake of his head and a pained sigh, he dismissed them from his thoughts in order to concentrate on Ballantry.

"Jocelyn, will ye stay with yer parents while I attend to the Ballantry matter?"

She pursed her lips and stared up at him, not at all liking the idea. "I can't face my parents just yet. Besides, I do feel a headache coming on. Would you mind terribly if I just stayed here and rested for a while?"

After the unexpected visit from her cousins, he was in no position to deny her anything. "All right, love. I'll try not to take too long. Lock the door and dinna open it for anyone but me."

He gave her a final, gentle kiss and then strode out.

However, he waited until he heard the click of the lock before heading downstairs.

It did not take him long to find Ballantry and Burling seated in the common room sharing a bottle of champagne. The pair were already celebrating.

Prematurely, they would discover.

They had gone through the entire bottle, he realized by their sloppy smiles of greeting. Malcolm frowned, for he never liked negotiating with a man in his cups.

Yes, it might give him an advantage. But the sot usually got angry when he sobered and realized what he had done.

Well, nothing would be signed today. He only meant to talk over the terms of a settlement. His Aberdeen solicitor would set the arrangement down in a formal document.

"Ballantry, I've reserved a private study for our discussion. Care to join me now?"

Ballantry shrugged and rose. "Why not? Did ye enjoy my little surprise?"

Malcolm knew he was referring to Jocelyn's cousins. "Delightful," he responded wryly.

"I thought ye might enjoy the happy family reunion. I've got ye by the bollocks, Camborne. I mean to bleed ye dry."

"If this is what ye think," Malcolm muttered, leading him to a private area that served as a reading room for the inn's guests. It had dark wood bookshelves and comfortable chairs. In the corner was a small table with more formal chairs around it.

Malcolm had reserved the space for an hour, although he doubted it would take very long to deal with Ballantry and send him back to

Burling.

He had barely shut the door and taken a seat at the table when the oaf laughed and settled in the chair across from his. "I meant it when I said I aim to bleed ye dry, Camborne. I want one hundred and fifty thousand pounds for the trouble and humiliation ye and the harpy that ye stole from under my nose have put me through. I will no' take a groat less."

"Yes, you will," Malcolm replied, casting the fool an icy look.

It took Ballantry a moment for the response to sink in. When it finally did, he snarled. "Do ye dare offer me less?"

"Very astute of ye. I'll offer ye much less and ye'll be grateful for it. After which ye'll leave here without so much as a whimper of protest."

"And why should I do that?" Ballantry's expression was once again smug, but Malcolm sensed a hint of uncertainty by the slight narrowing of his eyes. "I'm not leaving without my reward."

Malcolm leaned forward and regarded him with all solemnity. "Yer reward? Ye think to be rewarded for cheating on Jocelyn? Ye ought to get nothing for that alone."

"I want my one hundred and fifty thousand pounds!" Ballantry pounded the table. "Do not play yer Silver Duke games with me."

"No games played here." Malcolm's gaze never wavered from Ballantry. "Did ye think ye were safe from me? I know the secret that will destroy ye. The one ye've been hiding ever since ye inherited yer title."

Ballantry cursed him. "What secret? Ye're bluffing."

Malcolm heard the slightest quaver in the man's voice and had confirmation that his investigators had dug up the truth.

"Would ye like to know the particulars? Let me see if I remember this correctly. Yer mother was married to a man by the name of Abner Ferguson before she married yer father, who was the Earl of Ballantry. Problem is, Abner wasn't dead when yer mother and father married. Nor had her marriage to Abner Ferguson ended. Which means Abner and yer mother were still lawfully married when she wed yer father. I expect it was an honest mistake—she probably heard Abner had died and had no reason to believe otherwise when years passed and he dinna return."

Malcolm could feel the tomblike silence in the air. Indeed, it felt as though all the air had been sucked out of the room. He paused to await Ballantry's response.

"Ye'll never prove it, ye bastard!" Ballantry's hands were curled into fists as he set them on the table, but Malcolm could see they were shaking. "I'll kill ye for this, Camborne."

"It will do ye no good. All the documentation is in the hands of my solicitors, and this information has also been sent to others I trust. If anything happens to me, the world will know yer secret."

It had been ridiculously easy to discover it, in truth. An open secret just sitting there, waiting to be stumbled upon. Foolishly, Ballantry himself had led Malcolm's investigators straight to it after storming out of Arbroth. He had run to Edinburgh, probably stewed about what to do for several days, and then decided to go to the church where his mother and Abner had married, no doubt to bribe the clerics into destroying the proof or hiding it. Terrence and his investigators had come upon the clerics while they were in the midst of removing the registry book where his mother's prior marriage had been recorded.

It was almost *too* easy.

"Ye've told yer fellow Silver Dukes?" Ballantry asked.

Malcolm did not bother to answer. "What did ye think I was doing while in Arbroth these past two weeks? Merely entertaining my wife and her parents? Ye know me better than that. I was no' going to let ye get the better of me."

"No," Ballantry said, his voice shaking. "Ye were going to destroy me. Ye were always a heartless bastard."

"Aye, I am." While Malcolm did have it in his power to destroy Ballantry, this was not his aim. Marriage to Jocelyn had indeed turned him soft. He wasn't looking to destroy anyone, just free him and his wife from the entanglement of her prior betrothal. No court would uphold Ballantry's betrothal contract once they learned the intended groom had misrepresented his status as an earl. That the bride's father had also lied and misrepresented her dowry would be irrelevant and might possibly never come to light.

"But I can also be reasonable," Malcolm continued. "Here's my proposition to ye. I'll take yer secret to my grave on the condition ye leave Scotland, never speak an ill word about Jocelyn again, and live out yer days on the Continent. I dinna care where ye choose to reside. Italy. Spain. France. Portugal. Wherever ye wish, so long as it is not here. By here, I also include England. Wales and Ireland are out, too."

Ballantry's face turned red as his fury mounted. "How is this reasonable? Ye're banishing me from my own country!"

"Aye. I'll not have ye crossing paths with Jocelyn again. Admit it, Ballantry. Ye haven't been much use here anyway. Yer creditors are dunning ye wherever ye go. Yer friends are through giving ye handouts. Angry husbands are chasing ye, since ye've never been discreet in who ye bedded. Aren't ye better off making a fresh start?"

"Ye still haven't mentioned the most important detail. How am I to live overseas? Ye know I am destitute now. Why else would I bother to marry that harridan of a spinster who is now yer burden? How do ye tolerate her, Camborne? Or is it the fifty thousand reasons that make up her dowry that makes ye hard? It canno' be the ice maiden herself. Will ye be shoving her in one of yer remote properties and returning to yer old ways now that ye've gotten what ye want out of her?"

Malcolm ignored the question. He had the upper hand in these negotiations, he reminded himself as the urge to shut Ballantry's foul mouth with a solid punch overcame him. But he had already gone that route with Burling and wound up forced to marry Jocelyn to preserve her honor.

He was not going to allow himself to lose his composure again. Ballantry was to answer to him, not the other way around.

"I dinna suppose she'll care if ye banish her," the oaf continued. "She hates men, ye know."

"She isn't too fond of ye, that's for certain."

"And you, Camborne? Did ye stick yerself inside that cold witch? Did she freeze yer bollocks?"

Now, why did Ballantry have to say that? Malcolm wanted to leap to his feet and kill him.

But he held himself back, as difficult as it was. He had expected no less from this wastrel. The remark was designed to test his affection for Jocelyn. Ballantry's sole intention was to regain some of the advantage he'd lost. But the cur would never gain any advantage over him.

"That remark just cost ye five thousand pounds."

"Five that I dinna have in the first place," Ballantry said, snorting. "Ye've offered me nothing yet. And ye know my estates are not in good shape."

That was an understatement.

"How am I to live on nothing?" he insisted.

Ballantry's nephew was trying his hardest to restore the estates, but he could not keep up with his uncle's gambling and generally profligate ways.

"Here's the rest of my offer," Malcolm said. "I'll give ye twenty thousand pounds if ye meet my conditions."

"Twenty! The harpy is worth fifty!"

"Aye, but I am discounting the value of my silence about yer secret. The fact that yer father quietly married yer mother after Abner died is a tribute to his moral character, perhaps his love for yer mother. Yer parents did all they could to protect ye, even lying to the world to give ye undeserved preference over yer younger brother, who was born *in* rightful wedlock. They bestowed this enormous boon upon ye, and ye still turned out bad. They gave ye everything and ye treated it like rubbish."

"Getting moral on me now, Camborne? Ye're hardly one to lecture me. How did ye enjoy the harpy's cousins? I'll bet that pleased yer frigid stick of a wife. Did she toss ye out when she realized ye'd had them?"

"Mention Jocelyn again and that will cost ye another five thousand."

The lass had been devastated. It sickened Malcolm to know he'd played a part in this dishonor.

"There's my offer, Ballantry. Twenty thousand pounds and ye leave here forever. I have a solicitor in Aberdeen. I'll have him draw up the settlement agreement. The funds will be doled out to ye in installments upon performance of yer obligations. Five thousand immediately to allow ye to set up residence somewhere on the Continent. Ye'll receive the rest once ye've done so. If ye ever set foot here again, I'll kill ye. If ye ever disparage Jocelyn, I'll kill ye twice. Have I made myself clear?"

Ballantry looked mad enough to shoot him on the spot.

Indeed, Malcolm saw the cur reach below the table as he attempted to retrieve the pistol sheathed in the lip of his boot.

"I would no' do that if I were ye," he warned, and raised his hand to show his own pistol already drawn. "Ye'll forgive me for not trusting ye."

Ballantry spewed a string of curses before acknowledging his defeat with an angry grunt. "I'll take the twenty-five thousand ye first meant to offer."

"That is off the table. Ye insulted Jocelyn and that cost ye five. Ye'll take the twenty thousand and be grateful for it. I suggest ye grab it while I still have a mind to be generous with ye." Malcolm rose. "Well, that about does it. Oh, and another thing. My solicitor will have the settlement agreement ready by tomorrow afternoon. I'll be reducing my offer by five thousand pounds each day ye delay signing. Twenty thousand if ye sign tomorrow. Fifteen thousand if ye sign the day after. Ye get the idea. Any harm comes to me or Jocelyn and the parties holding the proof of yer mother's marriage to Abner will go straight to the gossip rags…and yer nephew, too. The lad thinks his father was second in line to inherit the earldom, when in truth, his father was the legitimate son and should have inherited, not you. Yer nephew is the rightful earl now that his father has also passed on. Do not tempt me to tell him."

"Bastard."

"Oh, and I think I will add another provision. Ye're to take it easy on yer nephew. If I hear that ye're running up yer debts again, I'll give him the proof and let him take the earldom out from under ye. He's a hard worker and deserves to inherit something more than the shambles ye've made of it. Ye're going to live well on the settlement funds and the money he'll be sending ye from the Ballantry holdings once they turn a profit."

Malcolm studied Ballantry's expression.

He had the look of a defeated man.

"I think we are done now," Malcolm said. "I suggest ye keep out of my sight this evening. Ye dinna want to rile me, or ye'll get nothing at all."

He strode out of the reading room and stepped outside for a breath of air, glad the worst was over. He had thought long and hard about how to handle Ballantry, knowing he could have saved himself the twenty thousand pounds by exposing his mother's bigamy. But that would have besmirched the reputation of a good woman and left him with no hold over Ballantry once that secret was out.

Malcolm wanted to maintain that hold. The man needed to keep away from Jocelyn.

The meeting hadn't taken long, so he expected she was still napping. He decided not to disturb her. Besides, there was something more he needed to accomplish, and there was no better time to do it than now.

After a quick visit to his Aberdeen solicitor to convey the settlement terms, he strode toward the main shopping street and the odd little duck of a jeweler who knew him quite well by now, Solomon Haggard.

A little bell rang above the door when he walked into the shop. "Good afternoon, Mr. Haggard."

The wizened old man tipped his visor up and straightened to his full, albeit diminutive, height. "Yer Grace, so nice to see ye. I have some lovely pieces to show ye," he said, speaking in a mix of accents that included Scottish, French, and perhaps a little bit of Prussian.

Malcolm nodded. "Yes, show me what ye have."

Smiling, the jeweler scampered into his back room and came out with several items that he set out atop a swath of black velvet. These were gaudy pieces, the sort Malcolm might have purchased for a paramour, but would never do for Jocelyn. "Show me something elegant, something less...obvious."

"Ah, not too expensive?"

"Something *tasteful*. This is for my wife."

"Yer wife?" The man regarded him numbly for a moment and then his eyes widened. "Ye've *married*?"

Malcolm arched an eyebrow and smiled. "Aye, Mr. Haggard."

"Felicitations and many years of happiness, Yer Grace! That is... Er, well... I dinna suppose ye had planned on it, being a Silver Duke and all. But ye're smiling, so I dinna think ye find the situation too objectionable. She must be someone quite special."

"She is," he admitted, his heart warming at the thought.

The jeweler gathered up the first samples and hastened into the back room as he called out, "I have a few pieces that will be perfect for yer wife. A price above rubies."

Dear heaven.

What did he mean? Something priceless? Malcolm would box the man's ears if he brought out a diamond necklace or another expensive piece. Such obvious trinkets would never sway Jocelyn.

To his surprise, Haggard revealed several beautiful brooches and lockets. Which one to choose? Malcolm had never bought *tasteful* jewelry for someone he *actually* cared about. "Are ye married, Mr. Haggard?"

"Aye, Yer Grace. Going on forty years now."

"A love match?" Malcolm asked, eager to pick the man's brain.

"Aye. Caught sight of her at a county fair in Dundee. She had lovely red curls that shone in the sun, and the most beautiful smile this side of heaven. *She's the one,* I said to myself. I knew it then and there—I would love her into our dotage. I dinna care if every last strand of her lovely hair turned gray, which it has now. She's more beautiful than ever, and still has the best smile this side of heaven."

"That's quite a love story," Malcolm muttered.

"It wasn't without its stressful moments. Took a while to convince her to marry me because I had stiff competition. The butcher's son was also courting her, and I was a mere apprentice at the time. I thought I had lost her for certain. He was richer, and she would have had an easier life with him."

"But she chose you. Has she ever told you why?"

The little man nodded. "Och, it was the first thing I asked her. Do ye know what she said?"

Malcolm grinned. "I would no' be asking ye if I had a clue."

"Nor did I understand it," the jeweler said, shaking his head. "But here is what she told me: 'Ye look at me, Solomon. Ye talk to me and care for my thoughts. Ye think of me in everything ye do.'" He paused, smiled, and shook his head again. "Well, it was true. I did think of her back then and still do. She was in my every waking thought, and remains so to this day. But I dinna realize it mattered at all to her."

"Apparently, it did."

"She will always be first in my thoughts. I was besotted, and still am."

Odd how this old, wizened fellow understood women better than Malcolm, a Silver Duke, ever had. But what Haggard said made a lot of sense. Jocelyn's cousins would have gone for the rich butcher, but not Jocelyn.

Perhaps developing a loving relation with his wife was as simple as remembering to put her first. It would not be difficult, for she asked so little of him.

"Which one of these pieces would ye purchase for yer wife, if ye were to do the choosing?" Malcolm asked Haggard.

"Och, that's an easy choice, Yer Grace. The gold heart locket because she is sentimental. I would say to her that I was giving her my heart to keep close to hers for all the years of our marriage and beyond."

Sadly, Malcolm did not think Jocelyn would believe him if he spoke those words to her. But she was sentimental and would be pleased to hear something romantic from him. It did not require flowery prose. This was not him, and she would never believe him if he spouted poetic nonsense. "I'll take the heart locket."

"I'll wrap it in a pretty package for ye, Yer Grace. If she is as softhearted as my wife, she will love it."

Malcolm was in better spirits by the time he returned to the Balgownie Arms. A little over two hours had elapsed since he left Jocelyn. Eager to see how she was faring, he took the stairs two at a time and strode down the hall toward their suite.

He tried the door and found it locked.

She was likely still napping, but it was a good two hours since she had taken to their bed, so he did not hesitate to rouse her. "Jocelyn," he called quietly while knocking on the door. She would hear him if she were awake.

It was not long before he heard footsteps pattering along the wooden floor of their suite.

"Jocelyn, it's me," he said, knowing she was probably close enough to hear him.

"Oh, goodness. How long was I asleep?" she murmured, letting him in. "The afternoon shadows are stretching across the balcony. How did your meeting go with Ballantry?"

"Productive, I think. He has to know he isn't going to get a better offer from me. I have every reason to believe he will accept the terms."

"What did you propose?"

He shut the door to afford them privacy, and then settled beside her on the parlor's settee. It was a feminine piece of furniture, blue silk and delicately framed. Jocelyn looked quite lovely seated in it. Her cheeks were pink and her hair tousled. Her lips had a rose blush to them, lips just aching to be kissed.

So he kissed her, a tender kiss, but did not linger too long upon her mouth. "May we speak of Ballantry later? I have something I'd like to say to ye first."

She eyed him warily, but nodded. "But you *will* tell me what happened, right? You are not merely stalling because you did something stupid, are you?"

He chuckled. "Lass, yer lack of faith in me cuts to the marrow. I did no' punch him, if that's what concerns ye. He walked out angry but unharmed."

She nodded. "Very well, tell me the other thing on your mind."

He reached into the breast pocket of his jacket and withdrew the prettily wrapped box. "This is for ye, lass."

She frowned. "Camborne, do you think I am angry with you because of my cousins and are now trying to buy me off?"

"No, it isn't like that at all. Just open the box, Jocelyn."

She eyed him curiously, still frowning. "What's in it?"

"Open it and ye'll see."

He watched her eagerly, hoping the gift would please her.

As she opened the box, he said, "This is my heart. I give it to ye freely and forever, lass."

He thought it would delight her, but she stared at the locket for the longest time and then burst into tears. "You clot! You big, wonderful Scottish clot! Why did you have to go and do this?"

He raked a hand through his hair. "I thought ye'd like it. I can take it back tomorrow, if it does no' meet with yer approval. You and I can go together and choose something ye'll like."

She clasped the locket to her bosom. "I *love* this locket. Don't you dare take it back."

He raked his fingers through his hair again. "Then why are ye crying?"

"Because I love it and I love *you*. I did not think you had it in you to be so…thoughtful."

Dear heaven. Was he that much of an inconsiderate dolt?

He knew he was arrogant. But so arrogant and full of himself to think about no one other than himself? This had probably been true at one time.

Not now. He was trying to be a better man.

She smiled at him, a smile as bright and lovely as a moonbeam. "It is the most wonderful gift I have ever received."

He breathed a sigh of relief.

"I will always wear it close to my heart. You could not have chosen a more perfect gift, Camborne. Thank you." Her smile turned impish. "Who knew you were quite the romantic?"

"Romantic?" He eased back on the settee and struggled to contain his laughter. That wizened old jeweler was the one with the soul of a romantic poet. Gad, the man looked like a broomstick with half the bristles fallen out.

Jocelyn threw her arms around him and hugged him fiercely. "It is a beautiful gift, and so considerate of you."

"Lass, I have to tell ye that I had help choosing it." He then explained what Haggard had told him about his own wife. "He helped me select the locket."

Jocelyn did not appear at all disappointed.

"So ye see, it was no' my doing."

She shook her head. "It was *all* your doing. Do you not understand?"

He groaned. "Explain it to me. Ye're smiling at me so sweetly. What did I do right?"

"You thought about me. You sought advice from someone who was in love with his wife, and you wanted the same for me. You understood me well enough to know that I would smash a vase over your head if you had given me something glittery and gaudy, as though I were a paramour of yours that you were merely trying to mollify."

She hugged him again, then drew away and cast him another impish grin. "I wouldn't really have smashed a vase over your head. You're too big for me to reach that high. Just don't tempt me by standing too close to ladders."

He laughed. "Thank ye for the warning." He drew her onto his lap and wrapped his arms around her lovely body that he had grown to know so well and adore. "Jocelyn, I've been an *idjit*."

He then kissed her soundly.

She held on to his shoulders as she leaned into the kiss and welcomed it, her inviting lips meeting the probing heat of his.

She sighed when he ended it, and leaned her head against his chest. "You haven't been an idiot. Are you still overset about what you did with my cousins?"

"That will always be to my shame. But that's not quite what has me bothered. I know we've only been married two weeks, a mere fortnight. In that time, ye've admitted that ye love me."

She sat up and tipped her chin in the air. "I am not embarrassed by it."

"Nor should ye be. It is the loveliest gesture imaginable. But I've said nothing in return to ye, lass."

"You weren't ready."

"But should I not be ready? I've taken ye into my bed and loved ye in physical ways. But I left open the question of what is to happen to us in the next month, in the next year...or for the rest of our lives. This has left ye to wonder whether I'll be leaving ye to return to my old ways. I've given ye my oath that I wouldn't, but I've also given ye so many reasons to doubt me."

He felt the tension flowing up her spine as he held her in his embrace. "I'm never going to leave ye, Jocelyn. That locket is a representation of my heart that I now freely give to ye. Ye already had my vow to protect ye and keep ye safe. But that is a vow I might give to anyone I felt a duty to protect. What I owe ye, what I wish to have with ye, is something different. With this locket, I give ye my heart."

Her eyes widened and then began to sparkle.

"Aye, lass. With this locket, I give ye all of me."

She cast him a warm smile. "Camborne, that's a lot of you to handle."

He laughed. "Think ye can manage?"

"I sincerely hope so."

"Och, lass. Ye can. Ye'll have me twisted around yer little finger in no time. I should no' have let on, but I dinna care. I'm actually liking this marriage arrangement. Ye deserve to be first in my thoughts."

"As you are in mine, Camborne." She handed him the locket and then turned her back and angled her neck so that he could fasten the clasp. "Will you help me put it on?"

"Of course, lass." He gave her a light kiss upon the neck before proceeding.

"I'm going to wear it every day from now on," she said, obviously pleased.

"It will no' go with yer more formal gowns. We'll get ye finer pieces for those once we arrive in London. Ye know how formal those *ton* affairs can be."

She shook her head. "Whenever I cannot wear it openly, I'll tuck it into my chemise and tie it with a ribbon so that it rests over my heart."

He laughed. "Jocelyn, it isn't necessary. I'm pleased ye like it, but I will understand if ye have to take it off on occasion."

She turned to him. "No, Camborne. I will *always* wear it."

"Ye're very sentimental for a harpy," he teased.

"I know, but so are you. Sentimental, that is. And I have one more thing to say to you."

He arched an eyebrow. "What is that?"

She reached up and pressed a kiss to his mouth. "You are the best husband, and I am so glad I happened to fall into your bed."

Chapter Thirteen

Jocelyn walked on a cloud for the rest of the afternoon and into the evening.

She met her cousins for tea and ignored all their snide innuendos to the point their game lost its fascination for them. Those shameless she-cats made excuses to end the intimate family gathering and left her to enjoy her tea and cakes alone.

She was ebullient at supper and showed her parents the heart locket Camborne had purchased. "It is lovely, Jocelyn," her mother remarked with a muted gush of approval. Her father muttered something complimentary, too.

They were not particularly impressed.

This surprised Jocelyn until she realized they were measuring Camborne's devotion by expense. She wasn't showing them a diamond necklace or rare sapphire ring. But she thought they would understand what a priceless gift this was because it represented Camborne's love.

Well, he hadn't actually come out and *said* he loved her. But was there a doubt she was on her way to winning Camborne's heart? The heart of a Silver Duke.

Was this not extraordinary?

She spared her husband a glance. He smiled and winked at her. Her bones melted.

As their supper progressed, the four of them spoke on many topics.

However, Jocelyn began to notice that Camborne was casually changing the subject whenever any of them mentioned Ballantry.

She also realized Ballantry was nowhere to be seen around the inn since his meeting with her husband. He would not have departed yet because he had a settlement agreement to sign and funds to collect.

Was it not odd that Camborne had yet to disclose the details of this agreement to her? Nor did he appear willing to disclose it to her father.

Perhaps she ought to press him on the matter before it was finalized. Had he given in to Ballantry's ridiculous demand of one hundred and fifty thousand pounds and was ashamed to admit it?

No, he couldn't have.

Could he?

Out of the corner of her eye, she noticed Burling seated at a nearby table. He was drinking heavily. "He's staring at us," she said, nudging her husband. "He does not look happy. Do you think he has had a falling out with Ballantry?"

"Does he make ye uncomfortable, lass?" He frowned and began to draw back his chair. "I'll have a word with him."

"No." Jocelyn placed a hand on his arm. "It isn't important. I merely made the remark in passing."

She did not want a repeat of what had happened the last time her dear husband offered to have "a word" with Burling. Punches were thrown and everyone found out she was a runaway bride who was possibly *not* married to Camborne, even though she was sharing his guest bedchamber. "Truly, let's just ignore him."

"All right," he grumbled, but Jocelyn knew he was not pleased.

"My mother's condition is still delicate," she whispered in his ear. "You know excitement is not good for her constitution. And how is starting a fight in the inn's dining room going to solve anything?"

"I'm not promising to behave, lass. If he comes toward us, I'll do whatever is necessary to protect ye."

She sighed. "I do not need you turning ape to protect me at every turn."

Although she probably did, because she was a bit of a disaster on her own. Even she recognized her failings. But she was not about to admit it to Camborne while his protective instincts were already on alert.

She switched the conversation to their plans after Aberdeen. It warmed her to know she and Camborne would remain together. The worry that they might not had weighed so heavily on her heart. "Do you still wish for us to go to your lodge?"

"I dinna know yet, lass." His gaze remained on Burling, who was glowering back at him.

"Camborne, stop looking at him. You are provoking him."

"Me? No, lass. I dinna like the way he's looking at ye."

"Then do not encourage him," she chided. "He'll stop looking your way once you stop looking his way."

"I'm not going to avert my eyes until he averts his."

What was it about men and their need to confront each other?

"Ballantry must have told him there would be no reward for him," Camborne muttered.

Jocelyn leaped at the opening to discuss the settlement. "Did you drive that tough a bargain?"

"Aye, lass. I did."

"Were ye ruthless?" her father asked.

Camborne nodded. "Aye."

Her father arched an eyebrow. "Then ye offered him a pittance? And he accepted?"

"Aye to both yer questions. It was still more than he deserved, but it came with the requirement that he leave the country."

Jocelyn gasped. "And he agreed? But he is a born and bred Scot. Where will he go? And did he accept?"

Camborne nodded. "He'll settle somewhere on the Continent. As to where, I dinna care so long as he is nowhere near us. Aye, he accepted."

Her father shook his head as he raised his wine glass in a toast. "Ye got him to accept an insignificant payoff and leave? Ye're a magician, Camborne. I dinna know how ye did it, but ye brought that bounder to heel. Hopefully, by tomorrow this unpleasant affair will be over, and the two of ye can embark on yer married life without further distraction."

Jocelyn studied her husband, noticing the glint of steel in his eyes. "Did you threaten to kill him? Is this why he agreed to what sounds like ridiculously poor terms?"

He smiled wryly. "No, lass. He wasn't compelled by threats of death. But I did assure him I would kill him if he ever returned and attempted to bother ye again."

Jocelyn took a healthy gulp of her wine.

She did not want anyone's death on her hands, not even the wretched Ballantry's. He was a womanizing hound, a gambler, and utterly worthless in so many ways, but that did not give Camborne the right to do him in.

Apparently, she was the only one who held this opinion. Her parents were smiling at her husband and toasting him again.

Silver Dukes were not considered sweet, soft men by nature. That hint of danger enhanced their appeal. Jocelyn could not deny this immediate attraction she had felt for her husband. She was as taken by his Silver Duke allure as any other of his conquests.

Still, she refused to believe he had it in him to be quite as ruthless as his reputation. The locket he had given her today had to be a sign of his true nature and meant everything to her. He had pledged his heart to her.

His heart.

When supper was over, they returned to their suite and Jocelyn began to question him again. "Camborne, tell me the truth. What really happened in that negotiation? How much money did you offer him?"

"Let me help ye to undress, lass."

She held him off. "Why won't you tell me what you offered?"

He sighed. "It's complicated."

"It is just a number and not complicated at all. How much? Fifty? One hundred? Two hundred thousand pounds?"

His eyebrows shot up. "Ye think I would ever give that wretch anything close to those sums?"

"How much, Camborne? Was it less than my dowry?"

"Aye, lass."

"Much less? I'm just trying to understand what you consider a pittance. Why are you being so secretive about it?"

"Because the entire reason this issue is resolved is that he needed it to resolve quickly. If people start poking around, this settlement will fall apart."

"People?" She clasped her hands to stem her irritation. "I am not *people*. I am your wife. Do you not trust me to keep a confidence?"

"Aye, I do. But it is not mine to reveal."

"Then it is Ballantry's secret?"

"Och, lass. Dinna ask more questions. I'm begging ye to leave it alone. Any other wife would. What do ye care about the terms when they do not harm ye? In fact, they are immensely helpful to ye because…"

"Finish the thought, Camborne. Go ahead and say it."

"Will ye no' leave it alone?"

"What you mean is that the terms are immensely helpful to me because I was the idiot who got into this mess in the first place and handled it incompetently every step of the way."

He reached out for her again, this time refusing to allow her to skitter away. "Those are yer words, not mine. I've never blamed ye for the broken betrothal. I've never blamed ye when I found ye in my bed. Ye're the only one blaming yerself."

"Because I was in the wrong. I know that agreeing to marry Ballantry was a terrible mistake."

"Then it's time ye forgave yerself for it."

Who was he to offer counsel when he'd spent a lifetime torturing himself over the death of his family that was not his fault? She ached so much for him because he had so unfairly burdened himself and suffered for so long.

She would never mention it, especially now that he was beginning the delicate process of healing. *Never.*

But he must have seen something in her expression, for his gaze suddenly turned icy. "Ye're going to toss this back in my face?"

She gasped. "I would sooner die than ever hurt you."

He turned her around and wordlessly assisted her in undoing her laces. She felt the iciness in his silence.

"Camborne, I'm sorry. Obviously, I am having as much difficulty dealing with my demons as you are with your own. The difference is that you were a child and completely innocent. I am a grown woman and completely guilty."

"Ye were not to blame," he muttered, finishing with the laces.

She turned to face him, probably looking a ridiculous mess as her lower lip wobbled and her gown slipped off her shoulders. "Why do you insist I am not at fault?" she asked, struggling not to cry. "No one coerced me into entering the betrothal. I did it out of sheer spite to prove to one and all that I did not have to be a spinster if I did not want to be. My actions were stubborn, prideful, and foolish."

He groaned and walked away from her.

"Camborne?" Her heart began to beat faster as he strode toward the door. Did he intend to leave? "Wait! I'll come with you."

But he had loosened her ties and she could not possibly follow him in her state of undress. She clutched her gown at the bosom to keep the thing from sliding down her body. "Wait for me."

He looked back at her in exasperation. "Jocelyn, I do not need ye underfoot. Leave me be. I'll be back in a few minutes." Without sparing her another glance, he strode out.

She let out a defeated breath as the door shut forcefully behind him.

She ached, wanting to cry. Could she have handled this *more* stupidly? Why had she pressed him about that settlement?

Was it not obvious he held something damaging over Ballantry that had the oaf cowering in his boots? It could be something criminal. A hanging offense? What else might put the fear of the devil in him so that he would accept leaving Scotland?

Of course, if the secret came out, then Camborne would lose all the leverage he had over Ballantry. And still, she had prodded him for answers he dared not give.

Fool. Fool. Fool.

She truly was a harpy. Doomed to wreak misery on her loved ones.

As the minutes stretched into hours, Jocelyn retired tearfully to bed.

Would Camborne ever return?

Would he ever hold her in his arms again?

Chapter Fourteen

Malcolm realized he had been walking along the harbor for over an hour to cool himself down. The sun had set and a chill wind was blowing off the water, but he kept on walking. The tide was in and he could hear the light clanging of fishing boat bells as the crafts bobbed upon the waves. The moon was a faint silver glow behind a wispy layer of clouds.

There was nothing more beautiful than the shimmer of moonlight upon the water.

He wanted Jocelyn to share this sight with him, but he was not about to return to the inn and drag her out now. In truth, he ought to be heading back before even the tavern lanterns dimmed and the streets became dangerous to walk alone.

He turned and strode back to the inn, suddenly aware someone was following him. He quickened his pace to put distance between him and the man dogging his steps. Was it some dockside ruffian thinking he was an easy mark? Or had Ballantry set a man on him in the hope of silencing him?

Doubtful it was Ballantry, for he had too much at stake to risk his secret getting out.

As the inn came into view, Malcolm spared a glance behind him and saw a darkened shape that resembled Burling's rotund form.

Was that a knife in his hand?

He saw the glint of something metal as the moon's reflection fell upon the man and Malcolm saw him clearly. "Coward," he muttered, dismissing the drunken sot. Burling would never summon the courage to attack him. The resentful oaf was just playing out a fantasy.

Well, perhaps he was drunk enough to lose all reason and put his thoughts to action. But it was too late now that Malcolm was nearing the inn. There were too many people around.

Burling snarled at him and lumbered away.

"Arse," Malcolm muttered, dismissing the wastrel as he strode through the entry and started up the steps to return to his suite.

He was still unsure what to say to Jocelyn. The lass thought he was angry with her, but he was not at all. What he felt was frustration in not being able to tell her all that he had discovered about Ballantry.

The church clerics, Terrence, and the investigators knew of Ballantry's secret. That was already too many people. He trusted Terrence, of course, and knew the clerics would keep the matter confidential. He hoped the Edinburgh investigators would do the same. He'd certainly paid them enough for their discretion.

The only value in this information was in its remaining secret.

Perhaps he would have confided in Jocelyn if not for one problem...in hiding the truth, he was also harming Ballantry's nephew. Not that he owed the lad anything, but Jocelyn would be angry when she found out he'd known of Ballantry's lies and yet never said a word to the nephew.

His first duty was to protect Jocelyn, was it not? This was what he had pledged to do.

But how would she be protected if Ballantry, having lost his title and all the privileges and protections that came with it, decided she was the cause of his ruin and came after her?

The situation was already a mess with Burling feeling resentful and trying to summon the courage to stab Malcolm. Not that this frightened him in the least, for the man was incompetent and truly a coward at heart. In truth, he was relieved that Burling had trained his anger on him and not Jocelyn.

But Jocelyn's former betrothed was another matter entirely. He did not want Ballantry's anger festering to the point that he went after Jocelyn, for it was clear he blamed her for his misfortune. However, the man would behave himself so long as he received his settlement.

The suite was dark when Malcolm walked in, but he knew his way around the furniture well enough not to bump into anything without light to guide him.

He contemplated stretching out on the settee for the night. An uncomfortable night's sleep was better than climbing into bed with Jocelyn and having her kick him out. But he was too big for the settee and would fall off it the moment he shifted position. Anyway, he did not like the idea of sleeping apart from Jocelyn.

What was his Silver Duke experience good for if he could not convince her to let him remain in their bed?

He let out a breath and decided to tempt fate. Walking into the bedroom, he quietly sat on the bed to remove his boots.

Jocelyn stirred as the mattress dipped and she began to slide toward him.

He heard the soft swish of the coverlet as she sat up. "Camborne?"

"Aye, lass. I dinna mean to wake ye."

She lit the candle by her bedside, and then turned to face him. "You didn't. I wasn't able to fall asleep without you beside me."

"Och, sweetheart. I'm here now." He set aside his boots and then began to remove his clothing, relieved when she merely watched him complete the task and said nothing as he slipped under the covers beside her. "Will ye let me hold ye in my arms?"

She emitted a ragged sigh. "Do you want to? I thought you were angry with me."

"I was angry with myself. It was never my intention to keep anything from ye. I would no' have done it, but there is no other way. It is not something I can reveal to anyone. Ye're the first person I would confide in, if I could. I wish ye would trust me."

"I do," she admitted, casting him a remorseful smile. "I should not have pushed you. It was wrong of me not to take you at your word and simply let it go."

"Ye had the right to ask. I dinna blame ye for it. Nor am I happy that I had to put ye off." He drew her into his arms. "Thank ye for understanding, lass. Are we all right?"

"Yes," she said, wrapping her arms around him as she nestled against his body. "I love you."

Those simple words were sweeter than an angel's chorus.

"Och, lass." He rolled her under him and kissed her with fierce longing.

And proceeded to show her just how much he desired her.

COME MORNING, MALCOLM awoke to find Jocelyn still nestled against him, both of them in a tangle of limbs and sheets.

He should have told her that he loved her.

And after their disagreement of last night, she was not going to press him on anything.

He'd accused Burling of being a coward, but was he not one also? How hard could it be to admit his feelings for Jocelyn? He'd given her the locket, claimed it came with his heart. But he had not said the actual words.

I love ye.

He stared down at her lovely face in repose, her long, sooty lashes delicately at rest, her lips still rosy and slightly puffed from his kisses.

Aye, she had his love. She had his heart.

She had always been responsive when they coupled, beautiful in her passion. Last night was no exception. Perhaps it was relief she felt in their not fighting upon his return. Whatever her reasons, she gave all of herself to him, and it was indescribably good.

Were he less of a cynical arse, he would believe they had achieved a "oneness" in their marital relations. A true blending of hearts and a union of souls that he had never thought possible to achieve in a lifetime, much less in a matter of weeks. This was the *bond* of marriage.

He understood what this meant now. This bond was a realization that nothing could ever come between them to break them apart. There would be no running away. They would face each challenge together.

The relief Jocelyn must have felt had him feeling ashamed.

He would tell her that he loved her…soon. He would tell her once they were through with Ballantry and the situation over her dowry, which was another secret he was keeping from her.

Would he lose her over these secrets?

He kissed her lightly on the forehead. She fluttered her eyes open and then smiled at him. "Good morning, Camborne…my dearest husband."

He chuckled lightly. "Ye're awake, then?"

She purred like a kitten while stretching her limbs, and then drew the covers around her when she sat up. "I'm awake. I seem to have lost my nightgown."

"It's somewhere here amid the sheets. But ye have no need of it yet, lass." He cast her a wicked smile. "I'm thinking ye look perfect just as ye are." He ran his fingers through her silken curls, loving the way they fell in a wild tumble over her shoulders and down her back.

She still wore her locket, which was the only item she had on her otherwise naked body. He'd accidentally licked it about a dozen times last night, flicking his tongue over the precious metal each time he put his mouth to her breast, meaning to suckle her soft bud instead of clanking his teeth against the locket.

Not that he was complaining.

They had both ended the night thinking the other one hated them and that matters were going to end terribly. Instead, they had strengthened their bond of love, both of them relieved the other one cared...and then gone at it like a pair of wild monkeys.

Best sex ever.

"Och, lass. Yer body's so soft and warm."

"Are you thinking of turning up the heat?"

"I was seriously thinking of it. But I had better not touch ye again this morning. Ye must be sore after what we did last night."

She blushed. "We did exert ourselves, didn't we?"

He grinned as he nodded, and then gave her a lingering kiss on the lips before rolling out of bed.

She sighed and searched for her nightgown. "Ah, here it is."

While he was slipping on his trousers and shirt, she donned her nightgown and robe, then went to the window to look out over the water. "Camborne..."

He looked up as he finished putting on his boots. "Aye, lass?"

She cast him a familiar, impudent grin. "The air is filled with sunshine and we have been married for fifteen days."

He came to her side and lifted her in his arms. "There'll always be sunshine for us, sweetheart."

She laughed and grabbed his shoulders. "I hope so."

"I know it will be so." He kissed her again and then set her down. "I'll be heading to the solicitor's office shortly. What do ye plan to do while I'm gone?"

"Other than spend the hours missing your splendid body?"

"Before it sags and turns wrinkled," he muttered with a snort.

She laughed. "I had no idea you Silver Dukes were such preening cocks. First of all, I doubt anything of yours is ever going to sag. You are not idle enough for that to ever happen. As for wrinkles," she said, placing a hand to his cheek and lovingly stroking it, "we shall probably wrinkle together, and our eyesight will fade so that we will never see each other's imperfections."

"Gad, I've a mind to take ye straight back to bed and not let ye out of it all day." He was going to take her into his arms again, but a knock at their door swiftly put that intention to rest.

"Who could that be?" Jocelyn said as she stared at the door. "Still a bit early for my parents, don't you think? But I'm pleased that Mama has been doing much better these past few days. I thought to take her for a little shopping along the high street while you were taking care of matters with Ballantry."

"Sounds like a good plan." Malcolm left her side to open the door. "Lord Granby." He was surprised to find Jocelyn's father already up and dressed. "Is it yer wife? Shall I summon a doctor?"

Granby shook his head. "She's fine. I'm sorry if I alarmed ye. The thing of it is, Camborne…I need to talk to ye."

Jocelyn came to Malcolm's side. "What's wrong, Papa? Can it not wait until my husband finishes his business with Ballantry?"

"No, lass. We won't be long."

Malcolm frowned, for he suspected the business Jocelyn's father wanted dealt with this morning was the same thing the man had been bothering him about these past two weeks—the matter of transferring fifty thousand pounds into the account set aside for Jocelyn's dowry.

He was not frowning over the fact that he had promised to give it over, or that her father was not letting up on reminding him until the matter was done. His irritation was in Jocelyn's father continuing to lie to *her*.

To put it more accurately, Malcolm did not like being complicit in this deception, and it worried him that Jocelyn might not forgive so easily this time…or forgive him at all.

He was not a praying man, but was heartily doing so now. He hoped their bonds of marriage were strong enough to overcome yet another disappointment on her part.

Assuming she ever found out.

He sighed. "All right. I'll meet ye downstairs in fifteen minutes."

"Thank ye, Camborne," her father said with a nod. "Ye're a good lad."

Lad? Malcolm hadn't been a little boy in ages. His childhood ended with the deaths of his parents and siblings.

"Bollocks," he muttered, stalking into the bedchamber to wash and properly dress while Jocelyn remained chatting with her father by the door.

He heard her ask about her mother's health.

"She's hale, lass. Take her shopping, as ye planned. The outing will do her good. Och, I needn't stand here while yer husband gets himself ready. I'll be downstairs waiting for him."

Jocelyn shut the door after her father and then joined Malcolm in their bedchamber. He'd tossed on some casual clothes when he awoke, thinking to take a quick look around the inn and then bring up a pot of tea and some scones from the dining room for them to share as they leisurely prepared for the day.

That plan had changed with her father's appearance. Was the old man worried about something more than Jocelyn's dowry?

He smiled at Jocelyn when she joined him in their bedroom and settled on the bed to watch as he began to shave. "You appeared impatient with my father."

"He thinks I want yer dowry, which I dinna want and couldn't care less about."

"*I* care about it. It is my contribution to the marriage and I am proud to provide it. But I think my father is more concerned with the entirety of our situation. Not merely the dowry but my marital settlement. His worry has to be that I will be given nothing should something happen to you or should we part ways."

"I'm not parting from ye, lass."

She smiled. "Oh, I know. We resolved that question rather thoroughly last night."

"Not quite, lass." He grinned as he lathered his chin. "I think it deserves more exploration tonight. *Much* more exploration."

She laughed, but then sobered after a moment. "Seriously, Camborne. He must want the matter formalized before he and my mother return to Granby."

"Aye, lass." But he knew it was mostly about that dowry and the fact it had all been spent. Her father had been fretting about it for days now, taking Malcolm aside at odd moments every day to make certain he was not going to renege on his promise.

Malcolm understood the root of this irritating behavior was her father's guilt over losing it all. But if he felt all that guilty, then why not simply confess to Jocelyn? The lass was all about sentiment and feelings, not wealth.

She still had not pressed him about what he was going to settle on her beyond the funds he had already placed in an account for her. It was a goodly sum, but a mere fraction of his wealth. He would add more once she had the chance to tour his properties and decide on her preferences. Of course, he could not give her the entailed properties. But he had plenty of unencumbered assets as well.

"Camborne," she said as though reading his mind, "I know you want me to set out a list of my demands, but I have none. The one hundred thousand pounds you've given me is an enormous sum. And you've already told me the fifty thousand pounds you'll receive as my dowry portion is to be added to it. Even with all that, am I expected to demand more? It is pointless when all I want is to be happily married to you. Frankly, I am a little irritated with my father for bothering you about it. You've already given me more than Ballantry ever agreed to provide for me under our betrothal contract. In fact, his obligation was far less."

"Because he is a wastrel who did not take care of his assets and therefore had far less to offer ye."

She paused to give the matter more thought and then looked up at him in dismay. "We've been worried about my mother's health all this time. Do you think my father is the one seriously ill and wants matters secure before he can no longer attend to them?"

"No, lass. He looks hale enough," he hurried to assure her, gazing at her stricken expression. "He has a tendency to fret, just as ye do. I expect ye inherited that trait from him."

He hoped she would not probe deeper.

"I do fret," she admitted. "It is a much prettier word than 'nagging,' which I hope I do not do."

"Och, lass. Ye're a worrier, for certain. But ye do not nag. Perhaps I am also a worrier, for I want to ensure ye'll always protected, especially if I am not around to see to yer safety. So, think seriously about what else ye would like in the marital contract. Yer father is right—it is important. And as I said, I have more to give ye than that lout Ballantry ever had."

"I'll delegate the matter to you, Camborne. Four gowns and a bulging bank account is more than I ever expected to receive. As far as I'm concerned, the only matter requiring discussion concerns what is to be settled on our children. But we don't have any yet, so is it not a bit premature to discuss this?"

He frowned. "If we have no sons, ye'll be set aside once my cousin inherits. Even if we do have a son, ye'll merely be the dowager duchess once he marries. I'll not have a greedy cousin, or some impudent slip of a girl who marries our son, thinking their status will ever be above yers."

Jocelyn laughed. "You really are being quite apish about this. If your cousin inherits, so be it. I'll be a rich widow and capable of caring for any daughters we might have. Same for the wife of our eldest son, assuming we have a son. She will be the reigning duchess. If she does not care to have me underfoot, then I will settle elsewhere."

"Ye'll do no such thing. I'll no' have any wife of mine reduced in standing. Ye'll live where ye like, and no one is ever going to kick ye out. As for that ingrate daughter-in-law, I want ye to be the dragon dowager she fears."

"Me? A dragon? I am not even a decent harpy." She shook her head and laughed again. "Well, none of it is relevant, since we do not have a son."

"Lass, I have not kept my hands off ye. I think the question is not *if* we will have any but *how many* we will have." He finished shaving and took a moment to wipe the remains of the lather off his face. He then dressed in proper business attire, asking Jocelyn for assistance in doing up his cuffs.

She scrambled off the bed and came to stand before him. She barely reached his shoulder, so he saw only the top of her dark tumble of hair while she looked down at his cuff.

She was such a pretty thing.

"Jocelyn, if ye take yer mother shopping this morning, I want ye to bring Terrence along with ye."

She glanced up at him. "Why? Do you think there is any danger? We are just going to walk up the high street, and not very far at that. We'll probably stay within sight of the inn because my mother still tires easily."

"I'm just being cautious, that's all. No specific threat from anyone. However, Ballantry and Burling have to be disgruntled. There's no telling what they might do."

"We'll be careful." She smiled at him. "I'm sure Terrence will be delighted to watch us try on hats or inspect bolts of fabric."

He finished dressing and started for the door. "Shall I send a maid up to help ye dress, lass?"

"No," she said with a shake of her head. "My mother can help me. I'm going to stop next door and look in on her once you leave."

He leaned forward to kiss her, loving the soft give of her mouth as he sank his lips onto hers. "Dinna forget to take Terrence with ye when ye go out."

He strode downstairs, shaking his head at the realization that he was besotted with his wife. He already missed her and they had not been apart for even a minute.

Gad, he was pathetic. That little jeweler, Solomon Haggard, would be laughing heartily if he knew.

Jocelyn's father was waiting for him by the entrance to the inn, pacing by the doorway. "What is the urgency, Granby? I've told ye a dozen times already that the arrangements for the transfer of funds from my account into the one ye held for yer daughter have been made. All I have to do is give the nod and those funds will be delivered. But that will no' happen before Ballantry signs the settlement. So, why are ye dragging me away from yer daughter when I'm merely going to repeat what ye already know?"

"I want to know what yer terms are with Ballantry. I'm Jocelyn's father. I have a right to be told."

"And I've told ye before, they are confidential and I am not discussing them with ye."

"But should I not be the one signing the settlement on Jocelyn's behalf? After all, the betrothal agreement was a Granby matter, and I am head of the clan."

"I am her husband now and responsible for her. The only signatures that matter are mine and Ballantry's. In truth, all I care about is Ballantry's, and he'll be signing this afternoon."

"How can ye be so certain? What if he fails to show up at yer solicitor's office?"

Malcolm frowned. "Do ye know something that I do not? Out with it, Granby. We're talking about yer daughter's safety. Ye had better not be holding anything back."

Granby glanced around nervously. "Walk outside with me. I dinna want us to be overheard."

Malcolm did not like this one bit, but agreed to follow him. "All right. Tell me."

"I overheard Ballantry and Burling fighting last night," Granby said as they walked in the direction of the harbor. "It was a while after supper. They were standing out here, talking low and looking around furtively. I had come outside to smoke. My wife detests the odor of cigars, so she does not permit me to smoke in our room. I honor the request, of course, for I am ever mindful of her delicate heart condition."

"Ye saw them whispering and scowling at each other," Malcolm said, prodding the man back to the point.

"They were so intent on their argument, they failed to notice me in the shadows. I meant to walk away, but stopped when I heard them mention Jocelyn's name."

Malcolm instantly tensed. "What did they say?"

"Burling was demanding money from Ballantry, but he refused. He said Burling could get it from Jocelyn, but there was none to be had from him. Burling retorted that maybe he would do just that because she was... I canno' repeat the vile terms he used to describe my daughter. He threatened Ballantry, too. But it was the way he spoke about my daughter that had me worried. I ran back to the inn and knocked at yer door last night, but Jocelyn said ye had gone out."

"So ye walked away and told her nothing?" Malcolm struggled to maintain his composure and not throttle the earl. How could he just walk away from Jocelyn and tell her nothing?

"I could never repeat such a vile thing and upset my daughter."

Malcolm raked a hand through his hair. "Ye left her knowing she was alone and defenseless."

"Och, calm yerself, Camborne. The pair were too busy fighting to plan anything last night. Ballantry stalked back to the inn, angry and disgusted with Burling. As for Burling, he just stormed off. I have no idea where he went, probably to some nearby tavern to get himself piss drunk. I knew Jocelyn would be safe enough. So, upon learning you were not there, I merely pretended I stopped by to invite ye for a drink and left it at that. But I had to tell ye now. Ye understand why I dared not speak in front of the lass."

Malcolm stopped, as they were now almost out of sight of the inn. They had walked far enough, and he needed to get back to Jocelyn to warn her and also relay this information to Terrence. "Ye canno' continue to shelter her, Granby. She is better off knowing of threats rather than being taken by surprise."

"She's my daughter. How can I scare her?"

"She will no' be scared. She'll appreciate being able to take whatever steps necessary to protect herself. Ye already know my thoughts on the matter. She is better off knowing *everything*," he said meaningfully, for it was time all of it, including the matter of her lost dowry, came to light.

But he saw by the stubborn set of Granby's jowls that he was not ready to reveal the truth to his daughter. "Jocelyn has a delicate constitution. Ye cannot tell her any of what I have told ye. Ye've given me yer oath."

"Not about Ballantry and Burling's discussion," Malcolm shot back, turning around and motioning for Granby to follow him back to the inn. If Jocelyn was able to endure three days on the run in a skimpy wedding frock and without funds enough for food, then she was not too fragile to be warned about Burling.

He already knew the sot was of a mind to hurt someone, since he'd been following Malcolm last night. It must have been shortly after he and Ballantry had their fight. "Terrence will be guarding your daughter and wife this morning while I meet with my solicitor. I'll alert him to be especially on his guard."

Granby gave an approving nod. "Aye, that will ease my worry."

"I'm going to alert Jocelyn, as well. She needs to understand why she is to keep away from both of those churls."

"But—"

Malcolm cut him short with a grunt. "Dinna give me that nonsense about her being yer little girl and too fragile to handle the information. She is a sensible woman and old enough to think for herself."

Malcolm hurried back to the inn and ran upstairs. Jocelyn's father lumbered a few paces behind him, struggling to keep up.

"Bollocks, the door's open," Malcolm muttered as the earl came up beside him. Taking but a trice to ensure no one was standing in the room with a pistol pointed at the door, he strode in and called for her.

His heart quickened when he received no response.

Nor would he get one, since she obviously wasn't there.

Nevertheless, he called out again with more urgency. "Jocelyn!"

Where was she? Her gown was on the bed. Was she still in her nightclothes?

"She might be with my wife," Granby remarked, noticing Malcolm's dismay.

"Aye." Malcolm followed Jocelyn's father to his guest chamber, which was only a few steps away from the grand suite he shared with Jocelyn. He waited just outside their door while her father stepped in to make certain his wife was decent for company.

"My love, I have Camborne with me."

"Oh, yes. Let him come in."

Malcolm entered and immediately surveyed the elegantly appointed room. "Lady Granby, have ye seen yer daughter this morning?"

"No, I haven't seen her yet. Why?"

Malcolm's heart surged into his throat. "She isn't in our quarters, and I dinna think she's dressed. The door was left open and her gown is laid out on the bed."

"Then she couldn't have gone out," her mother assured him with a light shrug, showing no concern.

Was he overreacting to the situation?

He did not think so.

But even if he was, so what? Was it not better to worry than to sit idly by while something dire might be happening?

His only comfort was that Jocelyn could not have been led out by Burling while still in her nightgown and robe without attracting everyone's notice. She had to be somewhere inside the inn.

He tore downstairs and called for the proprietor.

The man scurried forward. "Yer Grace, is something amiss?"

"I need the key to Lord Burling's room. Same for Lord Ballantry. Give them to me now or I'll break their doors down."

"I carry the master key on my person at all times. Follow me," he said, hurrying up the stairs.

"Burling first," Malcolm said. "Dinna knock. Just unlock it and then step aside."

The man's eyes widened, but he did as asked.

Malcolm cautiously stepped in. The drapes were drawn and the room reeked of spilled brandy and stale body odor. Burling was snoring in his bed and soundly asleep. A perusal of the room showed no one else present.

"Blast," Malcolm muttered, for Burling was in his nightshirt and nightcap. *He* certainly would have been noticed walking around the hallways dressed like that. "Take me to Ballantry's room."

The innkeeper hastily locked Burling's door and then scampered two doors down, pausing in front of the first room at the foot of the stairs. "Lord Ballantry's downstairs having breakfast, Your Grace. Perhaps we ought to ask him for—"

"Open it," Malcolm commanded. "I'll not be wasting time asking for his permission."

"Your Grace, what is it you are looking for? Perhaps I can help," the proprietor said as Malcolm stepped into Ballantry's room and raked a hand through his hair in frustration as he looked about the mess.

Where was Jocelyn?

"How long has he been seated downstairs?"

"Oh, about half an hour, I would say."

Malcolm had only left his wife about twenty minutes ago. "Duchess Jocelyn…"

The proprietor's eyes brightened. "Oh, she's seated with yer man, that Terrence fellow. They're having breakfast."

"What?" Malcolm shook his head, certain he had not heard right.

"She walked in just a few minutes ago. I doubt she's started eating yet. Ye'll catch up to her if ye—"

"She's there? Having her breakfast? In her nightclothes?" Malcolm was now utterly confused.

The proprietor frowned as they walked out of Ballantry's chamber and he locked the door behind them. "What makes ye think she is in her nightclothes, Yer Grace? She's wearing a pretty gown. But then, she's quite a beautiful lass, if I may be so bold as to remark."

Malcolm stifled a groan. "My apologies for disturbing ye. Seems my wife and I got our information crossed, and I worried needlessly."

"Were ye worried those two lords might have been up to mischief? We all noticed how they were scowling as they kept their eyes on ye and yer wife yesterday. Unhealthy, if ye ask me. Quite menacing. Do ye wish me to toss them out? I'll gladly do it. They're more trouble than they're worth."

Malcolm sighed. "I expect Lord Ballantry will be gone by tomorrow. Once he leaves, I doubt Lord Burling will have reason to stay on. My wife is downstairs, ye say? With my man, Terrence?"

"Aye, Yer Grace."

"Thank goodness," he mumbled, and then marched back downstairs along with the proprietor, who was staring at him in puzzlement.

Aye, he could have just asked the man whether he had seen Jocelyn and knew where she was. But he had gone apish over the possibility she had been abducted.

He found Jocelyn indeed seated with Terrence. Beside them was her father, who had remained downstairs while Malcolm was tearing through the inn, dragging the poor proprietor from chamber to chamber in the crazed belief she had been the victim of foul play. "Granby, ye might have mentioned ye'd found her," he grumbled, taking a seat beside Jocelyn.

"I happened upon her just now," Granby replied. "I was about to have one of the maids run up to tell ye. But ye're here and all is well."

Aye, all was well...if one overlooked that Malcolm had made a disruptive jackass of himself while scouring the inn.

Jocelyn noticed his frown. "What is the matter?"

He let out a heavy breath. "I turned into a wild ape when I returned to find our door open and yer gown laid out on the bed. Then yer mother reported she hadn't seen ye. I thought..."

She inhaled lightly. "Oh, I did tell you that I would knock at her door. Then I changed my mind because I thought it might still be too early for her to rise. A maid passed by as I was contemplating what to do, so I had her assist me with my gown. You thought I had been abducted?"

"Aye, lass. As I said, our door was open and yer gown was laid out on the bed...as though ye were interrupted before ye had the chance to dress. What was I to think?"

She cast him a gentle smile. "I'm so sorry I worried you. The gown you found on the bed was the one I decided not to wear because it was wrinkled. The maid who helped me took it to the inn's laundress to give it a quick pressing. She must have returned it."

"And left our door ajar for anyone to walk in," Malcolm muttered.

"It could not have been for more than a moment. She was going to clean our room while we were down here having our breakfast. Do not get her into trouble simply because she darted out a moment to fetch something."

Malcolm was not mollified. "That is no excuse. Anyone could have strolled in, stolen some of our valuables. Or lain in wait for ye."

"The poor girl was harried because the inn was short of staff this morning and she has had to be in three places at once. Besides, what valuables do we have? I'm wearing the locket you gave me, and you always carry your valuables on your person. What were they going to steal? My silk undergarments?"

"Jocelyn!" her father cried. "Ye are in company, lass."

"Forgive me, Papa," she replied, not sounding at all contrite. "I will not mention my *unmentionables* again. But my husband was obviously worried that I had fallen victim to foul play, so I hardly think my *unmentionables* are the issue."

She frowned at her father. "Is this the reason you asked for a moment of his time? I thought it was odd that you were up and about so early. Had you heard something worrisome and wanted to convey it to my husband? Why not tell me?"

Her father blushed. "I did not wish to frighten ye, lass. Ye're my little girl. It is my responsibility to take care of ye."

"And now it is my husband's. But you still should have told me." She turned to Malcolm, obviously not wanting to receive a watered-down version of the story from her father but the entire truth. "What did he tell you?"

Her father groaned as Malcolm began to relate the conversation between Ballantry and Burling with detailed accuracy. "Terrence, I need ye to stay close to Jocelyn and her mother today. I'll be busy with my solicitor much of the morning, and then Ballantry is to join us this afternoon."

"One hopes," Jocelyn interjected.

"Aye, lass." Malcolm nodded. "He has every reason to accept this fair deal."

She nibbled her lip. "But Burling appears to have been cut out by everyone and is angry. Is he the one we must worry about? I always thought he was an oily creature. Do you think he is desperate enough to commit violence? To what end? He only damages himself. He is not a peer and would have no privileges accorded to him."

"Who knows what might run through any man's mind if he feels trapped like an animal and has no other way out? But Burling has been ineffectual all of his life. Even when enraged, he is a bumbling fool."

She stared at Malcolm for the longest moment. "Perhaps he can be bought off cheaply."

"Bought off?" He arched an eyebrow in surprise. "Ye were adamantly against it until this very moment. Why should he be bought off? Ye know I am going to protect ye."

"So am I," her father intoned.

Malcolm frowned at him.

Jocelyn continued, unaware of the tension between him and her father. "Great, now both of you might get hurt. And Terrence, too. I would never forgive myself if harm befell any of you. Camborne, take whatever ye wish of my dowry and buy him off. Make him go away."

"No, Jocelyn. He is just a pig at the trough. If we give him anything, he'll only come around asking for more a month from now."

She resumed nibbling her luscious lower lip. "But this disappointment is fresh in his mind now and making him unreasonably angry. As you just indicated, we cannot reason with an unreasonable man. Give him something to mollify him."

"No. He gets nothing. Why are ye so insistent, lass?"

She tipped her chin into the air. "Why are you suddenly so against it when you were the one willing to bribe him when we were in Arbroth?"

"Ye weren't married to me then, and the threat to yer reputation was real. However, we are husband and wife now, so he has no secrets to relate to the gossip rags that can harm ye. He lost his leverage upon our marriage. I am not going to let him squeeze us now."

"Even if it leaves me in danger?"

"The man is a coward. He was following me last night, had his blade in hand, but was too afraid to confront me. Terrence will be guarding ye whenever I am not here to do it. Just stay close to the inn. Venture no farther than the high street, which is all ye planned to do anyway because of yer mother's frailty."

"I'll be with ye, too," her father remarked. "I'll not let anyone harm my little girl."

Jocelyn reached over and hugged him. "You are the best father. I'm so very sorry I put you and Mama through all this. You were not keen on my marrying Ballantry while everyone else in the family pushed me to move forward. I should have listened to you instead of being so contrary. Can you ever forgive me?"

"Nothing to forgive, lass," her father insisted, hugging her back. "We are family and must stand together no matter what mistakes are made. Is that not so?"

"Yes, Papa. Thank you." She hugged him again.

Malcolm groaned inwardly.

Jocelyn believed her father was speaking of her misbegotten agreement to marry Ballantry and then running away from her wedding. But the man was obviously thinking of her dowry that he'd spent down to nothing.

He stared at her father. Granby refused to look back at him.

"But, Papa," Jocelyn continued, "you really should have warned me of the threat last night and not waited until this morning to relay it to my husband. Promise me that you will not ever hide the truth from me again."

Her father mumbled something, then hugged his daughter again. "I love ye, my Jocelyn."

"Oh, Papa. I love you too."

Malcolm could take no more of the deception.

He excused himself to meet with his solicitor, but gave a final warning. "Lass, stay close to Terrence. Dinna stray far from the inn. I'll be back as soon as Ballantry signs the settlement."

Ballantry, seated at a table on the opposite side of the common room having his meal, had been staring at him and Jocelyn throughout.

Was he going to collude with Burling? To what end?

Burling had nothing to lose, but Ballantry had *everything* to lose if he stepped out of line. This also assumed he was thinking rationally.

What if he wasn't?

Malcolm considered taking Jocelyn with him to the solicitor's office to keep her close, but decided against it. If he did so, she would find out the terms of the settlement. She would realize Ballantry was not the rightful earl and then be furious that Malcolm had no intention of telling Ballantry's nephew he had been deprived of his rightful title.

Much as he wished to keep her close, she could not come along with him.

Terrence, he noted, already had his eyes trained on Ballantry. He would do the same with Burling when the sot woke up and made his appearance.

Malcolm had no doubt Jocelyn would be safe with his trusted companion. No one was sharper or more watchful than Terrence.

He strode out of the inn and made his way to the bustling center of town, where his solicitor maintained his bureau. But each step away from Jocelyn felt like a mistake and haunted him.

Had he been wrong in refusing to toss a few coins at Burling to make him go away?

The man could not be so deranged as to seriously threaten Jocelyn, could he?

Or did Malcolm have cause to worry?

Chapter Fifteen

Malcolm was surprised when Ballantry turned up at his solicitor's office at precisely the appointed hour. It was the middle of the afternoon, and he was pleased this matter would now be dealt with quickly and without rancor, judging by Ballantry's defeated expression as they took seats around the conference table.

"Read it over," he said as Gordon MacRae, his Aberdeen solicitor and kinsman, an intelligent man in his late forties, handed the document to Ballantry.

Ballantry spared no more than a glance at the parchment before signing. "There, now give me my money, ye bloody arse."

He followed the statement with several more vile curses hurled at Malcolm.

The solicitor's eyes widened in response to the earl's offensive language. "Now, see here," he said, rising with indignation to defend Malcolm.

Malcolm motioned for him to sit down. "Leave him be. Ye can see the man is a blight on humanity. Let him rant, for these slurs are all he has in his arsenal. He'll be on his way to the Continent shortly and will never set foot here again."

Malcolm turned to Ballantry and handed him two more documents. "Sign these, too."

Ballantry stared at the papers. "What are they?"

"Duplicates of the settlement agreement. I had Mr. MacRae prepare three identical sets as a precaution. Sign them."

"What if I don't?" he growled.

"Ye really need to ask me that? Ye know I dinna trust ye. Each original will be held in a secure but separate location. All ye have to do is honor the terms and I will no' bother ye. Cross me, and ye'll regret it."

Ballantry cursed him once again.

His kinsman rose to defend him, but Malcolm waved him down again. "He's merely flailing. Leave him be." He then turned to Ballantry. "Ye had better be gone from Scotland before the week is out or yer dirty secret will be all over the gossip rags."

"Just give me the money," Ballantry spat, his face red. "I wish ye nothing but misery with yer harpy of a wife."

Malcolm sighed. "Come along, the bank manager is awaiting us. Watch what ye say about Jocelyn, or ye'll never get the rest of the funds. That's part of the settlement terms and the one I won't hesitate to enforce if ye ever dare speak ill of her."

"I am only speaking the truth," Ballantry said, shoving his chair back and almost toppling it as he rose.

Malcolm rose with him. "It is *yer* distorted truth, and I would advise ye to keep those distorted thoughts to yerself. The terms are clear. Speak against her and ye'll lose everything."

He bade his solicitor good day and walked out onto the street with Ballantry, who was still fuming and resentful.

The Royal Bank of Aberdeen was but a few streets away. They strode apace amid the bustling crowd, passing one stately granite stone building after another until their destination came into view. The bank was another of those beautifully crafted buildings whose silvery granite stones shimmered in the afternoon light. This was a feature of Aberdeen, those gray quarry stones that gave the city its distinctive character.

The manager, another MacRae kinsman, was expecting them and

immediately rushed forward to escort them into his private office. "All is in readiness, Yer Grace."

The exchange was easy and rapidly done, since Ballantry also happened to have accounts at this same bank. The manager, an earnest but rather priggish distant cousin, was overly solicitous of Malcolm and eager to be of assistance. He believed a mere business transaction was taking place. Malcolm thought it better not to disabuse him of the notion.

Both he and Ballantry maintained the pretense of civility between them.

Once the transaction was completed, Ballantry began to complain bitterly about having to make arrangements for his travel out of the country. "Ye dinna give me enough time, Camborne. I'll need more than a week to make these preparations."

Malcolm regarded him stonily.

"I always said ye were a bastard," Ballantry muttered, and stormed out.

The manager turned to Malcolm, obviously rather shocked. "Not a friendly transaction, I gather."

"He's a lazy oaf who does not like to put himself out. Now, about the other matter I mentioned to ye?"

"Oh, yes. Lord Granby's account for his daughter. Shall I transfer the fifty thousand pounds into it now?"

"Aye. And ye're not to make mention of my hand in it when I bring Lord Granby and his daughter here tomorrow. Same for her personal account. How much was in it before Lord Granby withdrew the funds?"

"Oh, let me see. Easy enough to check the registers." The manager withdrew a large ledger kept at hand because he knew Malcolm wanted information on any accounts held in Jocelyn's name. "She has two accounts besides the one you recently opened on her behalf. One had a hundred pounds in it and the other had ten thousand."

"Had?"

"Aye, Yer Grace. They've had only ten pounds in each for several months now."

Dear heaven.

What would Jocelyn have done had she arrived here on her own only to find she had twenty pounds to her name? That was barely enough for a coach ticket and suitable lodgings and meals to get her back home.

Malcolm sighed. "Replenish those, too."

"If ye will but wait a few minutes, I shall return promptly with the receipts."

"Be quick about it," Malcolm muttered, not liking the idea of Ballantry on the loose and angry as blazes. He trusted Terrence to watch over Jocelyn, of course. But no one was going to be as attentive as her own husband.

Malcolm ached to get back to her.

The wait seemed interminable, but it was less than ten minutes before the manager returned with the receipts in hand. "Here, Yer Grace. All done. Complete discretion, of course. I shall see ye, Duchess Jocelyn, and Lord Granby tomorrow at the scheduled hour."

He escorted Malcolm out, casting him a conspiratorial grin as he repeated, "Complete discretion, Yer Grace. Ye may rely on me."

Which was exactly what worried Malcolm, for the man was still talking about being discreet as they walked through the bank. All this well-meaning but officious behavior would call attention to them and alert others that something was going on. Precisely what Malcolm did *not* want.

He bade the manager farewell and strode back to the inn.

Hours had passed since he had left Jocelyn's side. He doubted she would still be out with her mother, since Lady Granby had not the stamina for a full day of shopping. Likely, they were safely back at the inn now.

The proprietor eyed him nervously when he entered.

"Have ye seen my wife?" Malcolm asked, knowing the man was in fear of a repeat of this morning's performance. His hand had gone protectively to the set of keys he wore attached to his belt, as though he were worried Malcolm was going grab them and go on another apish hunt.

Well, he *had* behaved like an utter *idjit*.

He cast the proprietor a wry smile. "Ye can ease yer hand off the keys, Mr. Grant. I'll no' be asking ye to break into rooms."

The man grinned. "Aye, Yer Grace."

"Do ye happen to know where my wife is at the moment?"

He nodded. "She's in the dining room having tea with her parents and yer man, Terrence."

"And Lord Ballantry? Have ye seen him?"

The proprietor shook his head. "He went out earlier but has not returned yet."

Malcolm hoped this meant Ballantry had gone immediately to make his travel arrangements. It was true, giving Ballantry only a week to make those arrangements was not fair. But it could be done, considering he had only clothes to pack, since he had wasted almost everything else. The furnishings were not worth moving, and many Italian villas were offered to let with furniture included.

"And Lord Burling?" Malcolm asked.

"I dinna know, Yer Grace. He was in a foul temper when he walked out a few hours ago. Perhaps he has gone off to drink again."

"Let me know when he returns," Malcolm said, and then walked off to join Jocelyn.

Everyone at her table looked up at him in expectation.

"What happened?" Jocelyn asked. "Did all go well?"

He nodded. "The settlement is signed and done."

"Thank goodness," her father muttered, casting him an avid stare to ensure the dowry sum had been replaced.

Malcolm gave a quick nod.

"Good, good," Granby said. "Well, now it is time for me to release the dower portion. Shall we take care of this tomorrow morning, Camborne? Seeing as how nicely ye've taken care of my daughter, I am honored to turn it over to ye."

Malcolm merely grunted, not trusting himself to say anything.

Jocelyn's expression was soft and filled with love for her father. When she looked upon Malcolm, he saw pride shining in her eyes.

Aye, the lass was feeling a burden lifted off her shoulders.

She had come to him with nothing, and this had been a source of shame for her. Unwarranted, of course. But this was why she had delayed setting out terms for her own protection in the marriage. She did not want anything more from him because she already felt she was taking advantage of him.

He had told her repeatedly that it did not matter.

In truth, he wanted to give her the world. Falling in love did that to a man, he supposed.

That he was capable of falling in love at his age was a complete surprise and a kick in the arse for him. His head was still in a spin.

Jocelyn's smile was the sweetest thing. She was as happy as a meadowlark, and Malcolm silently prayed all would go smoothly tomorrow and this matter would be put behind them forever.

He smiled back, hiding his remorse for the deception he and her father were about to play on her.

Oh, how he ached to tell her the truth. But how could he break his oath to her father?

Later that night, when they returned to their suite after supper, Jocelyn confronted him. "Is there more going on than your worrying about Ballantry and Burling?"

"Why should there be?" he responded evasively.

"You were somber and unsettled all evening."

He shrugged. "It is nothing, just my cautious nature. I like to know where all the players are in this unpleasant game. Did ye notice Burling was not around tonight?"

Jocelyn nodded. "Now that you mention it, yes. Where do you think he might be?"

"I dinna know, lass. That's what has me concerned. I only hope he is off doing what he always does, drinking himself sick in some nearby tavern or trying to cheat some locals in a game of cards."

Jocelyn remained thoughtful for a moment. "It cannot be easy having to scrounge for every shilling, too proud to find work because he is a 'gentleman' and above such common exertions."

"The allowance provided by his brother would have been more than enough for a frugal man. But Burling has no restraint. If he isn't drinking, he is gambling, and is now so far in debt that he will never recover on his own. This is why he always has his hand out." He took Jocelyn in his arms and gave her a quick kiss on the nose. "Let's agree not to fret about him any further tonight. He isn't worth it."

She looked up at him with her big eyes clouded with worry. "You first. I'll stop fretting when you do. Perhaps we ought to rethink the matter of buying him off."

"Do not go soft now, Jocelyn. We are almost at the end. He will only take it as a sign to approach ye more aggressively next time and demand more. This is his character."

"And why you revile him?"

Malcolm nodded and kissed her again. "He could have taken on many respectful roles and still maintained his status as a gentleman, but he chose to do nothing but squander his life away. I would rather give alms to the needy. They are more deserving of assistance than that rat."

"But if pushed to desperation, do you think he will try something stupid? We know he was working up the courage to harm you last night."

"No, lass. I think he is all thunder and bluster, but his wind will die out soon and he will move on."

"I hope you are right."

So did he.

They retired to their bedchamber.

Malcolm had grown used to the way Jocelyn curled up beside him and nestled in his arms. In truth, he was growing to crave this affection. This was what he had been missing all of his life, this connection. This knowledge that someone cared whether he lived or died. This love she was giving him openly and generously.

This unconditional love.

Lord, he was an arse for holding back what he already felt in his own heart.

Come morning, Malcolm awoke early, as was his usual routine. But he lingered in bed waiting for Jocelyn to open her eyes and provide him with her weather report mixed with her endearing words of love.

His heart welled as she woke up and smiled at him. "Good morning, lass."

She scrambled out of bed and scurried to the window to look at the weather outside.

He thought she looked delectable as she stared out onto a gray sky and a darkening sea. "Oh dear. It is overcast, Camborne. We shall have rain today for certain, and…"

He arched an eyebrow. "And?"

She hurried back to his side and hopped onto the bed beside him. "And we have been married sixteen days now."

He laughed and took her back in his arms. "That long already?"

"Regretting it?" she teased.

"Not a minute of it, lass. But I think ye've made a mistake in yer weather report."

She cast him a look of dismay. "What mistake?"

"Ye're overlooking the sunshine ye bring into my life. Looks quite sunny from my vantage point." He liked lingering in bed with her, and admired her shapely figure beneath the gossamer fabric of her nightgown.

She playfully poked him in the ribs. "I did not think Silver Dukes were this sentimental. Careful, or you might just turn into a romantic poet."

He laughed heartily. "Och, no. I'm not one for flowery words."

"You think telling me I bring sunshine into your life was not flowery?"

"Dinna tease me about it, Jocelyn."

"I'm not. I love you with all my heart." She planted soft kisses all over his face as she continued speaking. "I'm delighted you feel this way. But we had better start to get ready or we'll be late for the bank appointment."

He drew her down atop him and held her in his embrace. "We could cancel it and just remain in bed all day."

"Not on your life, Camborne." She kissed him again before shoving off him. "You are to collect my dowry today. I will not have it put off any longer."

That infernal dowry.

He wished he did not have to go along with that lie.

They readied themselves for the day, and then went downstairs to join her parents for breakfast before heading to the bank. Jocelyn's mother was not going to join them, her excuse being that she tired easily and did not wish them to be distracted while they carried on their important business. "If the weather is not too foul, I'll sit on the terrace with a cup of tea and a book to read."

Jocelyn seemed to accept her mother's excuse for not attending the sham of a dowry transfer ceremony. Malcolm knew her mother wanted to remain behind so as not to look upon her husband as he continued to deceive his daughter.

Malcolm also ached over it. They were all in on the deception.

What made it worse was Jocelyn's pride in now being able to come to him with something. He set down his cup of coffee and gave her a kiss on the cheek. "Lass, just remember...I dinna care about yer dowry. It is yer heart that is the true treasure."

She laughed softly. "I knew it. You are turning into a romantic poet."

He groaned as he eased back in his seat. "Och, dinna say that. I have a Silver Duke reputation to uphold."

"Powerful and ruthless? Cold and aloof? Merciless in getting what you want? Camborne, perhaps it is true to an extent, because I think this is how you have dealt with Ballantry and Burling. But not with me. You have been so wonderful to me."

"Because ye are my wife."

"Is this the only reason?"

"I made a vow to honor and protect ye. I always keep to my vows. *Always*, lass. Even those I regret making and wish I could break."

Her smile disappeared and her lips began to tremble. "Excuse me," she said, and abruptly rose to leave.

"What was that about?" he muttered, and rose to chase after her. "Jocelyn, what in blazes? What happened to suddenly upset ye?"

He walked her outside onto the terrace, which was deserted except for them because the air was moist with the threat of rain and the sea wind had a bite to it. "Tell me, Jocelyn. What has ye suddenly threatening tears?"

"I thought you cared for me."

He shook his head. "I do. Is it not obvious?"

"But you wish you could break your wedding vows. You just said so."

He thought back to his words and groaned. "Ye thought I was talking about us, lass? Och, no. It never even crossed my mind."

"Then what vow are you regretting?"

"It is just something said in passing. Not important at all. And *not* about us."

"But it could be someday, couldn't it?" she asked.

He removed his jacket and wrapped it around her slight shoulders. "No, lass. That day will *never* come. Do ye think I kiss just any…"

He sighed, because this *had* been him until only recently, kissing just anyone who caught his fancy and then moving on without another thought or care.

"I know my reputation is no' the best. But ye are mine now. Mine to *honor* and protect."

He should tell her that he loved her.

Was she not his to *love*, honor, and protect? He felt this commitment deeply. But how could he be certain it was an enduring love after only sixteen days?

The urge to reveal what was in his heart went against the training instilled in him from a very young age. Never be too trustful. Never give someone leverage over you. Never show weakness. Never tip your hand to what you are feeling.

Never give your heart away in only sixteen days.

In truth, he had known he loved Jocelyn after merely two nights.

Perhaps even the very first night, when she cast him that impudent stare and admonished him for returning to his *own* room at the Arbroth Inn and disturbing her peaceful sleep in *his* bed that she had no right to be in.

"Come back inside, lass. We had better be on our way."

She nodded as she cast him a frail smile.

It tore him apart to see that her mirth had fled.

Terrence remained behind to quietly keep watch over Lady Granby. Although Malcolm felt she would not be anyone's target, why take the chance? Ballantry and Burling were still at the inn and no doubt seething over their unhappy outcomes. Who knew what that pair might do?

He had ordered a hack to be brought around. It was waiting for them when he walked out with Jocelyn and her father.

Malcolm climbed in last and settled beside Jocelyn. He took her hand in his, hoping she would understand their bond of marriage was unbreakable. She was not smiling as she glanced up at him, but did not remove her hand from his.

Well, she was not outright rejecting him. This was something, wasn't it?

They reached the bank, and the manager, Malcolm's kinsman, came running toward them. "All is in readiness," he said with a conspiratorial smile. "Come right this way."

Och, did the man have to be so obvious?

He escorted them into his impressive office and they all settled around an elegant table surrounded by cushioned leather chairs.

"We've come to transfer the account holding my daughter's dowry to her husband," Granby said, nodding toward Malcolm. "As ye obviously know, he is the Duke of Camborne."

The manager nodded. "Indeed, I do. We are cousins. Distant cousins, but still related by blood. Of course, I was delighted to learn the news of his recent nuptials. It is a pleasure to make yer acquaintance, Yer Grace," he said, nodding to Jocelyn.

She smiled and nodded back. "We have met before, Mr. MacRae. I often stop in when I am in Aberdeen, since I also have my own accounts with your bank."

"Ah, yes. Yes, of course," he said with a blush, obviously having no recognition despite the fact that Jocelyn was beautiful and would catch any man's eye. Perhaps the man had a fondness for blondes or redheads instead, Malcolm mused.

Malcolm was eager to get past the awkward moment. "The funds are to go directly into the account I established for my wife a few days ago."

The manager leaped to his feet. "I'll take care of it at once and return with the receipt."

He took off so fast, he did not notice Jocelyn about to ask him a question. "Never mind," she muttered to herself.

Malcolm shifted uncomfortably, eager to have this transaction finished and them out of here. "What is it, lass?"

"Nothing important. It can wait until he returns."

He wanted to press her, but decided it was better not to say anything. However, he could see that something was troubling her. It would come out once the manager returned.

Which he did not long afterward with the receipt showing the transfer of fifty thousand pounds into the account Malcolm had opened in her name as duchess. "Is there anything else I may assist you with?"

Jocelyn nodded, smiling at a young man who had just appeared at the door. "Yes, there is. I happen to have several accounts with your bank. They have run unexpectedly low, as I only discovered yesterday with the help of your Mr. Armbrewster. I would like them now replenished. I would also like to see the ledger entries, because there has obviously been a mistake made. I did not spend those accounts down to almost nothing."

She turned to Malcolm. "Those are my independent accounts. I already have established credit with most of the ladies' shops in Aberdeen. One of the shopkeepers showed me a bill that was returned unpaid."

Her father coughed.

"I was sure a mistake was made and needed to be cleared up immediately, since I had made additional purchases yesterday while out with my mother. Those bills will be presented shortly, and I did not want any problems. Let me introduce you to Mr. Armbrewster, the assistant manager here. He is the one assisting me with my personal affairs."

Malcolm nodded toward the string bean of a man who had thinning blond hair and wore thick spectacles. "Yer Grace," he said respectfully. "We are honored by yer presence."

He then turned to Jocelyn. "Yer shopping accounts are no longer in need of replenishment, unless ye spent more than ten thousand pounds yesterday."

She laughed. "Where on earth would I spend such a sum? No, there is definitely something odd going on. You and I checked those accounts just yesterday and saw they were almost down to nothing."

Malcolm glanced at Jocelyn's father, who was shifting uncomfortably in his seat, but clearly not about to make a confession.

Trouble.

Malcolm knew it at once.

Her father made matters worse with his obvious shifting and flustered manner. "Ah...um...secret is out. I had yer accounts refilled."

Jocelyn regarded him thoughtfully. "When? And how would you even know to do this? I only discovered the problem yesterday and said nothing to anyone about this mistake. I thought to address it at this morning's meeting. But you knew my accounts had already been emptied. Why, Papa? Was it because you were the one who withdrew my savings without telling me?"

"Jocelyn, ye canno'... Er... Enough, child! I am yer father."

"Which makes it all the more egregious," she countered. "It must have been during our last trip to Aberdeen. No wonder the haberdasher claimed I had not paid my last bill. Why did you not tell me? And why take from *my* accounts when you could have simply taken what you needed from the dower account?"

Her father gaped at Malcolm.

Oh, Lord.

This man was as bad a liar as his daughter.

A good thing, Malcolm supposed. Was it not better to be surrounded by people who did not know how to lie to him?

He refused to help Granby out of this mess of his own creation.

Of course, if he were the one needing to come up with a convincing lie, he could readily do it. Not that he ever would. However, he already had a dozen made-up reasons that sounded plausible whirling in his head.

He could have offered up one of those paltry excuses to help her father out. But this was Granby's problem, and he was not going to jump in to rescue him by making up more fabrications.

"Ye were betrothed to Ballantry by that time," Lord Granby blustered. "I dared not touch that pot on the chance he demanded to see it for himself."

Jocelyn glanced toward Mr. Armbrewster, who had turned red in the face.

She sighed and turned back to her father. "Are you certain, Papa? Or was that money gone before Lord Ballantry ever proposed to me? You drained that account first, did you not?"

Now her father turned red in the face. "Oh…ah, did I? Was it? Ah…let me see. Oh, well. Who remembers exactly? Perhaps I moved some funds around, but they are all put back now. So where's the harm? Ye can shop to yer heart's content, lass."

"Shopping? Is this all you think I am capable of keeping in my head? Did you withdraw the funds from my other accounts at the same time? To invest in those dodgy ventures I warned you about?"

"Yer other accounts?"

"Yes," she said more forcefully. "The ones you just admitted taking."

"Ah, did I? I dinna recall. Lass, why are ye giving me this inquisition? I am yer father and ye ought to be more respectful."

Her lips pursed as she stared at Malcolm a long moment before returning her attention to her father. "When exactly did you deplete the dowry account? If you do not tell me everything, I will demand to see all the registers."

Her father turned to Malcolm in alarm. "Who said I did? It is all there! Ye've just seen the receipt for yerself. And I will not give my permission for ye to look at anything."

"You are too late. Yesterday, when I stopped in here to inquire about the haberdasher matter, I overheard Mr. Armbrewster and Mr. MacRae discussing a transfer into the dowry account that had been drained to nothing."

Lord Granby glowered at the poor fellows. "Ye had no right to give my daughter this information!"

"They didn't. I happened to be standing nearby and they did not see me." Jocelyn moved to stand in front of the hapless Mr. Armbrewster, as though to protect him from her father's unwarranted wrath. "And had I directly asked these gentlemen, they would have had every obligation to tell me, since those funds belong to Camborne now that he and I are married. Do not give me that nonsense, Papa! I will not be lied to! Did Mama know about this, too? Of course she did. She hasn't read a book in years. Now all those odd looks she has been tossing at you these past few days are starting to make sense."

She let out a ragged breath and continued. "Why did you not just tell me? Do you think I would not give you the very clothes off my back if you needed them? And what were you going to say to Ballantry had I married him and he demanded this account that you knew was empty?"

Her father stared at her in silence.

Her eyes rounded in horror. "You were going to send me to that vile oaf knowing you did not have the funds available? Oh, how could you? Was the money already gone when you entered into the betrothal agreement?"

Her father sank heavily into his chair and buried his face in his hands. "Lass, stop asking questions. It's all taken care of. The money is in the account."

"How?" She nibbled her lip as her sharp brain began to put the pieces together. "Who loaned it to you? Papa, if you were so direly in need of funds as to take everything, even my own accounts, who was going to lend you so much as a groat? What did you have to give up to secure those funds?"

"Nothing," he said in a muffled voice. "I gave up nothing."

"How is it possible? Did your investments suddenly come through?" She shook her head. "No, it could not be. I read in the papers that the mining company you were so eager to invest in months ago just had its assets seized last month. I…"

She turned to Malcolm.

Oh, hell.

"Did you know about this?" She continued to stare at him. "You *knew*. You were in collusion with my father?"

"Granby, tell her all of it," Malcolm said, wanting to shake her father, who was still sitting with his hands over his face and refusing to admit anything. Aye, the man felt defeated and acutely shamed. But his daughter loved him and was not going to cut him out of her life unless he persisted in lying to her.

As for him, he had no idea what Jocelyn would do about him. He was merely her husband of sixteen days. He hadn't met her until the day before he married her. Two nights and one day was the extent of their relations up to then.

"Camborne, *you* tell her. I cannot. I canno' look my daughter in the eye."

Jocelyn's face was etched in pain as she turned to Malcolm. "*You* gave him the money? Of course, it had to be you. On what terms?"

A muscle twitched in Malcolm's jaw. "No terms. He needed it and I gave it to him."

"And you never thought to tell me? You hid the truth from me? You listened to me go on and on about my dowry and about paying you back for all you had spent on me? You said nothing while I stood there like a prideful fool, and all along you knew I had nothing to give you? You listened to me jabber like an idiot and never stopped me."

He took her gently by the shoulders. "Ye never made a fool of yerself. How can ye ever think that? When I sensed something was wrong, I went to yer father. All I ever wanted to do was protect ye, lass."

She snorted. "Because you thought me stupid."

"No! Because I thought ye worthy of my protection. I was only thinking of yer happiness when I gave my oath to yer father that I would no' tell ye. That's what I was talking about earlier today. That vow I wished with all my heart I could break. As for yer dowry, may it all go to blazes. I dinna want it. I never wanted it. All I ever wanted was—"

He broke off before he spilled his heart to her in front of everyone, for he could not bear the humiliation if he was rejected.

"What, Camborne?" She looked up at him with those big eyes of hers that tore at his soul. "What were you going to say? But you stopped yourself because you cannot bring yourself to say it, can you? Am I now supposed to believe all you ever wanted was *me*?"

She glowered at him as he remained silent and refused to respond. "I do not want any more lies from you. How many other vows are you bound to that you cannot break?"

"None, other than my vows of marriage." He raked a hand through his hair. "Jocelyn, ye know I will never break those."

She snorted again. "Oh, do I?"

"Aye, lass. Ye do. No matter how angry ye are with me at the moment, in yer heart ye know it is a good marriage." He sighed and stopped himself from saying more. He was not above groveling, but would not do it here and now. "I think we've put on enough of a show for these gentlemen. Let's return to the inn and yer father can tell ye the entirety of his story. Right, Granby? Ye'll tell her all of it."

Her father merely groaned.

"Come along, Papa," Jocelyn said, her voice filled with hurt. "It is time the truth came out."

They returned to the inn, the three of them so gloomy that one would think they were on their way to a funeral. Which brought up memories of Malcolm's own parents and siblings dying, and the pain of losing them all tore up his insides. He had never faced a greater agony than the deaths of his dear ones.

But he was about to face a similar agony now.

Would Jocelyn be too angry ever to forgive him?

He understood why she was hurt, but was her father not to blame for this? All Malcolm had done was attempt to preserve her father's stature in her eyes.

Would she absolve her father and then lay the blame squarely on *him*? Would she hold on to her resentment until it gnawed at her insides?

Her mother's smile faltered when they entered the inn and she rushed forward to greet them. Since Lord Granby could not look at his wife for all the shame he felt, and since Jocelyn was simply angry as blazes, Lady Granby turned to him for answers. "Camborne, what happened?"

He sighed. "Jocelyn knows what your husband did."

A light breath rushed out of the woman. "Thank goodness the truth is finally out." She drew Jocelyn into her arms to offer comfort. "Child, I know how disappointed ye must be in me and yer father."

"And do not overlook my husband," Jocelyn said as her tears began to flow. "He eagerly joined in the deception."

Her mother frowned. "No, ye are not to blame him. He was a most reluctant accomplice and wanted ye to be told the truth. It was me and yer father who insisted on keeping up the lie. He came to our rescue, his only intention to spare yer father any shame. Who else would have been so honorable as to do such a thing? Certainly not Ballantry."

"Jocelyn, let's discuss this back in our suite," Malcolm said, and asked her parents to join them.

Her mother declined.

Her refusal surprised him, for he was merely an incidental player in this game her father was playing and did not have all the facts before him. "Why no', Lady Granby?"

"Because I need to box my prideful husband's ears for creating this mess in the first place, and ye need to speak to my daughter with heartfelt candor. Things may be said between ye that we should not hear. Be warned—my daughter can be just as stubborn and wrongheaded as her father sometimes."

"Mama!"

"Do not give me that tone of voice, Jocelyn. Do ye think I am blind to yer foibles? It is yer husband who should be indignant that ye even *think* to blame him for this mess that was yer father's fault. And need I mention yer hand in it?"

Jocelyn gasped. "Mine?"

"Aye. Now, I'll admit I also had a hand in this because of my constantly pressing ye to marry. The weight of all the Granby relatives hounding ye could not have been easy for ye to bear. But ye were the one who got that flea in yer ear and accepted a man ye knew would be an unsuitable match for ye. Ye couldn't have found a bigger arse had ye searched under every rock in Scotland."

Jocelyn's face turned red, but she still had that indignant look upon her face.

Her mother—bless the gracious lady—was not finished chiding her. "Now, go up to yer suite with yer husband and listen to what he has to say. Really listen to him and do not let yer pride get in the way of sound judgment."

Aye, it was a relief to have found an ally in Lady Granby. Malcolm sensed he would need all her support when dealing with Jocelyn.

"Come along, lass." He reached out to wrap Jocelyn's arm in his, but she edged away and walked upstairs on her own.

He followed after her, completely at a loss as to how to handle arguing with someone he cared deeply about and feared to lose.

She stepped inside and strode to the window.

"Camborne," she said, watching the first raindrops that had threatened all day now begin to fall in earnest, "let's put an end to this farce."

"What are ye talking about?" he asked, shutting the door behind him.

"Getting out of this marriage. Isn't this what you really want?"

Thunder roared in his head and he felt the world around him collapsing.

Was this what *she* wanted?

Chapter Sixteen

Jocelyn heard her husband's gasp, but refused to turn around to face him.

"Ye think I want to be rid of ye?" he asked after a long moment of silence. "After all we've been through in these last sixteen days? Ye think I want ye out of my life?"

She nodded, unable to hold back her tears or her humiliation. "How could you not? My father lost his fortune on reckless investments, and it was not merely the dowry account or my shopping accounts that he must have lost. He would have touched those last and only in desperation. This can only mean he has nothing left."

"Is this what has ye crying, lass? That ye're worried yer parents will be destitute? They won't be. I'll take care of them, just as I'll always take care of ye."

His voice was so gentle that it made her feel even more ashamed of herself and her family. "Always, Camborne? Why ever would you? How can you stand me when I can hardly stand myself? I was caught cheating you out of your room at the Arbroth Inn. You must think we are horrid people. As detestable as Ballantry and Burling."

She clutched her stomach, now feeling ill as she continued to revile herself and her Granby clan. "And never forget my fortune-hunting, devoid-of-morals cousins, who were only too happy to join Ballantry here for the sole purpose of humiliating us. Perhaps they meant to be more hurtful to me because I was such an uptight, righteous prig who was quick to pass judgment on them. I'm sure they propositioned you before they headed off for who knows where to cause more mischief."

By his silence, she knew that they had. Camborne, being ever protective of her feelings, was not going to respond to her.

She began to fuss with the clasp of her locket.

She heard his sharp intake of breath, and then he came to her side and stilled her hand. "Do not take it off, Jocelyn."

"I only mean to give it back to you."

"I gave it to ye," he said, his voice shaking. "It is yers forever, and I'll not have it back."

She turned to argue with him, but stilled when she saw the stricken expression on his face.

He appeared stunned, as though she had just slapped him.

"Camborne," she said, wanting to throw herself into his arms and lose herself in his embrace, "all I have done is take from you."

"How can ye say this? Ye've given me the most precious gift of yer heart. Do ye think a dowry can compare?"

It was true, the love she had given him was from her heart.

She loved him so much.

This was why she wanted to return this beautiful locket. Did he not deserve to be free of her if he wished it?

"Everyone takes from you," she said, feeling her tears flow again. "And I am no better than those leeches and hangers-on. But don't you deserve a better wife? Should I not be more than a penniless burden?"

"Stop thinking of yerself that way! Ye're perfect. I would no' change a thing about ye," he said, his voice a harsh rasp.

"Perfect? Me? What a laughable statement. I've brought you nothing but scandal and chaos."

"Ye brought me hope and happiness. Ye married me, and I think that was very right," he said so gently, she was in dire risk of bawling like an infant again.

How could he care for her?

She started to unclasp her locket again.

He growled low in his throat. "Ye promised me ye would never take it off."

"But—"

"Dinna take it off, Jocelyn. My teeth clanked against it every time I made love to ye, but I dinna care because it was right that ye kept it on. That locket is my heart that I gave to ye. If ye dinna love me, then take it off. Throw it back at me."

She gasped.

"But if ye love me, lass…then leave it be. Leave it over yer heart. I dinna care how many teeth I lose knocking into it while attempting to worship yer breasts."

She laughed as her tears began to fall again. "Camborne, I knew you had the soul of a romantic poet."

"No, lass. I'm just a man with plenty of faults." Instead of taking her into his arms, as she was sure he would do next, he left her side and sank onto the settee. Her heart broke as she watched him place his elbows on his lap and bury his face in his hands.

"Camborne?"

Was it possible this incident was tearing him up as much as it was tearing her? Was it possible he loved her just as deeply as she loved him?

She placed her hand over her heart, wrapping her fingers around the locket that represented his own heart that he had given her.

Dear heaven.

It was not some glib gesture, some token he was giving her to acknowledge an unwanted and forced marriage.

Only, he hadn't been forced. He had wanted to marry her all along. Not because he felt honor bound to protect her reputation, although this was the reason he gave.

She could not believe she had just been so hurtful to her own husband.

This was too, too cruel of her, especially since her mother was right. She needed to calm down and think without her feelings clouding her judgment.

"I'm so sorry, Camborne. I lashed out in frustration, and it was not right of me."

"Jocelyn," he said, the sound filled with an ache that tore from his throat. "I know how hurt and angry ye must be. All I wanted to do was keep yer family together. I wanted ye to look upon yer mother and father with the love ye'd always had for them. I told yer father I would replenish the dowry account. Ye know I did no' marry ye for the expectation of enriching my coffers. Then I promised yer father I would never tell ye what we did. I regretted it the moment I uttered the promise."

She took a seat beside him. His wounds were palpable, and she could feel his heart ripping apart as she took his hand in hers.

He eyed her questioningly.

She kissed him softly on the lips.

It was all so clear to her now, for she understood what had compelled him, and ached all the more for attempting to take off the locket that represented *everything* to him.

His own family.

The loss he'd felt when they died.

The love regained when marrying her.

The fear of losing her, too.

Her thoughtless words and actions were the cruelest thing possible to him.

She was in danger of crying tears again, but this time for happiness because he loved her. This big, hard, arrogant duke loved her.

It no longer mattered that he could not bring himself to actually say the words. She only had to be patient and he would admit it in his own good time.

Smiling, she cleared her throat. "Camborne…"

He eyed her warily because he was naturally cautious.

She shifted closer to him so that their bodies touched from shoulders to toes.

He arched an eyebrow. "Lass?"

She cast him a fragile smile. "I wanted so much to come into this marriage with something to my name. You have given me everything, and all I could think about was giving something back to you. It was so important to me and still is. I feel as though I am no better than that cur, Burling. Always with my hand out. Always grasping. But—"

She held him off, as he was about to protest.

"You're going to insist that I haven't grasped for anything. But I have. Four new gowns. Four shawls. Silk and lace *unmentionables*. Not to mention you are paying for my parents to stay at this inn with us and will have to pay for a private coach to return them to Granby. But—"

She held him off again as he was about to respond.

"—every morning I've told you that I love you. And every morning, I have not heard it said back to me."

"That is my failing, not yours," he interjected, his eyes etched with pain.

She shook her head. "No, it is not a failing. That is *you*. This is who you are, a man who speaks with his actions and often finds it hard to put his tenderest thoughts into words. But it does not diminish what you are feeling. It just made it a little harder for me to figure out, especially as I wrapped myself up in a cloud of shame and could not see anything clearly because of it."

He gave her hand a light squeeze. "What do ye see now, lass?"

"A man who loves me. A man who would give everything to see me happy. Camborne, I will always be happy so long as I am with you. So, if you can put up with a reckless father-in-law, a delicate mother-in-law, Granby cousins who are completely immoral, and a harpy of a wife who is sometimes too stubborn and prideful for her own good, then I think we shall have a very long and exceedingly successful marriage."

A smile began to spread on his lips. "Are we all right, lass? Am I forgiven?"

"Yes, but will you forgive *me*?"

"For what? Ye've done nothing wrong."

She laughed and rolled her eyes. "Were you not listening to my mother? I did so many things wrong, starting with agreeing to marry Ballantry. But the point I would like to make is that I will never force you to say words or express feelings that you are not ready to reveal."

He stared at her.

Was she wrong in thinking he loved her?

No, she could not have misunderstood his agonized looks and the heavy air of desperation.

"I will understand if you cannot say the words aloud yet. How could you when you have only known me for sixteen days?"

"Bollocks," he muttered, raking a hand through his hair.

"Shall I stop?"

"Stop what? Stop talking?" He cast her an affectionate smile.

She snuggled closer. "Shall I stop telling you that I love you? Does it make you feel awkward? Is it too much? Too soon?"

He laughed. "Don't ye dare stop telling me. I want to hear those sweet words from yer lips every day. As many times as ye wish to say them. Morning, noon, and night. It does no' matter when. My heart was so empty until ye came along, lass. Yer words… Every day with yer lovely words, ye fill my heart with joy."

"Then you don't mind?" She was elated for so many reasons, but mostly because they had just made it through their first serious argument and come through it stronger. Hadn't they?

She was glad he wanted her to love him and express it. This was enough for her.

"No, I dinna mind at all. But there is something else important ye ought to know. I dinna think yer mother knew anything about yer father's financial problems until recently either. She only learned of them shortly before they arrived at the Arbroth Inn. Her heart palpitations…they were as much brought on by the financial strain as yer running away from yer wedding. That's all I will say about it, lass. But I dinna want ye blaming yerself for her ill health."

She nodded.

"She's a caring mother, and that is a precious thing."

"It will take me a little longer to forgive him," she said, although she never doubted her father's love for her. It was all the stupid things he had done to keep her from knowing of these disastrous decisions he'd made, and the fact he did not trust her enough to tell her. Perhaps it was hard for a parent to let their child know of the parent's failures.

What a misery her life would have been had she gone through with her wedding to Ballantry. Looking back on it, her father had tried hard to talk her out of it. But she still could not forgive him completely, because all he ever had to do was tell her he'd lost her dowry.

Done.

No betrothal.

No mad dash across Scotland.

On the other hand, she never would have met this wonderful Silver Duke seated beside her. Was this all a part of some grander plan? Fate? Destiny?

She scooted onto her husband's lap and wrapped her arms around him. "Camborne…"

"Och, lass. Yer smile is sunshine upon my heart."

"It is raining buckets. We have still been married for sixteen days. And…I love you, my husband."

"Lass," he said, and she felt his heart begin to hammer within his chest. "Lass…"

She smiled and kissed him lightly on his finely shaped mouth. "Say it, Camborne. You are a Silver Duke, after all. Use that silver tongue of yours and tell me what you are feeling."

"Lass…"

"I'm still right here." She placed her hand over his heart, which was still pounding.

"Lass…"

She laughed. "If you say that once more, I am going to hit you over the head with the nearest heavy object I can find."

He grinned. "All right, I give up. Willingly and with great relief. Just be patient with me, for it has taken me over forty years to get to a point I never thought I would reach. Not only that I never expected to marry, but that I never expected to fall in love with my wife. Yet here I am, madly, deeply, and quite unexpectedly…in love with ye. There it is. I love ye, Jocelyn."

He kissed her fiercely and then rose to carry her toward their bed. "I loved ye from the first moment I set eyes on ye, and will always love ye with my full heart and the breadth of my soul."

"You are a romantic, I knew it," she whispered, wrapping her arms around his neck and soaking in the warmth of his very fine body.

"Och, no. Despite my reputation, I'm not one for silvery words." He kissed her, then set her down on the bed and began to undress while keeping his gaze fixed on her. "I'll only speak true and plainly to ye. If ye deem it romantic, then so be it. Just know that I will always honor and protect ye. I will always lie beside ye and hold ye safe in my loving arms."

He removed his jacket, waistcoat and cravat. "And I will always love ye."

She cast him a warm but impish smile as she watched him, loving the manly way he shrugged out of his clothes. "Should I undress, too?"

His eyes sparkled like dark emeralds. "If ye wish, lass. It would be most convenient if ye did. Let me help ye with the laces."

"What are we going to do once you undress me, Camborne?"

"We'll think of something, lass. It might take us all afternoon and evening to figure it out. Do ye mind?"

"I don't mind at all."

She opened her arms to him, for she loved this man beyond measure.

>>>—<<<

COME MORNING, SHE awoke to find her husband still fast asleep beside her. He lay on his stomach, one muscled arm wrapped around her waist as though he needed to hold on to her even while lost in his dreams.

She eased out of his light grasp and hunted for her nightgown to put it on before looking out the window. The drapes were slightly open, allowing dapples of light to stream in. She quickly tossed on her nightgown and padded to the window, drawing the drapes aside to allow in a little more sunlight. She wanted to look at her husband under the gentle rays of the morning sun.

Last night's rain had moved north and left behind a sparkling day.

Camborne began to stir.

He noticed she was not in bed beside him, but smiled and rolled over to stretch on his back when he spotted her by the window. "Good morning, love."

Her heart beat faster as she recalled what they had done last night.

Oh, heavens.

Some would call their intimacies sinful, but she could not wait for him to teach her more tonight. There was something to be said for marrying a Silver Duke. Her husband certainly knew what he was doing.

"Good morning," she returned brightly. "We are married seventeen days now. The weather is sunny and perfect, and...I love you to pieces, Camborne."

His smile was beautiful and blinding. "Mutual, Jocelyn. I love ye too."

Jocelyn was still walking on air when they made their way down to the elegant common room set up for dining. Several of the inn's patrons were already downstairs having their breakfast, including her parents and Terrence.

A pretty maid fussed around Terrence, the big, stoic man who appeared quite receptive to her attentions. He actually smiled at the lass, and then whispered something in her ear before turning to greet Jocelyn and Camborne.

Her parents looked upon them with strain as they approached. Her father in particular remained unusually silent but cast her a hopeful smile, while her mother took the lead in greeting them.

"Good morning, my dearest." She gave Jocelyn a kiss on the cheek. "How are you?"

Jocelyn glanced at her husband, who winked at her. "Perfect, Mama. Quite happily in love."

"Aye, Lady Granby," Camborne said while holding out a chair for Jocelyn and then taking the one beside hers. "Yer daughter and I are good."

"Excellent news," her mother replied, releasing a breath.

"Aye," her father said with a nod. "All I ever wanted was for yer happiness, lass."

Jocelyn noticed her husband's gaze sweep across the room and realized whom he was searching for. "Are you looking for Ballantry and Burling?"

He nodded. "I dinna see them here. Most likely, they are still up in their rooms. Doubtful they are early risers and have already eaten."

Terrence took a sip of his coffee and then set his cup down. "The proprietor informed me this morning that Burling absconded in the night without paying his bill, just as ye were certain would happen. I took the liberty of settling it, as ye instructed, Yer Grace."

Jocelyn's eyes widened in surprise. "Camborne, I thought you were adamant on giving him nothing."

"Still am, but I am not going to have the proprietor denied payment for his services when Burling was only here sniffing around because of us."

"Thank you," she said. "I agree wholeheartedly."

Terrence nodded and continued. "Ballantry departed about an hour ago, muttering something about Italy." He turned to Jocelyn. "Yer cousins left with him."

Lady Granby shook her head. "Good riddance to those scandalous creatures. I am not surprised they decided to go with him. Not that either of them would care that one was leaving behind a dying husband and the other supposedly mourning her own recently deceased spouse. Shameful!"

"I'm glad they are gone, and they are welcome to Ballantry," Jocelyn muttered, holding out her teacup as one of the maids came around to fill it.

She stared into her cup, watching the vapors of steam rise from it. As each column of vapor disappeared into the air, she realized her worries were also disappearing. Ballantry had signed the settlement, grabbed the money Camborne had offered, and was now off to spend it—no doubt unwisely—on an Italian sojourn.

As for Burling, he had stolen off like a thief in the night. She hoped he would not return to bother them for a handout ever again.

She turned to her husband, who appeared more relaxed than she had ever seen him. He was sipping his coffee and smiling at her to acknowledge he had noticed the same thing. "Camborne, is it possible? Is it over? Are we entirely at our leisure today?"

"Aye, lass." He turned to Terrence. "Ye've been working hard on my behalf these past few weeks. Take the day off. I think there's a lass eager to spend it with ye." He nodded toward the pretty serving maid who had been lingering close to their table. She was removing her apron and appeared ready to go off duty.

Terrence's expression remained stoic as he excused himself and made his way toward the lass, who smiled up at him with a look Jocelyn recognized.

Yes, love was a breathless thing.

"Jocelyn," her husband said with a chuckle, "dinna concoct any romantic stories in yer head. He's just met the girl. For all we know, she may already have a husband."

"She doesn't," Jocelyn insisted, although she had no idea whether this was true. "I know the eyes of love when I see it."

"Do ye?" His lips curved in an appealing smile.

"Yes." She grinned impertinently at him. "It is the same way you are looking at me right now, Camborne."

He chuckled. "Maybe, lass. Maybe."

As he sat there in all his broad-shouldered glory, his deep green eyes sparkling with humor, and his beautiful mouth stretched in a magnificent smile meant for her, she considered herself beyond fortunate to have made this love match.

She truly loved him.

And he loved her.

He loved her.

What were the chances?

Her father cleared his throat to regain her attention, since she was obviously mooning over her husband. "Lass, yer mother and I are thinking of returning to Granby today. All's well now, and there is no reason for us to stay."

"Oh."

"Aye, Jocelyn," her mother said. "Ye have yer husband to look after now, and he'll be looking after ye. We aren't needed here."

Her father cleared his throat again. "Camborne, may I impose on yer kindness for another favor? We'll need coach accommodations."

Camborne nodded. "I thought ye might. I've made arrangements with the ostler. Ye'll have a fine carriage for yer ride home. Choose whichever one ye'd like."

Everything suddenly moved so fast.

Jocelyn's parents had little to pack and were ready to leave within the hour. Camborne stood beside her as she fiercely hugged her mother and father, finding it difficult to bid them farewell. She might not see them for months and months.

At first, she had been reluctant to hug her father because she had yet to fully forgive him. But she could not bring herself to part on bad terms.

Perhaps she was too forgiving of his deception. But was she any better with her headstrong ways that led her to so foolishly choose Ballantry?

There was such a look on her husband's face as he stood by and watched her with her parents…a yearning for all the good and the bad that existed within a family and had been denied him all his life.

"I love you, Papa," she whispered in her father's ear.

"I love ye beyond the sun and the moon, Jocelyn," he whispered back, struggling to hold back his tears. "I'm so sorry I disappointed ye, my sweet lass."

He was crying and smiling as he climbed into the carriage after her mother, who was there to console him as she had done throughout the years. Indeed, she was the steady hand in their marriage.

Jocelyn wished to be that for Camborne, but knew *he* would likely be the steady one in their marriage.

The coachman spurred the team and drove off with her parents.

In the distance, she saw Terrence walking toward the harbor with the pretty maid beside him.

The sun warmed Jocelyn's face, and all suddenly felt delightfully peaceful as she stood beside her husband. "Where are we to go next?" she asked him. "Fishing?"

"No, lass. I was only going there to contemplate the changes needed in my life. That got taken care of when I found ye in my bed." He smiled as he caressed her cheek, but his expression then turned serious. "I dinna have any close family, but I have two friends who are as close as brothers to me, and they will likely be in London for the month of September. I'll need to be there anyway, for there's parliamentary work to be done and Scotland's interests need to be represented."

Jocelyn knew there would be no one better to protect those interests than this big, handsome Scot who was now her husband.

As for those friends who were close as brothers to him, she knew he was referring to his fellow Silver Dukes, Bromleigh and Lynton.

"I'd like to introduce ye to them. They are my family. I think ye'll like them. Despite our bad reputations, we are at heart decent men."

"Sounds perfect," she said, her smile brightening. "They'd have to be fairly awful to be as bad as my own family, don't you think? I'm eager to meet them. Perhaps *they* will decide to marry once they see how happily wed we are."

He laughed and shook his head. "Och, lass. How likely is that?"

They decided to remain the week at the Balgownie Arms and explore the countryside around Aberdeen. They rose early and returned late to the inn, although there were a few rainy days when they did not leave their bedchamber at all.

But the day before they were to leave for London, Jocelyn went on her own to do a little shopping in the afternoon. She wasn't lacking much, only a few items she might need on the journey south. Her parents maintained a London townhouse, so she had a wardrobe there already sufficient to get her through most of the daily activities once they arrived. She would require some finer evening gowns, but this was not urgent and she would make do with those she already had. Her first task upon reaching London would be to have the Granby staff pack her clothes and send them to Camborne's residence. This was another coincidence, for his Mayfair home was only in the next square over from the Granby house.

How had they never met before?

She shook her head and laughed softly to herself, her mind whirling as she walked up the high street toward the shops.

It did not take her long to find what she wanted, and she was soon walking back to the inn clutching her few purchases, which included some fragrant soaps and a small bag to tuck her grooming essentials in. She had also decided at the last moment to purchase a pair of woolen stockings and a sturdy nightgown suitable for colder weather, and had that larger package neatly tucked under her arm.

As the afternoon shadows began to stretch across the roadway, she hurried along to the inn. Several shops had already shut and others were about to close for the day. This was a fairly quiet part of town, but suddenly felt too quiet.

But she shrugged off the prickles running up her spine. The area was by no means abandoned, and there was activity noticeable by the inn, carriages arriving and others departing. Camborne had spent the afternoon with his solicitor attending to matters concerning his estate and should also be returning about now.

A moment later, she saw him in the distance and recognized his confident stride as he walked toward the inn. But he did not notice her because she was approaching from the street above.

She was about to call out to him when someone suddenly grabbed her from behind and brandished a small pistol that he held at her head. "I've been waiting to catch ye alone, my prideful lady."

Burling.

He was drunk, for his breath was foul and reeking of spirits.

He had one hand around her neck, pressing his fingers against her throat so that she could hardly breathe, much less scream. The other hand held the pistol to her temple, and she dared not make a sudden move for fear his finger would slip and the pistol would go off. It was one of those small pistols a lady might carry in her reticule, not very powerful, but still quite deadly at this close range.

He stumbled as he began to drag her into a nearby alleyway. She saw her chance and immediately pushed against him, knocking him backward in the hope he would fall.

But even drunk, he was too heavy for her to shove to the ground.

Still, she managed to loosen his grasp and began to scream to draw attention to them.

"Ye stupid cow, I only wanted yer money!"

He shoved her hard against the rough stone of the alley wall. A blinding pain shot through her temples as her head struck hard stone.

He laughed, then grabbed her reticule and began to sort through it. "Where's yer blunt? Do ye carry nothing of value?"

It took her a moment to recover her senses, although it could hardly be called recovery when she was still fighting not to pass out.

All she could feel was relief he hadn't shot her, for he was a big, stupid oaf and not thinking clearly at all. Did he not realize she could identify him to the authorities? Did he not understand the rules of thievery? He was supposed to simply snatch and run, not linger and fumble through his mark's belongings.

Well, he was not spry enough to outrun a three-legged dog or even an old woman.

Her heart pounded savagely as she staggered out of the alleyway in the hope of taking advantage of his drunken distraction to edge away. Her head was also painfully pounding, and blood trickled down her forehead.

She ignored the discomfort and dizziness as she tried to run away, then released a breath of relief when she saw the blurred outline of two men who resembled Camborne and Terrence racing up the street toward her. "Thank goodness."

As she tried to run toward them, Burling grabbed her again. "Where are ye going, lass? I think I had better hold on to ye."

The drunken fool was attempting to use her as a hostage, and was now in obvious panic as her husband and Terrence approached.

"Don't do anything foolish, Burling. I won't press charges. Just let me go."

"Let ye go?" Burling said against her ear. "Aye, I'll let ye go and take *him* instead. Say farewell to yer beloved."

He aimed his pistol at Camborne.

"No!" Jocelyn screamed, at the same time shoving Burling's arm upward.

He angrily turned, intending to shove her away and run. But as she fell to the ground, landing painfully on her side and then rolling onto her back as the breath rushed out of her, he also stumbled and lost his balance.

His pistol went off.

Jocelyn felt a painful impact to her chest.

Her husband's anguished cry split the air just as everything began to spin. She felt herself absorbed into the cobblestones and dragged into a dark abyss.

"Jocelyn! Jocelyn!"

Camborne was calling out to her as she tumbled into the darkness.

"Dinna leave me, lass! Oh, Lord. Dinna leave me!" He held her in his arms. She tried to wrap her arms around his neck, needing to hold on to him, but he stopped her. "No, love. Dinna move. He shot ye. Lie still in my arms, my love. Someone get a doctor! Now! Bring him to the Balgownie Arms."

A crowd had begun to gather around them.

"Aye, Yer Grace!" Someone ran off to fetch the doctor, probably one of the inn's staff, since they knew who Camborne was.

"He meant to shoot you," she whispered, her throat so dry that her words came out scratchy and almost unintelligible. "I love you, Camborne. I couldn't let him."

"I love ye too. I love ye so much." His voice was thick with the pain of a thousand torments. He suddenly sucked in a breath as his fingers found the rip in the fabric at her chest where she had felt the impact. He groaned in agony. "Jocelyn, dinna move. Oh, Lord. Dinna move."

She couldn't even if she wanted to.

But she could talk, and meant to tell him what had happened, although it was all coming out disjointed. "He pushed me against the wall... I felt my head bleeding... I tried to run."

"Hush, lass. It's all right."

"Something hit my chest."

"I know, sweetheart. I...saw." His breaths sounded raw and ragged as he delicately sliced open the hole in the fabric with his knife, and then she felt the warmth of his hand ever so lightly upon her bosom. "Where's the blood? How could he...? Lie still, love. Och, Jocelyn. I love ye, lass. Dinna move. Oh, Lord. How can ye still be conscious? How can ye still be talking? How can it be? There's not a mark on ye, lass. It isn't possible. Not even a break in yer skin."

Was he crying?

Were Silver Dukes capable of tears?

"My heart is a little sore," she said, still feeling that impact to her chest.

Camborne's breaths were now coming fast, and she felt his fingers trembling as he drew the fabric further apart. "Jocelyn, my love. My sweet, sweet love. My miracle."

He removed his jacket and wrapped it around her before carefully drawing her back into his arms. All the while, he told her how much he loved her.

She raised a hand to his cheek.

He kissed her palm. "It's a miracle, sweetheart."

"What is?" She was a bit dizzy and confused.

"The locket. It stopped the shot that should have ruptured yer heart. The locket saved ye, lass. Ye've not a scratch on yer chest. It saved ye."

She swiped her thumb along his cheek to wipe away his tears.

"No, Camborne," she said as realization dawned on her. "It was your *love* that saved me."

"I canno' take credit, lass. Perhaps yer guardian angels saved ye, the same ones that led ye to me that fateful night in Arbroath."

She smiled and wrapped her arms around his neck. "That second night was the best. You made all my fantasies come true."

"Naughty girl," he said with a rush of relief. "Ye made mine come true, too."

He was about to carry her back to the inn when a constable hurried over.

"My man, William Terrence, has the culprit," Camborne said, seeming to be once more composed and speaking with authority. "Ye can speak to my wife after the doctor sees to her. We have rooms at the inn." He nodded in the direction of the Balgownie Arms.

"Aye, Yer Grace. I'll run the knave in and then return to speak to Her Grace at her convenience."

Camborne carried her up to their suite and gently set her on the bed.

His heart was still pounding so loudly through his chest, she could hear it without need to press her ear to it. And his eyes were once again clouded with tears.

"Oh, Lord. Oh, Lord," he said, his voice still raspy and his always-steady hands now shaking as he drew a chair beside her and gently began to wipe the blood from her forehead with a moistened towel.

"I did not realize Terrence was his family name. I would have called him William, or Mr. Terrence."

Camborne laughed. "This is what ye have to say, lass? Ye were almost shot through the heart, and ye're talking about how to address Terrence? Och, sweetheart. I thought I had lost ye. I should have stayed close. I should no' have let ye go out on yer own."

"You think this is your fault? I'm a grown woman and have been independent for years. I went up the street in broad daylight and remained in sight of the inn. Don't you dare blame yourself for something Burling has done."

"Ye told me to pay him off. I should have done it, lass."

"No, Camborne. I saw the hate in his eyes when he shoved me against the alley wall. No matter what we gave him, it would never have been enough. He would have squandered it and resented us for it when he came back for more and we refused him."

She started to sit up, but he wouldn't allow it. "Not yet, sweetheart. Let the doctor check ye over first." But he took her hand and pressed it to his lips. "I love ye."

Until this moment, Jocelyn had been certain that she loved him more. Hers was the greater love; it had to be. She was the first to feel it and recognize it for what it was. She was the first to admit it. She was always the one telling him that she loved him. She was the one mooning over him, sighing and swooning whenever he smiled at her.

Did any man have a more beautiful smile?

She was the one melting whenever he removed his clothes and settled in bed beside her. She was the one who sighed and *cooed* every time he drew her into his arms, *purred* every time he touched her and made love to her.

Ah, yes. She was a veritable font of contented animal sounds.

He was much less obvious about his feelings. She hadn't been sure until now that he loved her.

Yes, he'd told her. But he was never as effusive as she was. Mostly, he'd kept his thoughts so private that she honestly believed he was still in the midst of falling in love with her. Not quite *in* love yet. But she'd been confident he would eventually get there, and believed he was close enough to loving her that he felt comfortable telling her on occasion that he did.

But she was wrong.

He loved her so much, she was a fool for not realizing it sooner.

If there was any good to come out of this awful incident, it was the knowledge that his heart was fully invested.

He loved her completely. It was even possible he loved her *more* than she loved him.

The pain reflected in his dark emerald eyes was intense. His mask was down. His protective walls had crumbled. She saw into his heart, understood the depths of his sorrow, and realized he was reliving the agonizing loss of his family, the parents and siblings he'd adored and still missed to this day. He was looking at her and despairing that he had almost lost her, too.

The possibility devastated him.

"You must tell your jeweler about the locket's saving me," she remarked, hoping to lessen his torment. "Won't he be pleased? You must tell him, Camborne. He'll understand and appreciate that it was your love that truly saved me."

"Aye, I'll tell him." He emitted a shaky laugh. "Lass, do ye think the rest of our marriage might be a little more peaceful? I think I just lost ten years off my life. Indeed, I would no' be surprised to wake up in the morning to find my hair had turned completely white."

She laughed softly. "You would still be the handsomest man in all of Scotland."

The doctor arrived soon afterward and confirmed she was in no danger of dying but needed bed rest for the injury to her head. He then set about properly cleansing the scrape on her brow and bandaging it. "I'll return tomorrow to remove the bandage," he said while packing up his medical bag.

Camborne thanked the doctor, his poised façade back in place as he escorted the man out of their suite.

But the façade came down the moment he returned to Jocelyn's side.

"Lass," he said with a moan as he sank heavily into the chair beside their bed, "he says ye'll make a full recovery. Ye're to take it easy for the next few days, and ye're not to lift anything until the lump on yer head subsides."

"But we were leaving tomorrow."

"We'll leave at week's end instead. The constable will want to speak to ye, anyway. I left word with the proprietor that he's to come around tomorrow afternoon to take yer statement. But ye let me know if ye're not up to it and—"

"I'll be fine." She smiled up at him. "This also means Terrence will have more time with the pretty maid."

His eyes lit up with amusement. "Aye, lass. That ought to please him."

"Camborne, you have to promise me something," she said, her expression now serious.

"Lass, ye know making promises to ye Granbys is no' a good idea."

The comment had her smiling again. "We have been difficult, haven't we?"

He kissed her softly on the mouth. "Ye've been a blessing. I'm sure ye were sent to me by yer guardian angels. What happened today was a holy miracle."

"Perhaps those angels are your family and they sent me to you," she said, only half teasing. "They certainly could have chosen someone a bit less chaotic for you, don't you think?"

"No, lass. Their choice was perfect. Although we've experienced more excitement in these few weeks of marriage than most couples have in a lifetime." He raked a hand through his hair. "I should have been with ye. I should have been there to protect ye."

"I will kick you if say that again." She sighed and took hold of his hand. "Camborne, you weren't to blame for your family's fate, nor are you to blame for mine. Burling was not your fault. If anyone is at fault for bringing him upon us, it is me. But I do not blame either of us. He was an opportunist whose sole aim was to extort whatever he could, whenever he could, and from whomever he could. It was always going to end badly for him."

"He almost took ye down with him."

"But he didn't. So get that guilty, anguished look off your face or I will get out of this bed and kick you fiercely. I'll do it, too. My reputation as a harpy is not completely undeserved."

"All right, I surrender," he said with full-bodied laughter. But then his voice turned aching and raspy once more. "Just don't ever leave me, lass. I could no' bear it."

"No worries. I will not go meekly. I'm too happy with my situation and have no inclination to change it. You are stuck with me."

"The lump on yer head should subside in a day or two. That's what the doctor said."

She wanted to nod, but her head still hurt. "Oh, I just realized…"

"What, love?"

"I've lost my packages. In all the commotion, I dropped them and now they must be gone."

"They are easily replaced." He kissed her softly on the mouth again. "*You* are not."

"Will you sleep beside me tonight?"

"Aye, lass. Tonight and every night hereafter."

He helped her to undress and don her nightgown, since the doctor's orders were that she was not to get out of bed tonight. Then Camborne ordered supper brought up to their room.

"Only broth for me?" she muttered, peering under her silver salver.

"Aye, lass. And a soft bread to dip in it. The doctor felt ye should no' overdo it this first night."

"But you'll stay beside me?"

He nodded. "Wouldn't want to be anywhere else."

He'd propped pillows at her back, and she was at ease while he spooned the broth into her mouth. "I can do it myself, you know."

"Aye, lass. I know. Let me fuss over ye." He cast her a look that revealed he was still in pain over the incident.

As night fell, which it did late in the summer, he climbed into bed beside her and drew her into his arms. "Can ye manage? Am I hurting ye?"

"No, Camborne. This is perfect."

"Are ye certain, love?"

"Quite certain." She nestled against him, her thoughts drifting back to the night they first met.

She had been elated at the prospect of sharing two nights with this duke, and that second night on the eve of their wedding had been deliciously sinful.

But there was nothing better than a lifetime with him.

"I love you, Camborne."

"I'll love ye forever, Jocelyn."

She drifted off to sleep while wrapped in the warmth of his arms and soothed by the strong, steady beat of his heart…a heart that beat with love for her.

She was going to enjoy *every* night with this duke.

Epilogue

London, England
September 1817

MALCOLM STRODE INTO White's on the evening of his return to London, eager to meet Bromleigh and Lynton. They had sent word he was to join them tonight for the purpose of discussing an urgent matter, stressing that the matter was dire.

He had planned to decline, knowing it was mere curiosity about the rumors of his marriage and not any governmental crisis that had brought on this summons. They would have come to his townhouse in person had there truly been a problem that needed to be addressed immediately.

But Jocelyn would not hear of his refusing the invitation. "Invite them to dine with us tomorrow night. I'm eager to meet them. In the meanwhile, I'll be fine here on my own. There's plenty of unpacking to do now that my clothes have been sent over from the Granby townhouse. Truly, my love. You would only be underfoot."

So he had dressed in formal evening attire, kissed Jocelyn with all the love in his heart—something he would always do from now on after that frightening incident with Burling—and walked off to meet his friends.

The large clock in the club's entry hall bonged eight times to mark the hour. One of the liveried stewards rushed forward to greet him. "A pleasure to see you, Your Grace. Your friends await you in the green room."

Malcolm nodded and followed the elderly steward to one of the smaller rooms off the main sitting room that held the scent of leather and freshly oiled wood. The wall sconces were lit, casting a golden glow upon the richly paneled wood and picking up the gold threads of the oriental carpet. His friends were casually seated in the room's maroon leather chairs, but rose as he walked in.

His stiff collar chafed at his neck, for he had gotten used to wearing less restrictive attire while up in Scotland, even on occasion wearing a kilt. Aye, Jocelyn enjoyed seeing him in his traditional clan colors and getting an eyeful of his legs, which, she remarked, were nicely formed. Most of the time he was out of his clothes whenever alone with Jocelyn because he could not get enough of that sweet body of hers, and they often wound up in bed.

Such were the benefits of being newly married, although he looked forward to aging gracefully with his wife and building a life with her that encompassed far more than an occasional tumble in bed. He had never been much of a praying man, but he'd done so constantly ever since that Burling incident.

Please keep my Jocelyn safe.

Gad, his friends were never going to believe he was a married man.

Bromleigh and Lynton set aside their brandy glasses and came forward to greet him as he entered. They were also formally attired, no doubt intending to head off to one of the *demimonde* parties he would no longer be attending or ever wish to attend again. "What was so urgent ye had to pull me away from home?"

Bromleigh grinned at him. "My valet told me the most alarming story. We had to know if it was true."

"What story?" Although Malcolm expected the gossip of his marriage had spread like a wildfire throughout the elegant parlors of London.

Lynton regarded him thoughtfully. "You look different...happy. Then it's true. You're married?"

Malcolm laughed. "Come to dinner tomorrow night and I'll introduce ye to my bride. Her name is Jocelyn, and she's the Earl of Granby's daughter."

"Gad, you cannot even say her name without turning soft," Bromleigh muttered. "Are you that far gone?"

Malcolm nodded. "It is a love match, so ye had better watch what ye say to her, because I'll not be forgiving any insults."

Lynton was still grinning at him. "May we each bring along a guest?"

Malcolm nodded. "But they had better not be tarts. I'll not have some overly perfumed, overly rouged, bosom-spilling—"

His friends burst into gales of laughter.

"Oh, Lord. Eden's going to laugh hard when she hears this," Lynton said, holding his side.

Bromleigh was also laughing. "Cherish will find it funny, too."

Malcolm's ears perked. "Cherish Northam? The beautiful lass ye meant to match with yer nephew? What happened? Did that no' work out between them?" He studied his friend closely. "Och, I knew there was a spark between ye and the lass. Bromleigh, dinna tell me ye've taken her on as... What did ye do? Ye could no' have been so depraved as to take her on as yer mistress. How could ye be so cruel as to offer her nothing better? To bloody blazes with our Silver Duke reputations. Ye—"

"I married her." Bromleigh raked a hand through his dark hair that glinted with threads of silver by candlelight. "Have a seat and I'll tell you what happened. But for the record, ours is a love match, too."

Malcolm shook his head.

Had he just heard right? Two Silver Dukes tying the knot? He turned to Lynton, not certain what to say to the lone remaining bachelor. Nor did he understand why Lynton appeared so jovial.

In fact, the man was grinning like a hyena.

Then it suddenly dawned on Malcolm. "Och, laddie! Are ye telling me we've *all* been caught in the parson's mousetrap?"

"Without a struggle and quite happily." Lynton nodded. "I married my neighbor, Eden Darrow."

"The delightful lass with owlish spectacles and a shock of red hair with pencils always poking out of it?"

"That's the one."

Malcolm gave him a companionable slap on the shoulder. "She's a bright thing. I thought she was too smart to ever choose ye," he teased.

His friend took the jest in good nature. "My children have always adored her. My mother, too. Turns out I have always adored her, as well. Just too stupid to admit it. I refused to recognize the gem in front of me all along until I almost lost her to another. I think my mother and children would have disowned me and moved in with her. Fortunately, I came to my senses in time and proposed."

Bromleigh poured Malcolm a brandy, and then the three of them raised their glasses in toast. "To our wives," he said. "To these extraordinary women who tamed the Silver Dukes."

Lynton nodded. "Hear, hear."

Malcolm drank a little of his brandy and then set his glass down. "This is a joyous occasion, but it is also bittersweet, is it not? The end of the Silver Dukes."

Bromleigh shook his head. "Oh, it may be the end of *us*. But I'm sure there are others ready to take our place."

Malcolm shrugged. "Do ye really think so?"

⇛⇚

THE QUESTION WAS raised again at the dinner table the following evening among the three of them and their wives. "What do ye think, love?" Malcolm asked Jocelyn as they lingered at the table over the desserts that included a Viennese torte and a blancmange. "Is this the end for the Silver Dukes?"

She set down her fork and cast him a soft look. "I hope not. I think it would be lovely for three other gentlemen to take your place. We spinsters," she said, smiling at Eden and Cherish, who were close in age to her and had similarly believed they would never marry, "like to hope there are other handsome paragons out there ready to give their hearts to worthy ladies who have held out for love."

Cherish rose and held up her wine glass. "Eden, Jocelyn, will you join me? Close your eyes and make a wish that someone you hold dear—whether friend or relative or worthy acquaintance—will find true love with one of the next Silver Dukes."

The ladies eagerly joined in.

Malcolm and his friends watched their wives as they stood in silence for a moment, their eyes closed as they made their wishes.

Lynton shrugged.

Bromleigh chuckled.

Malcolm knew whoever took their places had not a chance of avoiding true love. "Are we allowed to know yer choices?"

Jocelyn shook her head. "It won't come true if we tell you."

Malcolm's eyes lit up with amusement. "Love, ye canno' believe that nonsense."

"*Camborne*," she said in that impertinently loving way he adored, "it isn't nonsense. Of all people, you should believe there is a higher force that guides us. You cannot disrupt it."

"What if we wrote down our choices?" Cherish suggested, glancing at her and Eden. "It wouldn't count as telling if our husbands merely happened to notice the list of names, would it?"

Eden agreed.

Jocelyn went into the parlor and returned with an armful of supplies from her writing desk that included parchment, quill pen, and ink pot. "You go first, Cherish, since you were the first of us to marry."

Malcolm arched an eyebrow, finding it all quite humorous. Cherish and Bromleigh had married a few days ahead of Lynton, who had only married Eden a few days before he and Jocelyn had wed. Their hasty ceremonies could not have been more than a week apart.

Was he too cynical?

Cherish smiled as she wrote down her choice.

Bromleigh peered over her shoulder and laughed. "I knew it. Perfect. I cannot wait to see what happens."

Malcolm and Lynton read the name next and laughed as well.

Cherish had chosen Bromleigh's cousin, Lady Fiona Shoreham. Obviously, she was not a duke, but Cherish was wishing for a Silver Duke for her best friend. Fiona was a widow, not a spinster, and had resolved never to remarry. She was also a bossy bit of goods, very quick witted and quite meddlesome, but all in all a lovely lady.

Eden was next and wrote down her choice.

Lynton frowned. "You chose him? The bloody fellow was in love with *you*, Eden. You think he's going to make an adequate Silver Duke? He isn't even a duke."

Eden frowned back at him. "But he will be. Apparently a granduncle of his passed away and his father is next in line to inherit the dukedom, which means *he* will be next in line after his father."

Malcolm did not know who they were talking about, but peered at the name. Lord Trajan Aubrey, also known as Viscount Aubrey, a courtesy title given to him by his father, who was an earl and now about to become a duke.

He smothered a chuckle, for this was the man who almost stole Eden from Lynton. No wonder Lynton was peeved.

Bromleigh was grinning, too.

They knew Lynton could not be jealous, for Eden had made her choice clear and loved her Silver Duke, Lynton, with all her being. Malcolm supposed he would be a little irked if Jocelyn did the same and chose a former beau.

When Jocelyn's turn came, he peered over her shoulder as she wrote down a name.

Lady Florence Newton.

"Who in blazes is that, love? I thought ye ladies were choosing Silver Dukes to replace us, but Eden's the only one who has done so."

"The name I wrote is that of my best friend since childhood," Jocelyn explained, noting his look of confusion, "and I am wishing for a Silver Duke *for* her. Spinsters are entitled to have friends, you know. She happens to run the Ladies' Ornithological Society in Lower Bramble, a charming village in the south of Devon."

"I'm an avid bird watcher," Eden interjected, and then suddenly gasped. "So is…" She pointed to the name she had written on the paper because to say the name aloud would ruin the wish. "Do you think…?"

Lynton groaned. "No. No, no, and no."

Eden ignored him.

Jocelyn rose. "Ladies, I think we ought to leave our husbands to their port while we retire to the drawing room."

"To plan out yer fiendish plots?" Malcolm teased.

She cast him a sugary smile. "No plotting required. The die has been cast. Fate has already intervened."

Bromleigh took a sip of his wine as he watched the three ladies scurry out with their heads bowed together and laughing. "Gentlemen, are you up for some wagers? If the ladies can make their wishes, we ought to do be able to do the same."

"Aye," Malcolm said, "and select actual dukes to follow in our footsteps. I think the ladies got sidetracked thinking about those dear to them whom they wish to see find happiness."

Lynton grumbled.

Bromleigh slapped him on the back. "Just remember, Eden chose you. Be a good sport about her choice. She only wants the man to find his own happiness."

The quill pen and parchment were still on the table. Malcolm took the parchment and cut three strips off it. "We each get to write down the name of someone we know who is most likely to take our place as a Silver Duke."

Bromleigh went first and wrote a name down on his strip of parchment.

Lynton went next and did the same.

Malcolm wrote his last. "All right, let's see the names."

They laughed upon realizing they had written down the same friend—Jonas Langford, the Duke of Ramsdale, perhaps the only one among their circle with a reputation as rakish as theirs and a determination to remain independent to rival their own. He was also intelligent, honorable, and a man of maturity, being that he was of similar age to them. These requirements made him an obvious choice to step into the role of Silver Duke. But Ramsdale was very much his own man and did not like to be labeled by anyone, much less the *ton* elite.

Bromleigh stared at the strips. "Who is going to tell him?"

Lynton shook his head. "Not I. In fact, none of us should say a word to him. He's no puerile youth. Let him fall into it on his own. Besides, do you really think this will work on him?"

"No," Malcolm and Bromleigh said at the same time.

"Ye mentioned placing wagers," Malcolm said.

Bromleigh nodded. "I'll open up a betting book and set down a list of wagers. First wager is, who of those named by our wives or us will marry first? Second, whom will they marry? Third, when will they marry? Fourth, which of them will *never* marry? We'll add additional wagers as needed. What say you?"

"Agreed," Lynton said. "But we keep the wagers private, only betting among ourselves."

Malcolm grinned wickedly. "Och, no. We open up wagers on

Ramsdale to the entire *ton*. The others we'll keep among ourselves for now, in deference to our wives."

Lynton laughed. "What you mean is, our wives will kill us if we put their friends in a betting book for all to see."

"Aye, that," Malcolm admitted, still grinning.

But Bromleigh groaned. "You do realize Ramsdale is going to shoot us when he finds out what we've done."

Malcolm shrugged. "He'll be angry for certain, but he's a good friend. Should we not wish for his happiness?"

Lynton nodded. "So be it. We open up the betting book on Ramsdale. Who are we to subvert the course of true love?"

They finished their ports and then joined the ladies in the parlor.

Malcolm's heart filled with a contentment he never thought possible as Jocelyn looked up and cast him the brightest smile as he approached.

"Love ye, my sweetheart," he whispered in her ear, taking hold of her hand as he settled beside her. Having almost lost her, he was never going take a moment of their time together for granted.

She knew it and felt it too, for he saw it in the open-hearted way she looked at him.

There was much to be said for the power of love…and finding a gorgeous stranger in one's bed.

THE END

Also by Meara Platt

FARTHINGALE SERIES
My Fair Lily
The Duke I'm Going To Marry
Rules For Reforming A Rake
A Midsummer's Kiss
The Viscount's Rose
Earl of Hearts
The Viscount and the Vicar's Daughter
A Duke For Adela
Marigold and the Marquess
The Make-Believe Marriage
A Slight Problem With The Wedding
If You Wished For Me
Never Dare A Duke
Capturing The Heart Of A Cameron

BOOK OF LOVE SERIES
The Look of Love
The Touch of Love
The Taste of Love
The Song of Love
The Scent of Love
The Kiss of Love
The Chance of Love
The Gift of Love
The Heart of Love
The Promise of Love

The Wonder of Love
The Journey of Love
The Treasure of Love
The Dance of Love
The Miracle of Love
The Hope of Love (novella)
The Dream of Love (novella)
The Remembrance of Love (novella)
All I Want For Christmas (novella)

MOONSTONE LANDING SERIES
Moonstone Landing (novella)
Moonstone Angel (novella)
The Moonstone Duke
The Moonstone Marquess
The Moonstone Major
The Moonstone Governess
The Moonstone Hero
The Moonstone Pirate

DARK GARDENS SERIES
Garden of Shadows
Garden of Light
Garden of Dragons
Garden of Destiny
Garden of Angels

SILVER DUKES
Cherish and the Duke
Moonlight and the Duke
Two Nights with the Duke
Snowfall and the Duke
Starlight and the Duke

Crash Landing on the Duke

LYON'S DEN
The Lyon's Surprise
Kiss of the Lyon
Lyon in the Rough

THE BRAYDENS
A Match Made In Duty
Earl of Westcliff
Fortune's Dragon
Earl of Kinross
Earl of Alnwick
Tempting Taffy
Aislin
Genalynn
Pearls of Fire*
*also in Pirates of Britannia series

DeWOLFE PACK ANGELS SERIES
Nobody's Angel
Kiss An Angel
Bhrodi's Angel

About the Author

Meara Platt is a *USA Today* bestselling author and an award winning, Amazon UK All-Star. Her favorite place in all the world is England's Lake District, which may not come as a surprise, since many of her stories are set in that idyllic landscape, including her award-winning fantasy romance (romantasy) Dark Gardens series. If you'd like to learn more about the ancient Fae prophecy that is about to unfold in the Dark Gardens series, as well as Meara's lighthearted, international bestselling Regency romances in the Farthingale, Book of Love, and Silver Dukes series, or her more emotional Moonstone Landing and Braydens series, please visit Meara's website at www.mearaplatt.com.

Printed in Great Britain
by Amazon